She might try to look like a guy, but the feel of her was all woman.

Gideon remembered those brief seconds when he had seized Sara by the waist. And all of a sudden, in the dark with nothing to distract him, his body responded to remembered sensations. A hungry ache zinged straight through him, reminding him he was a man— a man who'd been avoiding women for too damn long. Hell, he knew better. He'd sworn off Anglo women half a lifetime ago, and Sara Yates looked about as Anglo as they came. Irish showed in her slightly long upper lip and rose-tinted milky skin. The kind of skin that made a man think of cool misty mornings and gentle rain. Of long, lazy, sleepy dawns full of loving. The kind of loving he'd never found.

Hell, couldn't he find a likelier woman to get the hots for?

Dear Reader,

This month starts off with a bang—and with a book that more of you than I can count have requested over the years. *Quinn Eisley's War,* by Patricia Gardner Evans, finally completes the cycle begun in *Whatever It Takes* and *Summer of the Wolf.* Quinn is a commanding presence, and every bit the American Hero he's featured as. This is a story torn from today's headlines, and yet timelessly romantic. I have only one word left to say about it: enjoy!

The rest of this month is pretty spectacular, too, but what would you expect when we're celebrating the line's tenth anniversary? It's hard for me to believe we've been around that long, but it's true. And because it's your support that has kept us flourishing, it seemed only fitting to reward you with one of the best lineups we've ever published. We've got *Ironheart,* the latest in Rachel Lee's bestselling Conard County series; *Somewhere Out There,* the followup to *From a Distance* by award-winner Emilie Richards; *Take Back the Night* by yet another award-winner Dee Holmes; *To Hold an Eagle* by yet *another* award-winner (Does this tell you something about the line?) Justine Davis; and *Holding Out for a Hero,* the first of the stories of the Sinclair family, by Marie Ferrarella, another of our bestselling authors. In short, we've got six books you can't resist, six books that belong on your shelves—and in your heart—forever!

We're also offering a special hardcover tenth anniversary collection featuring the first books some of your favorite authors ever wrote for the line. Heather Graham Pozzessere, Emilie Richards and Kathleen Korbel are regular fixtures on bestseller lists and award rosters, so don't miss your chance to get this once-in-a-lifetime collection. Look for details at the back of this book.

And, of course, I'll expect to see you back here next month, when Silhouette Intimate Moments will bring you more of what you've come to expect: irresistible romantic reading.

Leslie J. Wainger
Senior Editor and Editorial Coordinator

IRONHEART

Rachel Lee

Silhouette® INTIMATE MOMENTS®

Published by Silhouette Books New York

America's Publisher of Contemporary Romance

SILHOUETTE BOOKS
300 East 42nd St., New York, N.Y. 10017

IRONHEART

ISBN: 0-373-07494-8

First Silhouette Books printing May 1993

Books by Rachel Lee

Silhouette Intimate Moments

An Officer and a Gentleman #370
Serious Risks #394
Defying Gravity #430
*Exile's End #449
*Cherokee Thunder #463
*Miss Emmaline and the Archangel #482
*Ironheart #494

*Conard County series

RACHEL LEE

wrote her first play in the third grade for a school assembly, and by the age of twelve she was hooked on writing. She's lived all over the United States, on both the East and West coasts, and now resides in Texas with her husband and two teenage children.

Having held jobs as a waitress, real-estate agent, optician and military wife—"Yes, that's a job!"—she uses these, as well as her natural flair for creativity, to write stories that are undeniably romantic. "After all, life is the biggest romantic adventure of all—and if you're open and aware, the most marvelous things are just waiting to be discovered."

To Paige Wheeler,
who is endlessly patient with my disorganization.
And to all my P* friends,
who are the best bunch of pals a writer could ask for.

Chapter 1

"We don't want any redskins in here," said a loud voice from the back of the room.

A whisper in the bar's sudden hush would have seemed deafening. The men at the tables forgot their drinks; the waitresses hesitated in midstep. The bartender froze in the act of wiping a glass. Every eye fixed on the doorway. Trouble had started brewing the instant the regulars spied the invader.

A tall, powerfully built man stood there, surveying the room with eyes that were the exact dark gray color of steel. His solidly muscled body was clad in a plain white Western shirt and faded jeans that clung snugly with the familiarity of long wearing. Beyond that, there wasn't an ordinary thing about him.

His boots were scuffed but expensive, hand-tooled leather with a pointed toe and the high, angled heel designed for a stirrup. The black cowboy hat on his head was decorated by a band made of silver conchos, each one unique. His leather belt, also hand-tooled, boasted an ornate silver-and-turquoise buckle. Hair as black as the limitless night sky flowed past his shoulders.

His face was harsh-featured, hawkish, an unforgiving landscape of angles and planes that warned people away and invited no one to come nearer. He was sun-bronzed ·and weather-hardened, and standing there he looked as enduring and immovable as the Rocky Mountains.

Slowly, almost lazily, he scanned the room. Not a muscle in his face so much as flickered while his hard, dark eyes touched on everyone and everything.

After a moment, apparently undisturbed by the silence his arrival had caused or by the hostile stares he was receiving, he walked across to the bar, his boot heels loud on the bare wood floor. When he reached it, he placed a foot on the rail and looked at the bartender.

Just then the voice from the back of the room broke the silence, this time more insistently. "I said, we don't want any 'skins in here."

Slowly, the stranger turned, his dark eyes seeking the man who had spoken. When one of the cowboys shoved away from his table and stood, the stranger looked him over from head to foot. "Too damn bad," he said, and turned his back on the cowboy.

"Not in here," the bartender said to the cowboy. "Damn it, Alvin, keep it outside."

Several more chairs scraped back from tables, but the stranger never flinched. He looked at the bartender. "Coffee, please. And a menu."

The bartender shook his head. "Just get out of here, man. No point getting your head bashed for a principle."

The stranger smiled suddenly, a humorless, dangerous expression. "You think not? Tell that to the marines."

Then he removed his black hat, revealing a thin leather thong around his forehead that held his dark hair out of his face, and handed the hat to the bartender. "Take care of that for me."

The bartender measured him for a moment, then nodded. "Sure." Accepting the hat, he placed it safely behind the bar. "I wish you'd hash this out in the parking lot."

The stranger shrugged. "It's up to Alvin. Something tells me he doesn't listen too good."

The bartender almost grinned. It was there, a faint twitch at the corner of his mouth, a small glimmer in his eyes. "You're right," he said.

Right then the stranger saw the bartender's eyes narrow and suddenly shift to one side. Instinctively he turned, just in time to block a punch from the cowpoke who'd first spoken. Alvin, probably.

"I'm gonna call the sheriff!" the bartender roared. "I told you jackasses—"

"Take it outside," someone said, and a crowd converged, forcing the two slugging, swinging men outside.

The Wyoming night air was chilly, the only light coming from the flashing red of the neon sign in front of the bar. A dark, silent circle of men formed, an ominous boundary to prevent escape. The stranger knew the ritual. He'd played it out countless times, always on the receiving end, because his skin was the color of copper and his heritage was native to this land. Men like these had stripped his people of everything, and had tried to strip him of dignity and pride with their fists and their words. Despite it all, his head remained unbowed.

There was a swift flurry of punches, and then one solid slug from the stranger threw Alvin onto his back. He lay there unmoving.

Crouched, hands spread, the Indian turned slowly, facing each man in the circle one at a time. "Who's next?" he asked. Red light flashed, and now a blue flash joined it. The growl of a truck came from behind, but the men ignored it. More important things were at hand.

"Me," said a brawny cowboy with a paunch that hung over his belt. Handing his hat to the man next to him, he stepped into the circle. He swung first.

The stranger blocked the blow and landed one solidly in the guy's paunch. Then he caught a hard slug himself, in the shoulder. It was a hopeless situation, and he knew it. He might manage to beat another one or two of these guys, but he was tiring, and eventually they'd have the edge. He'd get hammered to a pulp, probably. It wouldn't be the first time. But never, ever, was he going to leave a place because he was Cherokee. Never. They would have to carry him out, feet-first.

He took another punch in the arm, then threw one that connected solidly with the other guy's jaw. The man staggered backward, and the stranger waited, fists ready, giving his opponent a chance to quit.

The sharp report of a pistol cracked the silence of the night wide open, reverberating on the chilly air.

"This is Deputy Sheriff Yates," said an amplified woman's voice. "This party is officially over. Now."

"Aw, hell, Sara!" yelled one of the cowboys. "We're just having fun!"

"I don't call it fun when ten jackasses gang up on one fool with more guts than brains. I'm giving you thirty seconds to clear the area."

The unmistakable sound of a shotgun being pumped reinforced the order. "And take Alvin with you," she added, this time without the aid of the megaphone. "Otherwise I'll book him for disturbing the peace."

The circle of men scattered, sifting into the shadows of the parking lot. One after another, pickup engines roared to life and tires spun on gravel as they pulled away.

In thirty seconds the lot was empty of every living soul save the Indian and the Conard County deputy. The Indian stayed where he was, bent over, resting his hands on his knees as he drew deep, cleansing breaths.

"Are you okay?"

Her voice was a little husky, a black-satin-sheet voice, a whisper of dark nights and forbidden things. Slowly he lifted his head and looked at a woman who was none of those things. Clad in a khaki sheriff's uniform, her hair hidden beneath a tan Stetson, her waist concealed behind the bulk of her gun belt, with a shotgun cradled casually in one arm, she wouldn't make anyone think of satin sheets or forbidden pleasures.

And in the moment before he responded, he struggled with a sense of embarrassment at being rescued by a woman, even if she *was* a gun-toting, pistol-packing peace officer.

Somewhere along the winding trail he had traveled in his life, he had developed the conviction that it was a man's place to protect those weaker than he was, and women just naturally fell into that category. Such chivalry was outdated, he knew, but that didn't keep him from feeling he had just lost another little chunk of his masculinity because he had been rescued by a female.

Stupid, he told himself. Stupid. Would it have been *masculine* to be beaten to a bloody pulp and left for dead hamburger on the gravel? A wry smile twisted his bruised mouth. Yeah, that would have been the manly thing.

"I'm fine," he said, straightening all the way. "Thanks for helping out."

"Why didn't you just clear out? Did you really think you were going to be able to handle them all on your own?"

"I figured I was going to get my butt whipped," he said frankly, "but a few of them were going with me."

Sara Yates shook her head a little and studied him. The flashing red of the neon light didn't provide much illumination. All it seemed to do was heighten the harshness of his face and create a sense of mystery. "You're a damn fool," she said flatly.

"Maybe."

"Did you really think you'd change any of their minds about Indians by beating them up and letting them beat you up in return?"

"It wasn't *their* minds I was interested in."

Silence fell again in the parking lot. For long moments neither of them said a thing, each studying the other a little warily. Then Sara spoke. "You'd better move on before someone else comes out of that bar and decides to take exception to your ancestry.''

He settled his hands on his hips. "Wish I could oblige, Deputy.''

Sara stepped closer, wondering if she was dealing with a madman. In her experience, most people didn't argue with the law unless they were drunk, drugged or crazy—or just plain trouble. "You're not going back in there.''

"My hat's in there. It was a gift from my uncle. Custommade.''

Sara turned from him and strode back to her Blazer. "I'll get it for you," she said over her shoulder. Opening the door of the vehicle, she climbed up and turned the key in the ignition, not to start the engine, but to unlock the dashboard clamp where she stowed her shotgun. As soon as the gun was upright and in place, she removed the keys from the ignition. Nobody could get that gun now.

Climbing out again, she headed toward the door of Happy's. "What does the hat look like?''

"Black, with silver conchos on the band. The bartender's holding it for me. And thanks.''

Sara paused to look at him. "As far as I'm concerned, you're never setting foot in this place again.''

"Does that seem right to you?''

Sara heard the challenge despite his mild tone. "Look, mister, I don't know who you are or where you're from, but if you think you can walk into this county and change redneck attitudes in a place like Happy's just by being a stubborn cuss, it's your funeral. Just don't do it when I'm around. I get paid to keep the peace.''

"Is that an invitation to leave town?''

She faced him, unconsciously adopting an aggressive posture, her hands on her hips and her legs splayed. "Conard County, Wyoming, is a friendly place, and most of the folks are good people. You're welcome to stay as long as you like—as long as you don't cause trouble. I'm just recommending that you avoid getting your head bashed in. You can take that as friendly advice, or you can take it as a warning. Either way, maybe you ought to listen.''

She waited, but he seemed to have nothing more to say. Shaking her head slightly, Sara turned and headed into the bar. Just what I need, she thought. An Indian with an attitude.

Inside Happy's, the remaining regulars watched her arrival with pretended indifference. All of them knew Sara Yates. She'd lived every one of her twenty-eight years in Conard County, and her father had once been one of the regulars here. These days, she stopped in often enough herself, not to have a beer, but to hunt for her younger brother, Joey. The boy was trouble waiting to happen.

"Howdy, Sara," the bartender said, his greeting friendly. "Did anybody get hurt out there?"

"A few bruises is all, Ned." Reaching the bar, she leaned an elbow on it and looked around the room. Most everyone had gone back to their own conversations. "I came looking for a black cowboy hat with silver conchos."

"Yeah? I figured sure that Injun would come back for it himself."

"He would have. I . . . volunteered."

Ned gave a wheezy laugh. "I'm surprised he was smart enough to accept. He ain't the type to back off from a fight."

"Not by what I saw."

Ned reached behind the bar and brought out the black Stetson. "I haven't seen Joey, if you're looking," he told her as he passed her the hat.

"I'm always looking. He violates his probation at least twice a week. One of these days I'm going to run him in."

"Might do him some good, Sara," Ned said seriously. "That kid's got a chip as big as Wyoming on his shoulder, and some pretty dumb ideas about what makes a man. I'd sure hate to see your daddy's only boy turn out like Alvin Teague."

So would she, Sara thought, as she turned and left Happy's with the stranger's hat in her hand. Her dad had spent a little too much time in Happy's, but he'd been a good man, a hardworking man, until his wife died. The life had gone out of Ted Yates that day, but it had taken him two years to kill himself with booze. And Joey...well, Joey had been too damn young to understand. Sara had been nineteen at the time, and she wasn't sure she'd understood, either, but Joey had been barely seven.

And it's all just excuses, she told herself as she stepped out into the crisp spring night. Joey had had a better life than a lot of kids, a lot more stability, a home, plenty to eat.... It was all just excuses. There was nobody to blame for what Joey was doing except Joey.

The Indian was gone.

Sara froze, instinctively suspecting foul play. Then she saw him, squatting before the front of a long-bed pickup truck with a camper shell. Something made her hesitate, made her stay where she was. It was as if every instinct in her body screamed danger, but puzzlement held her still when fear never would have. And then she realized it wasn't her physical safety she was concerned about.

But she stayed where she was, anyway. "Trouble?" she called out.

"Yeah." The stranger straightened and turned toward her. Forty feet of gravel lay between them. "Somebody drained the oil and coolant from my truck. The bottom radiator hose is slashed, too."

Sara was a patient woman. Slow to anger, she habitually stayed calm past the point where most people were shouting and swearing. Tonight, though, she wasn't feeling any too patient. Her day had started at six with an auto accident out on the state highway and had been topped off by a domestic disturbance that had ended with a woman in the hospital and her husband in jail. She'd just been signing off duty at six-thirty when her grandfather called to say Joey hadn't come home.

Now here it was, after nine, she hadn't found Joey, and she'd gotten tangled up in this mess. For a moment she hesitated, thinking she ought to call someone else to come take care of this. She was off duty, after all. Let some other deputy write the report.

But she wasn't the type to ask others to do what she could do herself. Stifling a sigh, she looked at the stranger. "You want to file a report?"

He closed the distance between them and took his hat from her. Not caring that she stared, Sara watched him put it on, hiding the thong that held back his long, inky hair. He looked, she thought, like a warrior of old, a character right out of the American past.

"No point in it," he said after a moment. "It would just be a waste of paper."

"What are you implying?"

"What do you think I'm implying?"

There was no mistaking the challenge this time. Sara felt her back stiffen, and her slow anger began to simmer. "If that chip gets any bigger, mister, you're going to fall flat on your face."

He stared down at her, a tall, exotic man who looked as unyielding as granite. Sara was a tall woman herself and not accustomed to looking up at many men. Some corner of her mind noted that she ought to be nervous, facing him down like this, but she stood her ground. Sara Jane Yates always stood her ground.

And then he astonished her by giving a short, soft laugh. "You're probably right."

As easily as that, he defused the moment. Turning, he studied his disabled truck. "I don't suppose there's a tow service around here."

"Not at this time of night." And there was no way out of this one, she figured. If he left his truck here overnight, one of those yahoos who'd picked on him earlier might see it and decide to even the score a little. Then there *would* be hell to pay. Sheriff Nate Tate didn't stand for shenanigans like that in his county. "I've got a tow chain," she told the man.

He looked at her again, and this time he smiled. It was a faint, lopsided expression, almost reluctant. "Thanks. I didn't mean anything about the report, by the way. I just meant there's no way to prove who did it, so why waste the paper?''

"Oh." Sara felt a little foolish and wondered if maybe she was developing an attitude of her own. "I'll tow you into Conard City, but I have to make a couple stops along the way."

"No problem, Deputy." Suddenly he stuck out his hand. "The name's Gideon Ironheart."

Sara watched her smaller, paler hand vanish into his strong, warm grip. "Sara Yates."

She backed her departmental Blazer into place in front of his truck, then opened the tailgate to get at the tow chain. Gideon Ironheart was beside her instantly, his large hands stuffed into a pair of heavy leather work gloves, ready to take over. Standing back, Sara was content to let him do the work. Ranch-bred, she could do these things as confidently as anyone, but there was no point in arguing about it.

He knew what he was about. He moved with the ease and confidence of a man who was accustomed to hard physical labor. Nothing about the heavy chain or crawling beneath his truck to attach it to the frame caused him any hesitation. Glancing at his Georgia license plate, she wondered what he did for a living. A man didn't get a build like that from a desk job, and he didn't develop endurance from pumping iron a couple of times a week. And this man certainly had stamina. Not ten minutes ago he'd been well on the way to having the stuffing beaten out of him, but you couldn't tell it by looking at him now.

"All set," he said as he rose from the gravel.

She noticed he didn't brush off his jeans. Dirt didn't bother him, either. A construction worker, maybe. Or a farmer . . . he had the sunburned look of an outdoorsman.

"I need to stop at two places on the way into town," Sara said. "Then we can drop your truck at Bayard's Garage, and I'll take you on to the Lazy Rest Motel."

"Sounds good. Except that I haven't eaten since breakfast. I went in there to get a sandwich." He indicated Happy's with a jerk of his head.

"We'll be stopping at a couple of other watering holes. You can get a sandwich to go at one of them."

He gave a nod and turned to get into his truck.

Sara stayed as she was a moment, watching him climb into the cab of his pickup, noting again the catlike grace of his movements. Something about him was familiar. Or at least she felt as if something about him *ought* to be familiar.

Shaking her head a little, she climbed into her Blazer and switched on the ignition.

Gideon Ironheart. That sure was some name.

Towing the truck slowed her down considerably, and it was more than twenty minutes before she saw the next roadhouse she wanted to check out. Signaling early to give Gideon Ironheart plenty of warning, she turned slowly and easily into the rutted parking lot.

Neon flashed in four front windows, and a lighted arrow on a signpost pointed the way to the front door. There were more than a dozen of these places scattered around the county, all doing a booming business on Friday and Saturday nights when cowpokes came in from the range with their week's pay in their pockets.

Gideon climbed out of his truck and walked up to her as she locked the Blazer.

"Are the sandwiches here any good?" he asked.

"Good enough, I guess. Let me walk in first, and you stay behind me."

He shifted his weight to one foot, canting his hips to the side in a timeless posture of male arrogance. Barely able to swallow being rescued by her, he was in no mood to accept her protection, regardless of her badge and her gun. Besides, he didn't like the idea of her going into this place alone. "Lady, I've never yet hidden behind someone's skirts."

Sara drew herself up to her full five foot eight, a good eight inches shorter than he was, and glared up at him. "Look, *Mister* Ironheart, we do it my way or you wait out here while I get your damn dinner. I'm in no mood to deal with another brawl tonight. What'll it be?''

He folded his arms across his chest and looked down at her stonily. It was his very lack of expression that communicated his anger. "Is this Wyoming hospitality?"

That nearly did it. She'd been dealing with fools and idiots all day long, and now she wasn't even on duty. "This isn't a matter of hospitality, Ironheart. It's a matter of *reality*. You want hospitality, come out to my ranch. My grandfather will stuff you full of good home-cooking and I'll pour the damn coffee. These roadhouses are a different matter. They're loaded with redneck cowboys who've already had too damn much whiskey for their own good. If I go in first, nobody will pay any attention to you, and that's the way *I* want it, because I want to get home to my bed sometime tonight. Got it?"

His arms remained folded, and he continued to stare expressionlessly down at her. His stare was unnerving, Sara thought uneasily. Shadowed by the brim of his hat, his eyes were like two dark, glistening pools, drawing her deeper and deeper. They held her, mesmerized her, gave her the uneasy feeling that they were absorbing her and learning all her secrets. And gave her the even wilder feeling that if she just fell into those pools, a dark warmth would swallow her and shelter her.

"Who," he asked slowly, "made you ashamed of being a woman?"

It was a question to which Gideon Ironheart genuinely wanted an answer, but he knew he wasn't going to get it. Not yet. Without a word, Sara Yates pivoted on her heel and stalked toward the door of the bar. Gideon followed two steps behind, realizing what she apparently didn't: that her uniform might be scant protection in a place like this. When some men got drunk enough, they respected nothing at all. He would walk behind her if she insisted, but he'd be damned before he'd let her walk into this place alone. Happy's had been different, because the troublemakers were already gone when she went inside. Here, they were still inside and drinking.

The music from the jukebox was loud, the laughter louder. A haze of cigarette and cigar smoke filled the large room, and the bartender didn't look half as friendly as the one at the other place. Keeping close to Sara, Gideon escorted her to the bar.

The bartender nodded to her, glanced at Gideon, then dismissed him as a redskin. "Whaddya want, Sara?"

"My friend here wants some sandwiches to go. Have you seen Joey tonight?"

Kurt shook his head. "You told me the kid's on probation. He's underage besides. He comes in here, I throw him out. I don't want no grief with Tate." With visible reluctance, he looked at Gideon. "Yeah?"

Gideon ordered a couple of turkey sandwiches while Sara turned and scanned the crowded room. People were glancing surreptitiously their way, but apparently nobody was in a mood for trouble with the law tonight—except for two beefy guys in the corner who looked as if they couldn't quite make up their minds.

The bartender dumped a couple of plastic-wrapped sandwiches on the counter and threw Gideon's change down beside it.

"Walk out in front of me," Sara told Gideon as he turned toward the door.

"Damn it," he growled, keeping his voice low, "I—"

"My back is less of a provocation than yours," she said flatly. "All right?"

Over the top of her Stetson, he saw the two men who evidently had her worried. They were beginning to shove their chairs back from the table. There was no time for argument. Turning, he headed toward the door, dragging Sara right after him.

"I'm getting a really great impression of Conard County, Wyoming," he growled as he pulled her through the door after him and started tugging her across the parking lot. "I saw less trouble in dives in Chicago, Atlanta and Boston, I can tell you. What is it with these guys?''

Sara tried to yank her arm free of his grip. "Damn it, Ironheart—"

"Oh, just be quiet, woman. Those two cretins in there have got plans for both of us. I suggest you get behind the wheel and drive.''

"How come you didn't have the sense to clear out of Happy's before the trouble started?'' Sara demanded as she unlocked the door of her Blazer. "You're sure in enough of a hurry now.''

His face was completely shadowed beneath the brim of his black hat. Not even the neon light penetrated the darkness there. "Because," he said succinctly, "at Happy's I didn't have a woman to look after.''

Sara gasped, but before she could voice her outrage, Gideon pulled the Blazer's door open and lifted her onto the seat. "Drive, Deputy," he said. "I'll be right behind you.''

And, damn it, he actually smiled. She caught the gleam of his teeth even in the shadows.

He got behind the wheel of his truck just as the two men emerged from the bar. Sara didn't hesitate any longer but turned over her engine and pulled out of the lot. She would deal with Gideon Ironheart later.

Fifteen minutes later, they reached the last of the roadhouses Sara wanted to check out. After this, Joey was on his own. There were limits to what even a loving sister could or would do.

Before she climbed out, Gideon was there, opening her door and looking straight in at her. "Who were those two guys back there?'' he asked without preamble. "Local troublemakers?''

Sara shrugged. "I never saw them before. We *do* occasionally get strangers through here," she said dryly, wondering why she was no longer furious with him. She ought to read him the riot act for treating her like a helpless, defenseless female when she was neither. "I don't like the way you dragged me out of there, Ironheart.''

"Sorry, ma'am." He didn't look sorry, though, and his eyes never wavered from her face. "Who's Joey?"

Sara sighed and averted her face, staring out through the dusty windshield at the Watering Hole. "My brother."

"He's disappeared?"

"Not exactly. He's around somewhere, probably doing something he shouldn't."

"That bartender said something about probation."

"Yeah. Grand theft auto. He's supposed to come straight home from his job, and when he doesn't, he's violating his probation." Why was she telling him all this, anyway? It was none of his damn business, and he was a complete stranger besides. Catching herself, she turned and began to slide out of the truck. Gideon stepped back to give her room.

"You wait out here," she told him flatly. "I'll only be a minute."

He didn't bother to argue. He just walked right behind her every step of the way. Sara felt him there, like a severe irritation. She could have handcuffed him to something, she supposed, but that wouldn't be legal. She couldn't, after all, prevent anyone from going anywhere they damn well pleased, as long as no law was being violated.

Damn, she hoped he was on his way out of the county by tomorrow evening. In her entire life, she couldn't remember one person ever having irritated her so severely. Or so easily. Or so continually.

Suddenly she spun about and faced him, her jaw thrust out and her hands on her hips. "What is it with you, Ironheart? This is *my* business, and I'll handle it. By myself."

He didn't answer immediately. He stood looking down at her, hips again canted in that incredibly virile, incredibly cocky way, a tall, powerful, mysterious-looking man. After a moment, he tilted his head a little to one side, almost thoughtfully. "My grandfather was a medicine man. I didn't listen to him much as a kid, not nearly as much as I should have, I reckon. But a couple of things stuck with me. He told me a man answers only to himself, but he always answers. I don't want to have to answer to myself if you go in there alone and something happens."

There really wasn't a thing she could say to that. Whatever else he might be, Ironheart was evidently an honorable man, and an honorable man couldn't be deterred. Nor should he be. Sara felt the last of her irritation drizzle away. Without a word, she turned and let him follow.

The Watering Hole was usually a quieter place than the last one they had checked, and Sara didn't really expect any trouble. The bartender was a man she had gone to high school with, and he greeted her with a ready grin.

"No Joey," he said as soon as he saw her. "You know I'd send him home, Sara."

"I know, Bill, but you're not always here. Thanks, though."

The night was growing chillier, and Sara shivered a little when she stepped back outside.

"What now?" Gideon asked.

"I'll take you on into town."

"I meant, what do you do now about Joey?"

"Not much I can do except run him in when I find him." The thought made her sick to her stomach. "He agreed to the terms of probation, and I agreed to make sure he kept them. There's no alternative. Not anymore."

"Turning him in might get his attention."

"That's what my grandfather says."

Gideon held the door of the Blazer while Sara climbed in. "That's what my grandfather said about me, too."

As she reached for the seat belt, Sara paused and looked at him. "What happened?"

"He got my attention."

Two hours later, Sara sat at the kitchen table at home, her booted feet up on the chair beside her while she sipped a mug of chocolate milk and ate the dinner her grandfather had kept warming in the oven for her. She'd traded her uniform for soft old jeans and a faded sweatshirt, and had unpinned her long black hair, giving her scalp some relief.

The Yates ranch, known as the Double Y, occupied two thousand acres in westernmost Conard County, butting right up against the mountains. Sara could get on a horse on a summer afternoon and ride up into pine forests and watch mountain brooks tumble down rocky hillsides. It was some of the prettiest land in the county, and some of the toughest to ranch. Since her father's death, the Double Y had grown little but sagebrush and grass, and Sara had taken her job with the sheriff's department in order to hang on to it. Sometimes she wondered why she bothered.

But then she would think of the pine woods and the sound of rushing water, the way the fresh, clean air smelled, and she knew she could never let it go. Whatever it took, she would keep the Double Y.

The screen door behind her slapped shut, and she looked over her shoulder to see her grandfather come into the kitchen. "No Joey?" he said.

Sara shook her head. "How's Columbine?"

"She'll foal before dawn." Moving slowly, the old man rounded the table and sat across from her. In his seventies, Zeke Jackson still stood straight and proud, but his arthritis slowed him up a little. His face was lined and weathered from the elements and years, but his hair was still as dark as a raven's wing.

Sara had inherited his hair and a touch of his high Shoshone cheekbones, but apart from that she looked like her father's daughter: brown-eyed and ordinary. "Can I make you some coffee, Grandfather?"

The old man shook his head. "You worked hard today. You rest. I can look after myself. You'll have to turn the boy in, Sarey. A few weeks in the county jail might wake him up."

"But what if it makes him worse?" That was the fear that plagued her. The Conard County jail didn't house hardened criminals, as a rule, but just the fact of incarceration might be enough to harden his attitude rather than cure it.

Zeke shook his head slowly. "You've done all you can. We both have. Sooner or later, even a boy has to answer for what he does."

The words were so close to what Gideon Ironheart had said earlier that Sara found herself telling her grandfather about him. Zeke laughed when she told him that Gideon had said that his grandfather got his attention, but then he grew serious.

"There's nothing more you can do, Sara-child. Not a thing. You've given that boy all the loving and caring of a mother, and you've set a fine example in all you've done. You can plant a seed in the best soil, and it can still grow crooked."

Later, Sara stood at the open window of her upstairs bedroom and listened to the quiet whinnies from the barn where Columbine was in foal. Zeke and his old friend, a Sioux named Chester Elk Horn, would handle Columbine. She could sleep. She *should* sleep. But Joey was gone, out there somewhere getting into trouble, probably, and she couldn't help worrying.

And then she thought of Gideon Ironheart and wondered if he was just passing through. And hoped that he might stay a little while. He had been a splash of brilliant color in days that, for Sara, had grown increasingly colorless. Life had passed her by in some respects, but that didn't mean she was content.

Yes, it would be nice—in an interesting way—if he stayed for a while. There would be light and color and life wherever he went. He was that kind of man.

The motel room smelled like a motel room. Sickly sweet air freshener battled the odors of sweat, urine, tobacco and other things Gideon didn't want to think about. The rug looked clean enough, though, and the sheets smelled like laundry soap, so he ignored the rest of it as best he could.

The motel was located beside the state highway that ran just outside Conard City, and the otherwise quiet night was occasionally disturbed by the whine of a trailer truck as it passed at high speed. The last drunken cowboy had staggered into his room shortly after two, and since then only one truck had passed.

He was alone with the night and himself, and both were empty. Too empty.

With his hands clasped behind his head, he lay on the bed and stared up at the patterns of light on the ceiling—white from the porch light just outside the door, and green from the sign out front, softly diffused by the white curtains. The guy next door suddenly coughed, a smoker's hack, wheezy and sustained.

He'd stayed in a lot of cheap motels over the years and lived in a lot of furnished rooms, but he didn't want to think about that now. He didn't want to think about the past, and he didn't want to think about what he was intending to do tomorrow, so he focused instead on Sara Yates and the events of this evening. She was an easy out, a ready excuse not to think about important things. Not to think about all the things that had suddenly come to matter too much.

Something about her appealed to him. Maybe it was that tough exterior, that determined hardness of speech and manner that didn't fit her at all. She had all the words right and the postures down perfectly, but he didn't buy it. Someone or something had driven Sara Yates into hiding, and it was easier to wonder about her problems than it was to think about his own.

And suddenly, in the dark with no one and nothing to distract him, he thought about that brief couple of seconds when he had seized her by the waist and lifted her into her Blazer. Well, not exactly by her waist. Her gun belt had caused him to wrap his hands around her midriff. Just beneath her breasts. His thumbs remembered that all too brief sensation of warmth, weight and softness, and his palms remembered the fragile delicacy of her ribs. She might try to look like a guy, but her feel was all woman.

And all of a sudden, in the dark with nothing to distract him, his body responded to remembered sensations. A hungry ache zinged straight to his groin, reminding him he was a man—a man who'd been avoiding women for too damn long. Hell. Anyway, he knew better. He'd sworn off Anglo women half a lifetime ago, and Sara Yates looked about as Anglo as they came. Irish showed in her slightly long upper lip and rose-tinted milky skin. The kind of skin that made a man think of cool misty mornings and gentle rain. Of long, lazy, sleepy dawns full of loving. The kind of loving he'd never found.

Hell, couldn't he find a likelier woman to get the hots for?

But in the dark, with nothing to distract him except memories he wasn't ready to face, it didn't matter a damn.

Chapter 2

The sun was barely skimming the eastern horizon when Gideon left the motel and walked into town. Sleep had eluded him most of the night, and this morning he felt wired. It was the same feeling he got when he was working seventy stories up and something went wrong, the same rush of adrenaline, the same heightened senses, the same edginess of a close call. Until six months ago, he had been addicted to the feeling. These days he never wanted to feel it again.

But he was feeling it now, and it kept him walking at a brisk pace toward his goal, the Conard County Sheriff's Office. Downtown across from the courthouse, Sara had said last night. In a storefront.

He walked on the shoulder of the business detour from the state highway and into the outskirts of town. There he saw the usual businesses—gas stations, hardware stores, body shops, a veterinarian, and cattle pens and a railroad siding where market-bound steers were probably loaded.

Closer in, residential areas spread away from the business loop, older homes, mostly, with lawns and carefully nurtured trees. A nice little town, he thought. A town to grow old in, but not the best place to be young. Joey Yates probably needed a lot more excitement than Conard County provided.

Bayard's Garage still wasn't open, so he continued his way to the center of town. The courthouse was visible now, towering over the surrounding buildings, a Victorian gothic structure built of rough-hewn granite.

Maude's Diner was visible down a side street, busy even at this early hour, he noted. The coffee must be good. He'd stop there later. Right now he was too damn tense.

The courthouse lawn was large, a small park full of flower beds and benches to sit on. He found a bench right across the street from the sheriff's office and settled down to wait.

The sun rose higher and began to steal the night's chill from the air. A couple of old men, one of them leaning on a cane, took seats a little closer to the courthouse and began to read their newspapers. Pigeons strutted jerkily along the sidewalks, pecking at invisible morsels. A dog wandered by, pausing to sniff at Gideon's boots. Reaching out a hand, he stroked the dog's head absently, but he never took his eyes off the sheriff's office.

And then the day began. The first to arrive was a scrawny, leathery-looking older woman who unlocked the office and disappeared within. Only seconds behind her a sheriff's vehicle arrived, a sand-colored Blazer just like the one Sara had driven the night before. The man who climbed out was somewhere in his forties, sunburned to a permanent red and thickening around the middle.

Several much younger men arrived, all of them clearly deputies. Sara showed up but evidently didn't notice him sitting across the street. This morning she was wearing the mirrored aviator-style sunglasses that seemed to go with cop uniforms. Gideon almost smiled. Sara Yates wanted to be tough. He wondered if he would ever find out why.

The sun rose higher, and finally one more Blazer pulled up into a reserved slot. And this time Gideon tensed and sat up straighter, squinting in an effort to miss nothing.

A tall, powerfully built man climbed out. He, too, wore a deputy's khaki uniform, tan Stetson and mirrored glasses, but unlike the others, his dark hair flowed loose to his shoulders. He glanced toward the square, the quick, scanning glance common to men who never overlooked a detail of their surroundings, and then he turned to enter the office.

Gideon felt the shock of recognition like a hot punch in his stomach. He'd expected to be able to identify the man the way he would have identified any stranger who had been described to him. He hadn't been prepared for this gut recognition. It wasn't as if he'd ever met the guy.

The big man paused, scanning the square and streets again, as if he had sensed something. His eyes were hidden behind those mirrored glasses, but Gideon nonetheless felt the man's gaze scrape over him, felt it pass and then return briefly for another look.

Damn, was the man psychic? But then the big deputy turned and entered the sheriff's office. Whatever he had seen had been dismissed as unimportant. Gideon released a long breath, realizing for the first time that he had been holding it.

That was him, all right. No doubt of it. And now that he'd found Micah Parish, he had to figure out what he was going to do about it.

The sun rose a little higher and the street grew busier. The surrounding businesses opened; the courthouse parking lot filled with cars. Gideon couldn't have said why he continued to sit there. He had seen Parish, and that was what he had come here for, to identify the man. He could go down the street to the diner now and have some coffee and eggs. He could mosey on up to Bayard's Garage and arrange to get his truck fixed.

But he sat on, strangely paralyzed, and let the warm sun and cool, dry Wyoming breeze caress him. It was nice here, he thought, and he was finally old enough to appreciate it. Even six months ago he would have been impatient with the quiet, relaxed, aimless atmosphere, with the positively bucolic scene.

A battered old green pickup pulled into the last parking slot in front of the sheriff's department. Gideon watched absently as an old man with long, braided, raven-colored hair climbed out. Few full-blooded Native Americans turned gray with age, and the color of the old man's hair proclaimed the purity of his bloodline. Shoshone? Gideon wondered. Lakota? Such differences had once been critical, and to some they still were. In an Anglo world, though, they were kin.

A tall, dark-haired youth climbed out the other side, and suddenly Gideon sat a little straighter. If that boy wasn't Sara's brother, he'd eat his hat, conchos and all. Curiosity almost brought him to his feet, and then he remembered himself. If that was indeed Joey Yates, it was none of his business, and not even natural curiosity could justify his going over to the office to gawk.

Fifteen minutes later the old man came out alone and stood on the sidewalk, surveying the street as if he hadn't quite decided what he was going to do now. Then he saw Gideon.

Much to Gideon's amazement, the old man crossed the street purposefully, as if Gideon were someone he had been looking for. He came right up to the younger man and halted, staring down at him as if taking his measure.

Gideon returned the stare impassively. He knew that look. His grandfather had looked at him that way the day twelve-year-old Gideon had been brought to him from the orphanage. It had been a look that went past the surface and seemed to pry into the soul. It had made him uneasy then, but today he was a forty-one-year-old man who knew even the darkest corners of his soul. Having no secrets from himself, he didn't fear what others might see in him.

"You're Ironheart," the old man said finally.

Gideon nodded.

"Sara mentioned you. That's not any Indian name I ever heard."

"I chose it, old man."

Zeke smiled. "I'm Zeke Jackson."

"Funny name for an Indian."

"A missionary chose it."

Gideon felt a smile crease his face. "Yeah," he said.

Zeke stared down at him for another ten or fifteen seconds, then sat beside him on the bench. "Nice morning."

"Very. That boy who came in with you...Joey Yates?"

"Sara mentioned him, did she?"

"She was looking for him when we met."

"He's going to spend the next couple of days, maybe more, in jail. It'll get his attention, maybe."

Gideon looked at Zeke, and his smile broadened a little more. "Yeah. It can work that way."

Zeke nodded, the road map of lines all over his face deepening a little. "Leaves me shorthanded, though. You looking to stay in Conard County awhile?"

"Awhile. I'm not sure how long."

"What do you do?"

"I'm an ironworker."

Zeke turned and looked at him, his black eyes bright with interest. "One of those guys who builds the steel frames for skyscrapers?"

"That's right. I'm a connector."

"What does that mean, exactly?"

Gideon settled back and stared off into space, aware that his heart was picking up speed just a little. He didn't want to think about what he did. About what he *had* done. "A connector is the first guy up. He shinnies up the column from the floor below and hangs there like a monkey at the top until the derrick swings a ten- or twenty-ton beam his way. When it gets close enough, he grabs on to it, guides it into place and drives a couple of bolts home to hold it there."

"Then you're one of those crazy guys I've seen walking on those narrow I-beams up there."

"Yeah." Crazy was probably a good word for it.

"Then you're not afraid of heights."

Gideon turned his head and looked straight at him. "Old man, only a fool isn't afraid of heights."

Zeke nodded. "How high have you worked?"

"Ninety stories. My last job topped out at seventy."

"How high is that?"

"Around seven hundred feet."

Zeke gave a low whistle. "Beats me why any man wants to walk on a six-inch-wide piece of steel at that kind of altitude."

Gideon smiled. "It's almost as good as being a bird." Or had been.

Zeke studied him a little longer. "Know anything about horses?"

"A little. My uncle raises them, and when I was a kid I helped break them."

"Well, Ironheart, if you're looking for work around here, I'm shorthanded for a few days, and I've got a herd of mustangs I need some help with."

"Mustangs?"

"I can't let them all go to the glue factory, can I?" He rose and gave a nod of farewell. "Anyone can tell you how to find the Double Y, if you're interested."

Gideon hadn't learned as much from his grandfather as he should have, but he had taken a few things with him that had given him strength over the years. One of those things was the morning silence. His grandfather had called it prayer, and most other people would have called it meditation. Since Gideon didn't consider himself conventionally religious, he refused to think of it as prayer, and "meditation" sounded too New Age for his taste.

So he called it the morning silence, or going into the silence, when he called it anything at all. It was a place inside himself, an inner pool of stillness and peace, that he visited each morning before he began his day. It was like reaching inside and tapping some bottomless well full of serenity and strength. He always emerged from the silence refreshed, feeling centered in himself and ready for the day's trials. It didn't solve his problems or dull the edge of his pain, but it helped him endure.

Two mornings later, sitting in the center of the motel room on the floor, cross-legged and straight-backed, he emerged from the silence with an almost aching sense of loss. His grandfather had been a medicine man, a great shaman of the old ways, and he wished now that he had listened more closely.

"You have the power in you," the old man had told him once. "You have the gift, boy, and a responsibility. Learn to use it, and use it wisely."

But what had a fourteen-year-old boy cared for such things? A forty-one year old man cared, but now it was too late. He could only sit there in a dingy motel room and wish to God he had something more than a feeling that he had somehow lost his way, could merely think that if only he had listened to the wisdom of an old man, he might have had somewhere to look for answers and direction.

But he had only himself and the feeling that he hadn't done what he had been meant to do with the days of his life. Probably just midlife crisis, he told himself as he rose from the floor. It would sort itself out.

In the last two days, though, he hadn't learned a damn thing about Micah Parish, and learning about Micah Parish had been the main reason he'd come to Conard County. The locals, who probably gossiped avidly among themselves, were proving to be remarkably tight-lipped with the outsider. He would mention Micah casually in conversation, and all he ever got was, "Yeah. Damn fine deputy."

Two solid days, and he didn't know any more than the private detective had been able to tell him. Micah Parish had been with the Conard County Sheriff's Department for approximately five years, after retiring from the army, and just before Christmas he had married an old friend. It didn't tell Gideon a damn thing about the man. It did, however, explain why that expensive P.I. had been able to tell him so little. Judging by the way his neighbors closed their wagons in a circle around him, Micah must have made a good impression on them.

And if Gideon hung around this town much longer without some obvious reason to remain, he would probably become the subject of local speculation himself. In fact, it wouldn't surprise him if a Conard County deputy showed up at his door and started asking questions about his business. He'd already realized that people around here looked out for one another, and a stranger might be someone the community needed protecting from. Neighborliness was a far sight more than a casual wave in these parts—it was serious business.

That meant that if he wanted to stay around here without arousing all kinds of uncomfortable suspicion, he'd better take that job that Zeke Jackson had offered him out at the Double Y.

Dirk Bayard, at the garage, gave him directions, and soon he was on the road, heading out toward the western end of Conard County, driving straight toward the mountains that still bore a winter mantle of snow on their highest shoulders. Except for the six years he had spent on his uncle's ranch on the Oklahoma prairie, and a year spent building missile silos in eastern Montana, Gideon had been a city dweller because his job had demanded it. He had lived in caverns of steel and glass, and had been aware of a faint dislocation when he left them behind to travel to another city and another job across the continent, or even just when he took a week to go fishing or hunting with his buddies.

There was no way, he thought now as he drove down a long, empty county road, that you could overlook the isolation out here. Since leaving Conard City, he had passed two other vehicles, one a sheriff's unit, the other the mailman, who out here drove a white truck with the Postal Service emblem on the door. Different. It was different.

It appealed to him. Especially that line of mountains to the west, blue in the bright morning light. Everything looked so damn clean and fresh, and the quiet called to him, promising peace.

Being an ironworker had carried satisfactions that few people ever found. When Gideon had built something, he could look at it and see the actual fruits of his efforts. More, he could look at it and know it would still be there fifty years after he was gone.

People out here probably found the same satisfaction, he thought now. The seasons might come and go, but the land remained, and they passed it on to their sons and grandsons.

He could imagine making a life here, he realized. He could easily imagine it.

The turnoff for the Double Y was marked, as Dirk Bayard had promised. Almost as soon as he turned off the county road, the terrain changed, growing more rugged. The dirt lane he traveled now rose steadily toward the mountains, and the air grew gradually chillier. One of the prettiest spots in the county, Dirk had told him, and one of the hardest to ranch. Too bad there was no market for mountain goats, he'd added.

The road ended two miles later in a hard-packed yard between a house and a weathered barn. Behind the buildings lay a large meadow that rose gently toward the trees. Part of it had been fenced for pasture, and three horses grazed there now. An idyllic setting, he thought.

In a corral behind the barn, Gideon saw the old man holding a restless stallion by his halter. The roan had the compact, sturdy build of a mustang and the temperament of a wild male. His eyes were rolling a little as Zeke Jackson tugged on the halter rope and moved closer.

Damn old man, Gideon thought, climbing out of his truck. He wasn't big enough to hold that horse down, or strong enough. If that stallion reared . . .

Suddenly, the stallion did just that, then pivoted in an abrupt, unexpected movement that knocked the old Shoshone to one side in the dirt. Pawing at the air with his front hooves, the horse screamed and then came down hard.

* * *

Joey wouldn't even speak to her. That glum thought had been the first one in Sara's mind that morning when she awoke, and it was still haunting her as she performed her weekly household chores. Today was her day off, so she needn't go into Conard City for that reason, and thinking of Joey's sullen silence, she told herself she wouldn't go in to see him, either. He could just sit there and sulk.

Tough words, but they didn't do anything to ease the ache in her heart. Eleven years ago, when their mother had died, Sara had stood beside the raw dirt of the grave and hugged her weeping five-year-old brother. Two years later she had done it again when they buried their father. In all the ways that counted, she *was* Joey's mother, and like a mother, she suffered for him and with him. At least a dozen times a day she wanted to race into town and tell Nate Tate to let him out. Nate might even do it, but in the long run, it was Joey who would pay for the leniency. Somehow they had to get his attention.

No, Nate probably wouldn't let him out. The sheriff had been preaching tough love for Joey for the last six months, and he wasn't likely to go all soft because Sara asked him to. When Zeke had brought Joey in the other morning, Nate had looked at the boy and said, "Well, it's about time." And maybe it was. Better a few days or weeks in the county jail than years in the penitentiary.

Hearing the approach of a truck engine, she set her dust mop aside and went onto the kitchen porch to see who it might be. Emma and Gage Dalton, maybe. Emma had been her good friend for many years, and since their marriage, Gage often joined her when she came out to visit Sara.

She recognized Gideon Ironheart's truck immediately. What had brought him out here? she wondered, and then looked down in dismay at her worn jeans and the old khaki shirt she had put on for cleaning. She hadn't even done anything with her hair, had simply pulled it out of the way with a rubber band at the nape of her neck.

And it didn't matter, she told herself sternly as she watched him pull to a stop in the yard. It didn't matter a damn what she was wearing or what she looked like. It hadn't mattered in nearly ten years, and it wasn't going to start mattering today.

Just then the mustang shrieked, and Gideon leapt out of his truck as if propelled. Sara couldn't see the corral beyond the barn from the porch, but the sight of Gideon racing full steam in that direction told her that her grandfather was in trouble. Dropping the mop, she took off at a dead run.

By the time she rounded the barn, Gideon was in the corral, holding the mustang tightly by its halter. The horse jerked his head back sharply and twisted, trying to get away, but muscles honed to steel by years of hard labor jerked right back, telling the animal who was boss.

Sara climbed the rails and dropped to the dirt beside her grandfather.

"Grandfather? Grandfather!"

The old man's eyes opened, and he drew a deep, shuddering breath. "I'm okay, child. Just got the wind knocked out of me."

"Oh, Grandfather..." Relief left her weak. When he sat up, she hugged him wordlessly as her throat tightened in reaction.

He patted her shoulder. "It's all right, Sarey. It's all right."

She helped the old man to his feet, wincing sympathetically when the pain of his arthritis flickered across his face. He was too old for this, she thought angrily. Joey should have been here helping. At that moment, she could have cheerfully boxed her brother's ears.

"I'll get someone out here to help with the horses," she told him. "I don't want you doing all this work, Grandfather. I told you—"

"I think we already have someone to help with the horses," Zeke interrupted. He indicated Gideon with a jerk of his chin.

The mustang was still sidling nervously, but he had calmed considerably. Sara watched in amazement as Gideon Ironheart murmured to the horse, standing close enough that, had the stallion taken a mind to, he could have bitten off half the man's face. But the horse didn't bite. Shivering, shifting from hoof to hoof, he listened to each and every liquid syllable that Gideon murmured.

Without missing a beat or changing his intonation, Gideon spoke to her. "Sara? Get Zeke out of here."

"I'm fine, I'm fine," Zeke muttered stubbornly, refusing to accept even a hand from her. He'd always been cussedly stubborn, Sara thought. Always.

When they were safely outside the gate, they both turned to look back at Gideon and the mustang. Horse and man seemed to have reached some kind of agreement, for now the stallion stood still, head down, and docilely accepted Gideon stroking his neck.

"Look at that," Zeke said softly. "Just look at that. There's a man who knows horses, Sarey. I'm damn glad I offered him a job."

"A job?" Sara stared in surprise at her grandfather and then looked at Gideon. "Here? Can we afford him?"

"Reckon so. He didn't ask what I was paying."

"Then maybe you'd better discuss that with him."

Zeke gave her a smiling glance. "Don't worry, gal. I'll take care of everything."

Not certain that reassurance made her feel any better, Sara looked over at Gideon. He was still talking to that damn mustang, a soft, seductive murmuring that slipped over the ears like satin over skin, enticing, mesmerizing. Promising.

And he had once again fallen into that pose of sheer male arrogance, legs splayed, one knee bent, hips cocked rakishly and thrusting slightly forward as if to draw attention to his virility. Since he was intent upon the horse, she gave him the benefit of the doubt and decided that the pose must be unconscious. He wasn't George, after all.

Thinking of George, as she had been trying not to for ten years, turned her mood instantly sour and waspish. As if he sensed it somehow, her grandfather looked at her.

"I'll take care of it, Sara."

She nodded and turned back to the house. Twenty-eight years old, and she was still taking orders as if she was a child. But that was a problem, living in a multigenerational household. To her grandfather, she would always be a child who would do as she was told.

Gideon looked away from the horse and stared at her departing back. She had a figure, that woman, he noted approvingly. Without her gun belt to conceal it, she had a waist, a tiny waist accentuated by the way she had knotted her shirttails. The ragged denim of her jeans clung lovingly to long, slender legs and a full, round rump. And her hips...well, they weren't a model's skinny ones at all. Nope, they were a woman's hips, meant to cradle a man and bear children with ease. Her hair was long, he saw, too, and he felt a stirring in places that shouldn't be stirring in broad daylight.

He glanced toward Zeke. "You didn't say she was your granddaughter."

"I don't recollect you asking."

Gideon felt himself grin in response. Damned if he didn't like this old coot. The mustang had calmed down now, and the stench of the animal's fear, while still strong, was beginning to fade in the open air. "What were you trying to do when I drove up?"

"Right foreleg looks a tad swollen just below the knee, and he's been limping. It's probably nothing, but it took me three days to coax him into the corral, and I'd like to be sure there's no real hurt."

Gideon nodded, speaking soothingly to the horse. The mustang's ears were pricked, attentive to every sound the man made, and his nostrils were still flared, but the whites of his eyes were no longer wildly showing. Not afraid any longer, Gideon judged. Just naturally wary.

Murmuring nonsense syllables in a cadence he had learned from his uncle, he stroked his hand lower and lower by small degrees, until the horse was tolerating touches to his shoulder and chest. Slowly, very slowly, Gideon squatted and began to run his fingers over first one foreleg and then the other, comparing the two as the best measure of injury.

"It's swollen, all right," he said a few moments later. "Not a lot, though, and it's not feverish. The skin's not broken anywhere."

"Probably just a strain," Zeke said. "Guess I'll keep him corralled for a day or two."

Gideon straightened slowly, murmuring soothingly again as the horse shied a little. Then he released the halter and stepped back. For several heartbeats the mustang didn't move; then he darted to the far side of the corral. Gideon laughed softly. "Reminds me of some of the street toughs I've known over the years."

He climbed the fence and joined Zeke on the other side. For a while neither man spoke. They stood and watched the horse posture threateningly and whinny at the mares who hung back near a pine-covered ridge. The breeze stirred, carrying the scents of pine and grass and horse to them.

"How many mustangs?" Gideon asked.

"Just these. I'd take more—certainly have enough room for 'em—but we couldn't afford to keep 'em in hay all winter. Sarey works hard enough as it is."

The younger man nodded.

Zeke indicated the mustang with a jerk of his chin. "What did you say to him?"

Gideon shrugged. "Nothing but the truth."

"And what's that?"

Steel-gray eyes met obsidian ones. "That I didn't want to steal his fire or his freedom."

Zeke continued to stare intently at him for a few seconds; then he looked toward the mustang again. "So you want some work?"

"A little. A few days, maybe. A few hours here and there."

"What kind of wage?"

Gideon had already figured that one out. "Whatever will keep you from feeling you're taking a favor."

Zeke laughed. "I think you were wasted working with all that steel, Ironheart."

Maybe he had been, Gideon thought as he watched the stallion paw the dirt. Certainly now, whenever he looked back, all he saw was a vast wasteland where his past should have been.

Sara saw them coming toward the house and immediately recognized the indefinable aura that existed between men who had reached a friendly understanding. Gideon Ironheart would be working for them, which meant she was going to be seeing a lot of him.

The thought made her at once uneasy and excited. He affected her as no man had since George, and even George hadn't given her the electric feeling Gideon did, as if the very air around him tingled and snapped with energy. Her hand flew to her dark hair, freshly brushed and loose around her shoulders. At least she'd caught herself before she had changed. That would have been too obvious.

At the very last possible moment, though, she turned and fled from the kitchen. Gideon Ironheart made her feel vulnerable, and she had to shore up her defenses before she faced him.

In her bedroom, she listened to the men come in, heard the deep rumble of their voices as they settled at the kitchen table, heard the clink of crockery as her grandfather poured coffee.

Anger flickered briefly as she recalled the way Gideon had manhandled her last night. She hadn't been a deputy sheriff for the last nine years without learning how to handle herself in tough situations, or without learning how to judge them. He hadn't needed to drag her out of that bar and thrust her into her vehicle. He certainly hadn't needed to make that remark about women needing protection. He might be eight inches taller and outweigh her by seventy or eighty pounds, but that didn't necessarily mean he could protect her any better than she could protect herself.

The memory made her steam, even as a traitorous warmth touched cold places. Apart from her grandfather, it had been a long time since anyone had wanted to protect Sara Yates from anything.

But everything else aside, she wanted nothing to do with any man who made her feel vulnerable. She was never going to be vulnerable again. Nearly a decade had passed, but she hadn't forgotten the humiliation of waiting in a church packed with people for a groom who was finally discovered to have fled to another state in order to escape marrying her. Sara Yates had awakened that long-ago morning a blushing, fresh eighteen years old. It had been both her birthday and her wedding day. By the time it was over, her heart had felt as if it were eighty. And it had been months before conversations no longer halted whenever she entered a room. No, she wasn't going to make a fool of herself again.

When Sara returned to the kitchen, Gideon and Zeke were on a second cup of coffee and making inroads on the coffee cake she had taken from the oven only an hour ago. Since she had baked it only to satisfy her grandfather's sweet tooth, she didn't mind.

She *did* mind the way Gideon's gaze followed her as she moved around the kitchen, fixing her own coffee. Her stomach was suddenly full of butterflies, and her knees felt rubbery, almost exactly the sensation she had felt during her one foray into acting in a high school play. Stage fright, all because a man was staring at her? Get real, Sara!

She reminded him, Gideon thought unexpectedly, of a sweet, small brown mouse. Evidently she dropped the tough act around her grandfather, and she even moved differently—gracefully. More like a woman and less like a boy.

She joined them at the table with her coffee, giving him a polite, casual smile. "Grandfather says he offered you a job. Did you come out to accept it?"

"Yes, I did."

Zeke spoke. "I told him he's welcome to stay in the bunkhouse and eat with us."

"That was the big inducement," Gideon said, watching Sara for any sign of objection. "That fleabag motel is charging me thirty bucks a night."

Since Zeke did all the cooking, Sara couldn't much object to that, but she wasn't too thrilled at the prospect of cleaning out the bunkhouse, which hadn't been opened in almost five years. "What if the roof leaks?" she said, feeling strangely helpless.

"We'll fix it," Zeke said. "I don't reckon it does though, Sarey. I've been going in there a couple of times a year to make sure it was still okay in case we needed it. Now we need it." He looked at Gideon. "You'll bring your stuff up here today?"

"Yeah, in a couple of hours. I need to check out of the motel and give my uncle a call to tell him where to find me if he needs me."

Sara suddenly remembered him mentioning that his black hat had been a gift from his uncle. "You're close to him, aren't you?"

Gideon didn't evade. "You bet. By the time he took me in, he'd already raised six sons of his own. You'd have thought he'd have been too tired to bother, but he was never too tired for me. Now he's old and none too well, and all his boys are scattered to the four winds."

"You can call him from here," Sara said impulsively. "You can always call him from here. Anytime."

Gideon smiled, a warm expression that touched Sara almost physically. "Thanks, Sara."

"And now maybe you'll satisfy my curiosity," Zeke said.

Gideon suddenly looked a little wary, Sara thought, and was uneasy with the realization that this man might not be what he seemed. "Sure," he said, sounding almost offhand about it.

"Last night you told Sara your grandfather got your attention. What were you up to?"

"Grandfather!" Sara was appalled. That simply wasn't a question you asked anyone.

"It's okay, Sara," Gideon said unexpectedly. "He's got a right to know what kind of man he's hiring."

Which meant that Gideon Ironheart didn't have anything really serious to hide, Sara thought hopefully. Either that or he was a bigger con artist than she wanted to know. And that was unfair, she scolded herself. Why should she be suspicious before she had cause?

Gideon and her grandfather were looking at one another with a kind of seriousness that seemed odd considering that Zeke had already hired the younger man and, until a moment or two ago, had seemed quite favorably impressed. Now, suddenly, it was as if somehow another factor had been thrown into the equation. What had happened?

"I was a real troublemaker for a while," Gideon said slowly, never taking his eyes from Zeke. "Drugs. Booze. Fast cars. A little shoplifting for the thrill of it. I was lucky. I didn't get caught with weed on me, but I got caught with an expensive belt buckle I hadn't paid for. I got grand theft and sixth months on probation. Three weeks into my time, my grandfather found me out behind the barn rolling a joint. One thing led to another, and he eventually took me into town and turned me in. I did the rest of my six months in jail, fell behind a year in school, and came out a wiser man. I haven't been in trouble since."

Zeke nodded, satisfied. "Not everyone learns that quick."

"What I learned, old man, was that I can't stand to be caged. I can't stand being kept locked up away from the sun and the wind, and I can't stand having other people control me. I barely survived it once. I wouldn't survive it a second time. So I learned to get my thrills in legal ways."

Again Zeke nodded, as if he found this perfectly comprehensible. "A young man who is wild often grows into an old man with wisdom."

One corner of Gideon's mouth quirked. "I'm a long way from wisdom, Zeke. Believe me."

"A long way from old, too," Zeke said on a chuckle.

"And your grandfather?" Sara asked. "Is he still around?"

Gideon shook his head. "He passed on twelve years ago. Before I got old enough to really listen to him."

Something about the way he said that told Sara how much he regretted the loss, and she warmed a little more toward him.

"Well," said Gideon, pushing back from the table, "I'd better go check out before they charge me for another night. I'll be back in plenty of time to help with the chores, Zeke. Don't get started without me."

Sara watched him go, only half-aware that her grandfather was watching her. All man, she thought with a delicious, frightening inward thrill. Gideon Ironheart was *all* man. And he probably had a string of broken hearts behind him to prove it, she reminded herself. Still, it couldn't hurt to admire his rear view as he strolled to his truck.

"Seems like a good man," Zeke remarked.

"Maybe." She was determined to reserve judgment, and faced her grandfather with her chin stubbornly set. "Time will tell. Now I need to get out there and clean the bunkhouse. That place must be layered under inches of dust and dirt after all this time."

"I'll do it, Sarey. I offered it to the man."

"Forget it," she said, softening. "Your arthritis will give you fits, and it won't take me long at all to do a little dusting."

Zeke rose from the table and came over to wrap an arm around her shoulders. "We all depend on you too much, child."

They were nearly of a height, and Sara had to tip her head only a little bit to meet his eyes. "I wouldn't have been able to do any of it without you, Grandfather, and you know it perfectly well. I couldn't have taken a job if you hadn't come to live here and look after Joey. I would have lost the ranch for sure, and maybe I would have had to give Joey up."

And suddenly she gave a soft laugh. "Right now, that doesn't sound so awful, does it?"

Zeke joined her laughter and squeezed her in a warm hug. "No, Sarey, right now it doesn't sound bad at all."

The bunkhouse was dusty, all right, and there were plenty of cobwebs, but otherwise it was a sound and sturdy structure. It had four rooms, three with beds, and a front room with a wood stove, a couch and a couple of overstuffed chairs. A mouse had gotten into one of the chairs, pulling out a little stuffing, but the damage wasn't too bad. The plank floors needed a good dust mopping, and then a swipe with the wet mop.

A couple of hours later, she reached the last bedroom and noticed the stack of boxes and a trunk in the corner. Zeke's things, she thought. He'd stored them in here when he had come to live with her and Joey. Maybe he would want to bring them up to the house now.

Absently, not really paying attention to what she was doing, she flipped open one of the boxes. Her attention was immediately snared by a gold-framed portrait, and she lifted it with slow hands and a wondering heart.

This was her grandparents' wedding portrait, she realized, and sank onto the edge of the bed so she could study it. That would have been 1941, she thought. Just at the beginning of the war. Zeke would have been about nineteen, and his bride, Alma Dietz, would have been barely seventeen.

The photo was sepia-toned, but there was no mistaking that Alma was fair and Zeke was dark. Zeke wore an army uniform proudly, and his raven hair was trimmed close, revealing the proud shape of his skull and cheeks. Alma, with wispy blond hair and eyes so light they barely registered in the photo, looked as fragile as Zeke looked strong. Her dress was white, and her veil was trimmed with rosebuds.

Why, Sara wondered, had Alma's missionary father blessed this union? Prejudices had been even worse then than they were now, and they were bad enough now. Had

Alma been so persuasive? Or had the war made other matters seem unimportant? Or had her great grandfather simply been a man of principle without prejudice?

She was tempted to ask Zeke about it, then hesitated. This photo was out here, after all, hidden away with things he evidently had no need of. Maybe it was better left hidden. Perhaps the memories were still too painful for him in some way.

Sara devoted another couple of minutes to looking at the face of the grandmother she had never known, then slipped the framed portrait back into the box. Maybe she would just mention the boxes casually and see what Zeke said. Maybe he wouldn't want them out here where Gideon could rummage through them.

And maybe he would tell her why they weren't in the house with him.

The bathroom took a little longer to clean, partly because it had been years since anyone had scoured the scum from the tub, and partly because Sara kept coming face-to-face with memories of her father. Ted Yates had worked nearly a solid month one summer to bring water and modern facilities to the bunkhouse. Sara, ten at the time, had worked right alongside him, getting her first lessons in plumbing, soldering, welding and good, old-fashioned ditch digging. The ditch, to lay pipe from the well, had taken most of the time, needing to be pickaxed out of rocky ground and made deep enough so the pipes wouldn't freeze in the winter. Looking at her hands now, Sara remembered her blisters and her wonderful sense of accomplishment.

And remembered her dad hugging her to his side, saying, "You're a great gal, Sarey. Some man's going to love you to death."

But George had panicked at the mere thought of loving her and marrying her, and Sara, at twenty-eight, had given up hope of any man loving her at all, never mind loving her to death.

Then, slowly and softly, as easily as the words he had whispered to that damn mustang hours ago had slipped into her ears, the memory of Gideon Ironheart slipped into her mind. A woman would give a lot to be loved by a man like that, Sara thought. A whole lot.

But not her. Damn it, she was never again going to be any man's fool. Never!

Chapter 3

"Steady, boy. Steady." Gideon spoke soothingly to the wary mustang, patting the horse's shoulder reassuringly. In the four days he had been working for Zeke Jackson, he had spent some time coaxing the roan stallion to accept him. It was important, he thought, to get the horse to tolerate at least one person, because if the animal ever got truly sick or badly injured, he was going to need human help. So far, Gideon thought, he seemed to be gaining ground. The horse no longer shuddered so violently at his proximity and now didn't even attempt to evade his touch.

The horse had fire in his eye, Gideon thought. He'd survived the wilderness, capture and the BLM corrals, and yet he hadn't sacrificed any of himself.

"You sure haven't, boy," Gideon murmured, stroking the sleek neck and shoulder, and almost fancied the horse snorted an affirmative. "Still just as free and independent as day one, aren't you? Still you, through and through."

The stallion bobbed his head and whinnied, then butted Gideon's shoulder. Gideon chuckled.

The horse, he thought, with a deep, private pang, had achieved something that he himself had failed to. It was hard to put into words, this sense that the horse had fulfilled itself while he, Gideon, had not. Hard to explain even to himself the feeling that his life had somehow been bent out of shape, that he had sacrificed himself to goals that hadn't mattered. Hard to find words to tell himself that this horse had become the best horse he could be, but that Gideon Ironheart was a long way from being the best man he could be.

He clucked soothingly to the animal and let liquid syllables tumble over his tongue, the sounds and cadences learned so long ago and somehow never forgotten. And thinking of his uncle brought his reverie around to his grandfather, and the old man's warning.

"Boy, a life is a portrait. It's a picture you paint every day, every minute, every second, with the palette you were given at birth. It's an expression of yourself, whether you want it to be or not. Make sure it's a picture you're proud of."

Well, Gideon thought now, he sure as hell wasn't proud of his portrait. Not that he was ashamed of it. No, he hadn't done very much that he was ashamed of, because he'd realized a long time ago that he had to live with himself first of all. But he hadn't done a whole hell of a lot to be proud of, either. What did a few skyscrapers amount to, after all? They sure didn't measure up to a Sistine Chapel, or a *Mona Lisa*. They didn't even measure up to a guy who could raise a good crowd for his funeral.

Suddenly his lips quirked and he almost laughed out loud. God, talk about sinking into self-pity! What had gotten into him? He was almost never like this.

"You've got that damn mustang mesmerized."

Gideon glanced toward the fence and saw a man he didn't recognize. Tall, lean, well-built, the guy was dressed like everyone in these parts—jeans, Western shirt and straw cowboy hat. Gideon himself had traded his black felt hat for a straw one, in concession to the warmth of the day.

"Howdy," Gideon said quietly. "Something I can do for you?"

The man shook his head. "I'm here to see Sara, but I caught sight of you and couldn't resist watching. Where'd you learn to whisper a horse?"

"My uncle taught me when I was a kid." Realizing that his time with the horse was over for now, Gideon gave the stallion a friendly pat and then headed for the fence himself. "Does Sara know you're here?"

"Not yet. I'll go up to the house in just a minute. I don't recall seeing you around here before. You're new in these parts."

Gideon nodded. "Lately from Georgia." This guy was good-looking, he thought, just the kind of man women seemed to go for. What was he to Sara? "The name's Ironheart."

"I'm Jeff Cumberland." He stuck his hand out and shook Gideon's briskly. "I own the Bar C, up north from here."

Gideon had heard of the Bar C. It was the biggest, most successful ranching operation in the county, and Zeke must have mentioned it at least twice, as had other people around town when they thought he might be looking for work.

Jeff continued speaking. "I don't have a man who can talk a horse that way. In fact, I don't think I've seen anyone do it in a dozen years or more. If you get tired of the Double Y, come see me."

"Trying to steal my hired hand, Jeff?" Sara asked. She had come up almost silently, and both men started a little at the sound of her voice. The first thing Gideon noticed was that she was annoyed. Not at him, but at Cumberland.

Jeff smiled and shook his head. "Nope. Forget I said anything."

Sara put her hands on her hips in a posture Gideon recognized. Sara, who hadn't shown him the tough side of herself since he started working here, was showing it to Cumberland now. What had this man done to her to make her feel she had to be tough around him?

"What brings you up here?" she asked Jeff.

"I wanted to make our usual arrangement about summer pasturage. Are you agreeable?"

Sara nodded. She needed the money, even if she hated dealing with a Cumberland. Of course, it wasn't Jeff's fault that George had turned tail like a yellow-bellied skunk. In fact, Jeff had been as sympathetic as a big brother, had even offered to date her for a while to save her face. No, she told herself, she shouldn't be mad at Jeff. But every time she saw him, she remembered George and her humiliation at his hands.

"I brought the papers with me," Jeff said. "It's the same as always, except the fee has been upped five percent, if that's agreeable?"

"That's fine. Come on inside and I'll give you some coffee while I look it over."

Gideon watched them walk to the house, wondering what the story was between those two. And he was surprised to feel a rather hot irritation at the idea that Sara had a past with that man—the biggest rancher in the county.

He looked down at himself, at his dusty jeans and scuffed boots, and tried not to remember that he wasn't even a connector anymore. Tried not to feel as if he were falling, tried not to see the flashing, splintering images of spinning blue sky and wildly careening beams.

Dizzily, he reached out and grabbed the fence rail for stability. It would pass. The vertigo always passed, because it wasn't real. It was imagined. It was just a psychological reaction, that was all.

Breathing deeply, he kept his eyes open to counter the vivid, spinning mental images and the sensation of tumbling end over end. Nausea welled in the pit of his stomach, and he swallowed it.

It would pass. Everything passed eventually.

In the kitchen, Sara poured two mugs of coffee and carried them to the table where Jeff Cumberland sat. "I wish you'd refrain from stealing Gideon Ironheart, at least until

Joey is back out here to help my grandfather. Zeke can't handle it all alone.''

"I got the feeling Ironheart isn't in a mood to go anywhere." Jeff smiled and gave a little shrug. "Maybe I can borrow him for a few hours here and there?"

"That's up to him." She took a seat across from him and reached for the contract.

"What about Joey?" Jeff asked. "How long will he be locked up?"

Sara shook her head. "I guess it's up to Nate, from what Judge Williams said when she revoked Joey's probation. With the way Nate feels about it, I guess Joey's going to spend some time there."

"I'm really sorry, Sara," Jeff said. "I know how hard you've worked and how hard you tried to bring him up right. I guess not everybody turns out okay. Like George."

Sara drew a sharp breath and looked at him. She and Jeff had studiously avoided mentioning his brother for nearly ten years now. "George?"

Jeff grimaced. "He left his wife. Can you believe it? He left her and their kid because it wasn't what he wanted. I could kill him."

"What—what will she do?"

"I've asked her and the kid to come stay with me. Just because my brother is a reprehensible, good-for-nothing jackass doesn't mean his wife and kid should suffer."

"Is she coming?"

"I don't know. I think she's in pretty much of a state of shock." He shook his head. "She loved him, Sara. Just like you did. What the hell is the matter with him?"

"I can't imagine, Jeff. I really can't." And for the first time it occurred to her that she might have gotten off lightly when George left her at the altar.

"Well, I didn't come up here to saddle you with my troubles," he said after a moment. "I guess I just wanted you to know that you were never the problem."

Just as Sara turned her attention back to the contract, Gideon opened the screen door and stepped in. "Just wanted a mug of that coffee, Sara."

"Help yourself." As soon as he had moved into the bunkhouse, she had told him he was welcome to come into the kitchen anytime for coffee or a soft drink. So far, apart from mealtimes, he hadn't availed himself of the invitation, but here he was. Helplessly, Sara watched him saunter across the kitchen to the coffeepot. There ought to be a law, she thought, against men who looked like that walking like that. It was an almost animal prowl.

Glancing away, she found Jeff regarding her curiously. Before a blush could betray her, she fastened her attention on the contract.

Gideon poured a cup a coffee and leaned back against the counter as he sipped it. He was acting like a fool, he thought, coming in here this way, but he couldn't seem to make himself walk out. Well, he admitted, Sara was a damn attractive woman, at least according to his lights. He'd been trying to ignore the attraction because he was only passing through, but right now that didn't seem half as important as making sure Cumberland didn't put the make on Sara, especially considering how she had bristled. Since she had something against the man, it seemed wise to be protective.

"What brought you up here from Georgia?" Jeff asked him while Sara read.

"Vacation," Gideon replied promptly. He'd answered the question so many times that he had a stock answer. "I finished off my last job and decided it was as good a time as any to do some of the sight-seeing I've always wanted to do."

"Last job?" said Cumberland. "Where was that?"

Sara answered without looking up from the contract. "Gideon's an ironworker. I think he's only here because he likes Zeke and Zeke asked for his help." She scanned the last page, then looked at Jeff. "Looks good to me. My only qualification is that I don't want your cowboys crossing the fence line at the falls. That meadow up there is one of my favorite places. If their horses chew up the ground, the place will get full of sage and maybe choke out the wildflowers.''

"I'll make a point of telling them, Sara. If you have any trouble about it, let me know."

Declining an offer of more coffee after they had signed both copies of the contract, Jeff said his good-byes and left. Gideon was still standing against the counter with his coffee, and Sara glanced at him.

"Something wrong?" she asked.

Only with him. He shrugged. "Just wanted some coffee. What's this about him leasing your pasture?"

"I don't have a lot of grazing land, but I've got a lot of water. Come June, Jeff moves part of his herd into my pasture so he doesn't overtax his own water supplies and grazing."

"If you've got the water, why can't you raise your own herd?"

"Because I don't have enough good grazing to raise enough cattle to make it economically worthwhile. I could raise a few head, maybe, but not enough to make this a going concern."

"You've sure got some beautiful land here. I can see why you don't want to part with it."

Sara almost smiled at him. Most people thought she needed her head examined for working so hard to keep a nonproductive piece of land. "This place is part of me," she admitted. "Leaving it would be like cutting off my arm. But it sure would be nice if I could figure out some way to make it self-sufficient without sacrificing the beauty or the privacy."

"You could board horses," Gideon said, the words popping out before he considered them.

"But everyone around here..."

"Not everyone around here," he corrected her. "People in town, for one. They have no place to stable them. People who might want their horses broken before they take them to more convenient stables nearer their homes. Maybe some people who'd like to save a mustang but have no place to put one.''

She instinctively opened her mouth to disagree, but then she stopped, reconsidering. ''Maybe,'' she said after a moment. ''It's an idea. I'll give it some thought.''

''Good.'' He put his mug in the sink and headed toward the door. ''Zeke wants me to go to town and pick up some stuff for him. I'll be back before dinner.''

They couldn't possibly, Sara thought as she watched him go, be paying him enough to work as hard as he worked. Gideon Ironheart evidently preferred not to be idle, and jobs that had needed doing for years around here were beginning to finally get done.

The woman was getting under his skin, Gideon thought as he drove into town with Zeke's list in his pocket. For a minute there, when she had opened her mouth to object and then had changed her mind, he'd had an almost overwhelming urge to bend over and plunge his tongue into the warm, silky depths of her mouth.

He didn't like this at all. He was forty-one, not sixteen. It had been almost that long since the last time his hormones had ruled him, and he didn't like the idea that some woman could make a mockery of his restraint and self-control. He didn't like the feeling that some complete innocent, with no such intention at all, could cause his loins to stir and his heart to race.

If she'd meant to attract him, he wouldn't have minded half so much that he had responded. But Sara Yates honestly wasn't interested in attracting a man. She didn't send significant looks or make tempting little gestures, didn't put on makeup or do any of those other things a woman did to advertise her availability. He couldn't quite make up his mind whether she was unaware of such things or just wasn't aware of him as a man.

No, he thought after a moment, that wasn't quite it, either. A couple of times he had caught her gaze following him. She knew he was a man, all right, and flickers of interest showed from time to time. Sara just didn't want to be interested. Fine. He was willing to let it rest.

For now.

He had hoped that his frequent appearances in town would start putting him into the category of a familiar face, but while shopkeepers nodded and chatted with him, they still didn't respond in any detail to his gambits about Micah Parish. He'd better let that drop for a while, he decided, or somebody might notice his interest and get suspicious.

And maybe he was going to have to break down and meet the man. That was something he'd wanted to avoid, because, once done, it was irrevocable. Once Micah became aware of him, matters would no longer be under Gideon's sole control, and he wasn't at all sure he wanted that to happen. And then there was the matter of meeting him. He couldn't just walk up, introduce himself and tell the truth. No, he would need some kind of cover.

And there was always Sara, he found himself thinking. She worked with Parish and would be the likeliest person to introduce him if he decided to go that route. So maybe, if he worked at it, he could just get her to talk about the man.

Columbine, a sorrel mare, and her new foal were frisking together in the pasture near the barn, while the roan mustang stood in the corral and watched them, hooves planted widely, ears pricked forward and nostrils flaring as he sought their scent. When Gideon pulled his truck into the yard, Zeke and his lifelong friend, Chester Elk Horn, were standing at the fence and watching.

Gideon joined the two men at the fence and gave Chester, whom he'd met the other day, a nod. "What's up, Zeke?"

Zeke chuckled. "Boy meets girl. Same old story. That mustang has been putting on quite a show trying to get Columbine's attention."

"And she ain't giving it." Chester grinned.

Columbine wouldn't be interested for some time yet, but that didn't seem to faze the mustang, who now reared a little and then pranced along the fence, tail held high.

Shaking his head a little and smiling to himself, Gideon went to unload his truck. Zeke and Chester made a pair, he thought. Something about those two would never be old.

After he unloaded the truck, he went to wash up at the faucet out behind the bunkhouse. A cup of coffee was sounding real good right about now. Maybe he would venture into Sara's territory and get one.

It was as he stood shaking water off his hands and arms that a flash from the trees farther uphill caught his attention. Sort of like sun catching on glass.

There. Again.

That wasn't right. A piece of glass lying on the ground would have made a steady reflection. Whatever was reflecting the sunlight was moving.

Somebody was up there.

Without giving it another thought, he started trotting in that direction. A hiker probably, gone astray. As the weather warmed, every bit of wilderness in America became overrun by hikers and campers from all over the world. He would just check things out, make sure everything was okay. Sara and Zeke wouldn't mind a hiker or two crossing their spread.

What they didn't like was dirt bikers. "They tear up the ground, kill the vegetation, pollute the atmosphere with fumes, and ruin the peace and quiet with their racket," Zeke had said. "They scare the horses, drive the deer and elk away... damn vandals, that's all they are." The Double Y was posted against trespassers primarily because of off-the-road vehicles.

They also didn't like poachers, and from time to time they had trouble with out-of-season hunters who wanted to bag an elk or a moose.

So he would just go up and check things out.

Before he got halfway across the meadow, however, his quarry figured out he'd been spotted. With a roar of his motorcycle engine, he took off into the trees, giving Gideon a view only of a flash of sun off metal.

Dirt biker, Gideon thought, listening to the engine roar fade with distance. He stood there for a minute, clenching and unclenching his fists, angry at the intruder. For a long time he'd lived in cities, and he'd never owned property, so his territory had been limited to his personal space. Suddenly the Double Y seemed to have become his territory, and it irritated the hell out of him that some idiot had flouted the signs and ridden his bike all over Sara and Zeke's property. What was it with people like that? he wondered. Why couldn't they respect other people's rights?

He turned at the sound of boots moving through the grass and saw Zeke approaching. "Dirt biker," he said.

Zeke nodded. "I heard him. Don't go after them yourself, Ironheart. You never know when one might be armed. It just isn't worth it."

"Makes me almost want to string wire here and there as a lesson."

Zeke shook his head. "Think of the horses. They'd be the ones to suffer. Come on. It's just one biker. Let's go get some coffee."

"Where's Chester?" Gideon asked as they walked toward the house.

"He headed back to town."

"Why doesn't he just stay up here in the bunkhouse? I sure wouldn't mind."

"Chester hasn't taken a dime from anybody in his life," Zeke said. "He'd feel like he was taking charity, and he wouldn't like it. Besides, he'd miss playing checkers over at Bayard's Garage."

That was another one of the local charms, Gideon thought. A bunch of old coots settled on chairs beneath the tree at the corner of Bayard's Garage and played checkers with each other by the hour, weather permitting. On the couple of occasions he'd gone by, he'd stopped to watch them play. They sat there, chewing tobacco, telling tales as tall as the Rockies, and laughing the hearty, wheezy laughter of old men. Dirk provided a spittoon and kept the price on his soft-drink machine at cost for them.

Just another one of those things that got a man to thinking that Conard County wouldn't be a bad place to grow old.

The house was quiet when they entered, no sound issuing from the other rooms or the upstairs. Sara must have decided to take a nap, Gideon thought. He'd been a little surprised to see her up and about at noon when Cumberland had arrived, because she'd worked the graveyard shift last night.

He didn't like her working graveyard. He'd stewed about it the last two nights while she did it, and it hadn't helped to tell himself that it was none of his business and that she'd been doing it for years. It didn't help to remind himself that she was a trained, experienced cop and that she carried a gun she knew how to use.

Simple fact was, Gideon Ironheart was old-fashioned in some ways. Some women might even consider him a male chauvinist, though they would be wrong. He was perfectly willing to acknowledge that a determined woman could do anything a man could. And Sara was a determined woman. He had no doubt she was a damn good cop, too. That wasn't the problem. The problem was, he had been raised to believe that a man owed a woman his protection. The nuns hadn't been plagued with any notions of female equality. They'd raised the boys to be chivalrous and protective. His uncle and grandfather had done little to disturb those ideas. Men were the warriors. Period.

All of that made it hard to stand back and be silent when a woman went ahead and did something dangerous. Something a *man* ought to be doing. That was all.

But he kept his mouth shut, because it really wasn't any of his business, because he knew that women felt differently about such things, and tried to ignore his discomfort.

Zeke made a fresh pot of coffee and then joined Gideon at the table. With little in the way of livestock, the pace at the Double Y was sometimes downright lazy.

"You getting restless yet, boy?" Zeke asked.

Gideon shook his head. "Not at all, old man. I don't get restless that easy."

"Then how come you never settled down?"

Gideon turned his head a little, looking out the screen door, across the porch and yard to the mountains behind the barn. Wildflowers bobbed their colorful heads along the corral fence, adding color to a green-and-blue world.

"Did you know," he said slowly, "my people—the Cherokee—had a democratic government and a constitution before Jackson drove them from Georgia? One of my people created an alphabet for our language without even being able to read English. All he did was understand the *idea* of written language. We built brick homes and schools. We had our own newspaper. We married and intermarried, farmed, and trusted Andy Jackson because he was our friend."

He turned and looked at Zeke. "Then they drove us out of our homes and sent us on the long walk, the Trail of Tears. They drove us clear to Oklahoma, and we died in the thousands on that march. But some of us survived, and we built homes and farms and married and had children.... And then came the discovery of oil. They drove us out of our homes again, and we rebuilt again. We're not restless by nature, old man. We're builders, survivors. Adaptable and strong. But not restless."

"And you?" Zeke said.

Gideon shrugged. "I moved on because I never found anything that made me want to stay once the job was done. I hate to be idle."

When the coffee was ready, Gideon rose to fill their mugs. He hadn't missed the stiffness of Zeke's movements, and while the old man didn't let his arthritis keep him from doing a single thing, Gideon couldn't see any reason not to spare him some of the little stuff.

"Thanks," Zeke said.

Gideon returned to his seat, crossing his legs loosely and fixing his attention on the world beyond the open windows and screen door. He didn't know why he'd brought up all that stuff about Cherokee history except that it was about the only thing he had that gave him a sense of his place in the scheme of things. He sure as hell didn't know a damn thing about his European half. The half that was probably responsible for the way he moved on when the job finished. The half that was undoubtedly responsible for his inability to feel that he belonged anywhere.

Zeke startled him out of thought. "You need a vision quest, boy."

Gideon turned, facing Zeke directly. "You've done it?"

"Many times. I had my first vision when I was ten, and my second one before I asked Alma to marry me." Zeke gave a faint, rueful smile. "A man has to give serious thought to what he's about to do when he considers marriage to any woman, but most especially when she's of another race and culture. My mind and heart were both troubled, so Chester took me to a *wichasha wakan*—holy man—and I followed the Lakota rite."

"You've known Chester all this time?" The thought of a friendship spanning more than fifty years was rather awe-inspiring.

"We were orphans together in the mission school. I don't know if you know anything about it, but most of the Lakota religious practices were outlawed in the last century. In fact, the massacre at Wounded Knee came about as an attempt to prevent a Ghost Dance. Then, in 1923, Congress passed the Religious Crimes Act, which outlawed the practice of all Indian religions, so things got even worse. I was a small child at the time, but the primary effect of it for me was that I needed a friend to direct me in secret to a holy man, one who wasn't even of my own people. All of it was done in such secrecy."

"And you married her?"

Zeke smiled. "I married her. I guess the most surprising thing was that her father didn't raise any objections. There are times when the strands of destiny weave together seamlessly, and without the least struggle your dreams come to pass. But first you must dream."

First you must dream. Maybe three or four times in a lifetime, if a man was lucky, he heard a truth that he recognized in his soul. This was one of those times, and Gideon sat perfectly still as he let it fill him and settle in. When had he last dreamed? he wondered suddenly. When had he last dreamed anything at all?

"Just let me know," Zeke said presently. "I can arrange it all."

The sound of footsteps alerted them to the fact that Sara was up and about again. A few moments later she appeared in the kitchen, her cheeks still flushed from sleep and her long, inky hair caught back in a loose ponytail. Smothering a yawn, she bent to kiss her grandfather's cheek, then joined them at the table with a mug of coffee.

"Where's Chester?" she asked her grandfather. "I thought you were going to ask him to dinner."

"I did, but he had other plans. You're stuck with just the two of us again, Sarey."

She gave her grandfather a teasing smile. "I don't know if I can stand it."

Zeke chuckled and reached over to pat her thigh, while Gideon wrestled with a sudden surge of the desire he was trying to ignore. She looked so sweet just now, softened by sleep, and her black-satin voice was even huskier than usual, brushing over his nerve endings like the seductive touch of warm, smooth skin.

Maybe, he found himself thinking, he ought to ask her out. Just one date, on which he could kill two birds with one stone. He could tease himself a little, which always felt good, however frustrating, and maybe he could get her to talk about Micah Parish. His conscience objected a little at his mixed motives, but he reminded himself that having mixed motives was a far cry from dishonesty.

Sara looked at him. "You look like you're pondering the fate of the world."

"He's giving some thought to *Hanblecheyapi*," Zeke said, using the Lakota word for the ceremony, speaking of it as if it were a natural thing, not an embarrassing one at all.

Sara looked at Gideon with renewed interest. "Really? You're thinking about crying for a vision?"

Gideon squirmed uncomfortably. After a lifetime in the Anglo world, some things just didn't feel comfortable. He wanted to change the subject—fast. "Partly. And partly I'm thinking about asking you to have dinner with me."

Over the years, Gideon had experienced all kinds of re-actions from women when he asked them out, everything from borderline ecstasy to utter indifference, but he didn't think he'd ever made a woman turn as white as bleached cotton.

Sara felt as if something inside her were about to splin-ter. No man had asked her out in ten years, and she had come to believe she was completely unattractive. She had also come to believe that she liked it that way. Abruptly, she knew she didn't like it that way at all, but she also couldn't suddenly believe that she *was* attractive. That any man could be interested. That Gideon Ironheart could be doing any-thing except making fun of her.

"I... No!" Rising swiftly, she left the room, and her footsteps could be heard mounting the stairs.

Gideon looked at Zeke. "What the hell did I do? Apart from maybe moving too fast, that is."

"That's for her to explain," Zeke said impassively, dark eyes almost watchful.

"Then how about some advice, old man?" He was trou-bled by Sara's reaction, by the inexplicable feeling that he had harmed her in some way. A partly guilty conscience didn't help.

Zeke chose his words carefully, betraying nothing. "Maybe you haven't given her any reason to think you find her attractive."

Gideon's mouth opened to answer, but no words emerged. He had been about to argue that a dinner invitation was ipso facto a declaration of interest but he realized that wasn't necessarily so. "Does she date at all?"

"No."

Well, that didn't shock him. He wouldn't date at all himself, except it was part of the mating game, and a man had a biological urge that had to be satisfied occasionally. He tended to avoid women like Sara, though. Women who didn't know the rules. Maybe he ought to just drop this now.

But he remembered her shocked expression and the way she had paled, and he knew he couldn't drop it. He had hurt her somehow, however unintentionally, and he just wasn't capable of leaving things that way. He looked at Zeke. "She's upstairs? In her bedroom?"

The old Shoshone nodded.

"What will you do if I go up after her?"

The faintest of smiles touched the corners of Zeke's mouth. "I'm an old man. What would you expect me to do?"

"Fight like a warrior to protect your own."

Zeke gave a small nod. "But sometimes true protection is not always doing the obvious thing."

Gideon pushed back from the table. "I'm going up."

From the kitchen he walked through a dining room that was graced by a scarred but polished cherrywood table and eight chairs with worn embroidered seat covers. Probably as old as this house, he thought as worn carpet silenced his steps. The dining room opened directly onto a living room furnished with the overstuffed pieces of another era, and everything—everything—showed signs of age, wear and care. Poor but proud, that was the history of the Yates family.

The staircase rose at the far end of the living room, along the wall right beside the front door. As soon as his booted feet hit those wooden treads, they were no longer silent. Sara could hear his approach, and he wondered if she would lock her door. Damn, why hadn't he thought this through a little more before he blurted out that invitation? What had seemed like a good idea five minutes ago suddenly looked like the ultimate in stupidity.

She didn't lock him out. She hadn't even closed her door. Maybe she didn't really believe he would have the gall to follow her. Maybe she had thought those footsteps on the stairs were her grandfather's. Whatever, he found her in the first bedroom on the left. She stood with her back to the door as she stared out the window. Sheer curtains waved lazily in the breeze, wrapping from time to time around her jean-clad legs. Her arms were tightly wrapped around herself, a defensive posture he felt as much as he saw.

"Sara?"

She sighed, a heavy, sad sound, but didn't turn around. "I'm sorry, Gideon. I was unforgivably rude."

"Not to worry." He stepped into the room and looked around with quick curiosity. If a woman lived here, no one would ever guess. The room was sexless and sterile—except for the tiny pink stuffed cat tucked away on the corner of the dresser. "I guess I took you by surprise."

"Mmm." Still she didn't face him. "Did my grandfather tell you to come up here?"

"Not exactly."

"Well, I apologize, but I'm not going to change my mind, so you might as well go."

He stared at her stiff back, noticing its graceful, slender line, noticing just how small the bones beneath her creamy skin were. She was a woman, all right. A woman in hiding for some reason.

"Thanks for telling me," he said quietly. "For a minute there, I thought I was going to have to beg."

It took a moment, but at last a chuckle rose in her, shaking her shoulders and spilling over her lips, a gentle cascade of sound. God, he thought, that laugh was an aphrodisiac! She turned, still chuckling, to face him. Her cheeks were flushed, and her eyes sparkled with amusement.

"Nothing throws you, does it?" she remarked.

"Very little." He stepped closer. "I have to admit, it throws me a little when I ask a woman to dinner and she turns as white as a sheet."

Her smile faded. "Are you asking for an explanation?"

She was looking wary again, he noticed. A lot like that mustang outside. "Naw," he said casually, easing closer, keeping his voice soothing. "It's none of my business."

"That's right."

"But I wondered if maybe you have something against Cherokees."

She blinked, obviously astonished. "Why would I? And how was I supposed to know you're Cherokee?"

He shrugged and moved a little closer. "You're at least a quarter Shoshone, right? Well, for all I know, there's bad blood between our tribes."

She was watching him in helpless fascination, so distracted by his crazy suggestion that she was utterly oblivious to his close approach. Sleight of hand, that was what it was, and she was falling for it.

"I never heard of any bad blood," she said. "And really, I didn't know you were Cherokee until just now, when you told me."

"Actually, I'm *half* Cherokee."

"Like Micah Parish. He's half Cherokee and half European."

"Yeah?" He was only a foot away from her now, and he halted. "So you didn't turn me down because of my blood?"

She blinked. "Good Lord, no!"

"Then why?"

"Because I don't want to be a fool again." The words were out before she could stop them, and before she could take them back, he covered her mouth with the hard, callused palm of his hand.

"Shh," he said, calming her as he had calmed the mustang. "Easy, Sara. I don't want to make a fool of anybody. Not you. Not me."

"Then why...?" The words vibrated against his hand, and her wide brown eyes never left his face.

"Because you turn me on, lady," he said bluntly, watching color flood her cheeks all the way to the roots of her hair. "I figure that's worth looking into." He dropped his hand, but she didn't attempt to speak. "Maybe it'll wear off in a couple of hours and I can forget about it. Maybe it won't. There's only one way to find out. Go out with me tonight, Sara Jane Yates."

Sara stared up at him, unaware that every bit of her yearning, every bit of her uncertainty, was showing in her eyes right now. Gideon Ironheart said she turned him on, and her insides clenched when she thought of him saying that. This incredibly virile man, so much older and more experienced than she, wanted to take her out because she turned him on. Oh, God! It was at once a dream come true and a terrifying threat. Whatever it was that men really wanted, Sara Yates knew she didn't have enough of it. George's defection had made that clear.

She licked her lips. "I don't think—" She couldn't finish. She couldn't bring herself to say no.

"Please?" He coaxed her the way he would have coaxed a shy horse. He didn't mind asking. A man too proud to ask never got anything.

Finally she nodded, apparently unable to voice even so much as a yes.

"Good," he said with a broad smile. He turned and walked to the bedroom door, where he paused and looked back. "Tonight at seven," he told her. "Wear jeans and bring a warm jacket."

Chapter 4

The whole damn county was going to hear about this, Sara thought unhappily as she waited for Gideon that evening. Being a deputy had brought her into contact with nearly everyone in the county, and there wasn't a restaurant or a diner for a hundred and fifty miles in any direction where she could be sure she wouldn't be recognized. By this time tomorrow, everyone would know that Sara Yates, who hadn't dated since George Cumberland had left her standing at the altar, had been seen dining in the company of a stranger.

She could just imagine the curious looks, the speculation, the outright smirks she would get from some of the lowlife she had to deal with in her job. And come Sunday, the Bible Study Group would probably give her the third degree. Oh, Lord, why hadn't she refused to go out with him?

This close to the mountains, the sun vanished early, leaving the ground in twilight while the sky remained bright overhead. There was still plenty of light to see by when Gideon's truck pulled into the yard, returning from his sec-

ond trip to town that day, but the shadows that gave depth
were gone.

Taking Gideon at his word, she had dressed in fresh jeans,
a chambray shirt and her denim jacket. Stubbornly she had
refused to use even a dab of makeup, and she had plaited her
hair into two braids that fell to her breasts. Nobody was ever
going to say that she had gussied herself up for a man.

Gideon climbed out of his truck and walked toward her
across the hard-packed earth with surefooted ease and grace.
Watching him, Sara suddenly imagined him walking along
one of those incredibly narrow beams at those incredible
heights. His every movement was controlled, she realized.
Fine-tuned and accurate. Ready to deal with any unexpected obstacle or change of terrain. She had never seen a
man move that way before, so fluidly and precisely.

He reached the porch and stayed at the bottom of the two
steps, looking up at her. "I really didn't think you'd be
here," he said.

Sara caught her breath as she unexpectedly saw all this
from his point of view. She had been looking at it from her
own perspective as a possibility for him to humiliate her, but
she had utterly failed to consider just how much he had exposed himself to embarrassment. He had laid himself open
by asking her out in the first place, then had done it again
by coming to get her when he thought she might have fled.

"It's just a date, Sara," he said quietly. Reaching out, he
caught her cold fingers in his warm hand and tugged gently. "We'll eat and we'll talk, and maybe we'll start to become friends."

Why? The question was there in her eyes as she looked at
him and hesitated.

Why? Damn it, he thought, it was too early for questions
like that, all those complicating questions he'd managed to
avoid for nearly twenty years. What he wanted, *all* he
wanted, was a simple, uncomplicated evening in the presence of a woman who somehow turned him on. Maybe he
would steal a kiss or two and get himself really hot and
bothered, but that was as far as it would go. Ever. A woman

her age ought to be able to handle that, surely. But, as he looked up into her uncertain gaze, he knew she was no ordinary woman, and her age had nothing to do with anything.

"Okay," he said, and let go of her hand. Turning, he headed back to his truck. "Tell Zeke I'll see him in the morning."

Sara felt again that painful splintering sensation, as if somewhere deep inside she knew she was making a mistake, even though her mind told her she was avoiding one. Watching Gideon walk away, she suddenly saw the long years stretching in front of her, years that would grow increasingly empty unless she filled them with friends.

"Gideon?"

He paused and looked back over his shoulder. "Ma'am?"

"I thought we had a date."

He turned to face her then, settling his hands on his hips and cocking his pelvis to one side. Sara felt her breath catch, and her hand suddenly tingled with the memory of his warm, dry touch.

"We do," he said, "as long as you understand that I don't put out. One good-night kiss is as far as I'll go, Sara Yates."

The laugh rose from the pit of her nervous stomach and popped from her lips like a bubble breaking the surface of a still pool. His remark had been outrageously absurd, so absurd she couldn't prevent the laughter. But she had also taken his point. She was leaping to conclusions, crossing bridges they might never reach. Taking too seriously what was only meant to be a little bit of fun.

This time when he held out his hand, she stepped down from the porch and joined him.

"It's a beautiful evening," he remarked as he handed her up into his truck. "Is that jacket going to be warm enough against the chill later?"

"It'll be fine. It's lined."

"How's Joey handling his incarceration?" he asked as he guided the truck down the rough, rutted private road.

"Not well. He hasn't spoken a word to anyone since Zeke brought him in."

Gideon glanced at her, giving her a slight smile. "That's a good sign, Sara. He's thinking, not shooting his mouth off. Give it time."

"Is that how you acted when your grandfather got your attention?"

He shook his head. "I think I was a lot further gone than Joey probably is."

"Why?"

"Well, from what I see, your brother comes from a pretty good home. I grew up in an orphanage until I was twelve, and I had a serious attitude problem."

Sara turned on the seat to better see him. "Were you adopted finally?"

"With that attitude? Not likely. About the time I turned eleven, Sister Mary Paul came to the orphanage. She was one of these energetic types who could hardly hold still and could never leave well enough alone. She was looking through old files one day and saw my birth certificate, which showed that my mother had been born in Oklahoma. She was off and running with that, and finally, more than a year later, tracked down my uncle, William Lightfoot. He came for me before the week was out."

"Why—" Sara bit back the question before it fully emerged. It was none of her business, and he would tell her what he wanted her to know.

"Why did it take him so damn long? You know, I used to ask myself that question. It was all explained to me, but at that age I didn't listen very well. I'm a hell of a lot older now, and I understand some things a hell of a lot better. My mother was disowned by my grandfather when she insisted on marrying my father, who was Anglo. The old man told her she was dead to her family, and she believed him."

"How awful!"

"Oh, it gets better yet. The marriage didn't work. When they split, my mother didn't go home to Oklahoma but took me to Atlanta instead. No one knew where she was, and I guess my grandfather was still insisting she was dead. By the time he got over that, she and I had both vanished into smoke."

Sara had the worst urge to reach out and touch him. "What about your father?"

Gideon's hands tightened around the wheel. This was the part of the subject he didn't want to discuss. Still couldn't discuss fairly. Too many years of hurt, anger and bitterness lay there. "Who knows?" he managed to say finally. "Who knows?"

He turned them onto the county road and headed away from town.

"Where are we going?"

He glanced at her and smiled. "That's a surprise. It took a lot of ingenuity, I want you to know, to come up with someplace we could go where the whole county wouldn't be discussing the lady deputy's date."

A laugh escaped her. "You've figured this place out."

"I lived in a place like this once." Years ago, miles ago, when he'd been cocky and too angry to recognize the good things that he *did* have.

The road wound higher into the mountains, and the air grew chillier as day faded even more. Sara knew there was nothing up this way for fifty or more miles, but she was content suddenly to let the evening unfold as it would.

"You must have been so angry," she remarked.

"I spent a lot of years being angry. Too many. My grandfather lived to regret what he'd done, and he made it up to me by straightening me out when everybody else gave up. My uncle loved me like a son. Still does. But I'll admit, understanding has been a long time in coming."

He pulled off the highway on a narrow track Sara recognized well. It led to a small glade through which a mountain brook tumbled and where, at this time of year, wildflowers made a thick carpet.

"It's your land," he remarked. "I guess you can throw us off if you want to."

"Why would I want to? This is my favorite place. How did you ever find it?"

He flashed her a smile. "An old Shoshone whispered in my ear."

Gideon Ironheart was a truly exceptional man, Sara thought as he parked the truck. He just kept right on shattering all her expectations.

Since he wouldn't let her help him, she wandered in the glade, admiring the Indian paintbrush blooms that seemed to glow in the twilight like tiny fires. The brook tumbled wildly over rocks, hissing and splashing with spring vigor, still icy cold from the snowfields that had given it birth.

"Ready for supper?" He had to raise his voice a little to be heard over the noisy rush of the water.

Sara turned to him with a smile. "I'm famished." And she was. Her nerves had settled down finally, probably because he had gone to the trouble of bringing her to her favorite spot on earth.

And then she looked beyond him and gasped with pleasure. The darkening glade had become a fairy-tale setting. He had lit a campfire, and beside it dinner had been laid out on a colorful blanket. She had expected paper plates, but not champagne served in plastic goblets. She hadn't expected to see fresh strawberries heaped in a bowl, or that he would actually be planning to cook over the fire. She had anticipated sandwiches, or cold chicken from Maude's, not T-bones freshly cooked and foil-wrapped potatoes baking in the fire.

Gideon liked the expression on her face as she surveyed his efforts. She looked...enchanted. Until this very moment he would have sworn the expression could have appeared only on the face of a five-year-old on Christmas morning. And it was the first time in all his forty-one years that he had ever brought that look to someone's face.

Uncomfortable suddenly, he cleared his throat. "Grab a seat," he said roughly. Damn, what was so special about a stupid picnic? "Eat some strawberries. It'll be a while before those potatoes are done."

A little startled by his sudden gruffness, Sara glanced at him but couldn't tell what had disturbed him. Forcing herself to shrug it away, she sat cross-legged on the blanket and reached for a strawberry. "This is fabulous," she told him sincerely.

"It's nothing." He squatted and poked at the potatoes. "I travel a lot, because I have to go where the work is, and when I'm on the road, if the weather's good, I like to camp out and cook over an open fire."

"I would have thought there would be enough work to keep you in one major city."

He shook his head. "It comes and goes. And when you top off a job, there may not be another one ready to start just then. Guys with families pretty much stay put, but a lot of us travel like Gypsies. There's always another job, another thrill, another big one over the horizon." He sent her an almost amused look. "You can finish a skyscraper one day and the next start building a bridge. Or maybe you can work on a nuclear power plant. Or you can work on a radio telescope, or the launch tower at Cape Kennedy, or a missile silo...just all kinds of opportunity out there if you know how to walk the iron."

Sara popped the last of a strawberry into her mouth and then drew her knees up, wrapping her arms around them. "You must have seen all kinds of things."

"I've seen a lot of the country," he agreed easily. "And a lot of interstate highway."

"I've never even left Wyoming," Sara admitted.

"I don't see any reason to leave. Seems like you've got everything that matters right here, and I don't recommend city life. When I was a lot younger, I thought it was exciting, but these days..." He shrugged. "It just irritates the hell out of me."

He lay back on the blanket, propping himself up on one elbow to keep an eye on the fire. From time to time he glanced at Sara and smiled, but she was grateful that he didn't look steadily at her. She was far more comfortable with the feeling that he was only casually aware of her.

Because she was not casually aware of him. There was nothing at all casual about the way her gaze kept returning to his long powerful limbs, his broad chest, his long dark hair. Something about him kept pricking her with a sense of familiarity, but there was nothing familiar about the heat he stirred in her. Her blood felt as if it were turning to warm molasses, and she was developing a pulsebeat in the most unusual place.

Frightened, she tried to look away, to calm herself and her own treasonous body, but her eyes just wouldn't behave. He was a harsh, hard-looking man. His flowing black hair only added to the warriorlike power of him. It didn't matter that he might never have fought in a battle. He had been born to be a warrior, and while modern times had made him into something else, there was no doubt he had everything he needed to be one.

So why, Sara asked herself uncertainly, had this hard, harsh, *experienced* man, who was at least a decade older than she, asked her to spend this evening with him? Because she turned him on? That was what he had said, and it was probably the last thing she could really believe.

He looked so utterly relaxed lying there, sipping champagne from a plastic goblet too small for his large hand. The strawberries were huge, but he popped them whole into his mouth as he ate them. He couldn't possibly lie there eating and drinking if he felt one-tenth of the arousal he elicited in her just by being there.

And thinking about those things was making her condition worse. Desperately, she forced herself to speak.

"You told Jeff you're on vacation."

He glanced at her. "Yep. A *long* vacation. I'm . . . getting too old to connect anymore."

"Too old? You?" The thought was stunning. She had never seen a man more in his prime.

"Most connectors change to something easier by the time they hit thirty. It's a young man's job, and I've lasted longer than most by far."

"How old are you?"

"Forty-one."

Forty-one. Thirteen years her senior. He couldn't possibly be interested in someone her age. Lord, he must look at her and see a child. He was up to something, but she couldn't imagine what in the world it could possibly be. "What's so hard about connecting? I mean, what exactly do you do?"

He gave her a half smile. "Well, on an average morning I'll shinny up a few columns, guide a few ten- or twenty-ton beams or headers into place, line them up by levering them with a two-foot-long connecting rod or hammering with a sixteen-pound hammer, and drive a bunch of bolts home. In between I'll do my tightrope walk along the headers and beams with fifty pounds of tools strapped to my waist. It's physical, it's wearing, and you need to be absolutely sure in everything you do. Finally..." His voice trailed off, and he looked away briefly. "Finally you realize you're not as fast as you used to be. Not as sure. Not quite as strong or enduring. A smart man comes down then. Before he *falls* down."

Sara was troubled by some indefinable sadness in his expression. "I suppose," she said softly, "that people do fall."

"Oh, yeah," he said quietly. "People fall."

He sat up suddenly and reached for a long-handled fork. Prodding the potatoes baking in the fire, he tested their doneness. "Soon," he said a moment later. "More champagne?"

Sara shook her head. "Thanks, but I don't have any head for alcohol."

He smiled then, an expression that creased the corners of his hard eyes in the most attractive way. "Time to break out the soft drinks, huh?"

He had an ice chest full of them, and a selection nearly as good as the supermarket's. Sara felt an urge to laugh again. Really, he was the most surprising man!

He took other things from the ice chest: a lettuce salad in a clear plastic bowl that was chock-full of good stuff like cucumbers and tomatoes. Two different bottled dressings. Another foil-wrapped package that he set near the fire.

From his truck he brought a rack on legs and set it directly over the fire, turning it into a barbecue. Then he put the steaks on to cook, and the most delicious aromas filled the glade.

"You're prepared for just about everything," Sara remarked.

"I just do this a lot, mainly by myself."

They dined on perfectly cooked T-bones, broccoli that had been steamed in foil, baked potatoes with sour cream, and the crispy salad that he admitted he'd coaxed Maude Bleaker, of Maude's diner, into preparing for him. When they finished, he burned what trash would burn and stuffed the rest into a garbage bag for later disposal.

And then there was no longer the excuse of a meal to eat to keep them lingering by the fire. Gideon showed no sign of wanting to leave, and Sara grew quietly anxious, wondering what came next. Her entire experience of dating had been with George, when they had both been little more than children. Never had George gotten any more forward with her than a few careful kisses. Gideon Ironheart, however, was a man, and she was sure he didn't play children's games.

"You're getting tense, Sara," he said. The low rumble of his voice held a teasing note. "I told you, I don't put out, so quit thinking about pouncing."

But this time she couldn't laugh. This time she could only feel embarrassed and achy, and certain that he must see every humiliating longing she'd ever tried to hide from herself.

"C'mere, Mouse," he said suddenly, his voice a rough whisper.

Before she knew what was happening, he had her stretched out on her side facing the fire and he was pressed warmly to her back. One arm settled around her waist, and the other pillowed her head. Her heart started beating double time as nervousness battled with need. She ought to get up right now, she thought, but it felt so incredibly good to be held like this. Surely this couldn't hurt?

She had totally forgotten these sensations, she realized. Had forgotten the tentative, nervous thrill of wondering what would happen next. Had forgotten the warm, edgy satisfaction that came from being held. Had forgotten that the brush of old denim against skin could be so pleasant, or that the subtle scents of a man could be so good.

"There," he said. "It's a beautiful campfire and a beautiful night, and they deserve to be enjoyed. That's all we're here for—the fire and the night."

He could feel the hammer of her heart with the palm of his hand, which rested just below her breast. She was frightened and excited all at once, and confused about it.

He had enough experience to tell, to read her, to know. The thought of all that experience sickened him a little, and he wished, too late, that he could capture a little of the innocence and excitement he'd once had. Wished he could remember the time when getting this close to a woman would have had his hands shaking and could forget all the game-playing women between then and now. He was kind of soured on women, he guessed, but Sara Yates didn't fit into that category. Tonight he would hold her a little and excite her a little, and maybe he'd remember, just a little, what it was like when life was still a miracle.

And she hadn't once tough-talked him in the last few days, he realized suddenly. That tough, little sheriff's deputy he'd met the other night in a dark parking lot hadn't been in evidence once since he'd started working with her grandfather. She was out of her depth with him, he realized. She knew how to handle people on the job, but she had no idea what to do with a man in a social situation. The understanding tickled him.

But he wasn't here to get tickled, he reminded himself. He was here to get a little hot and bothered by toying with something he could never have, and to get her to talk about Micah Parish.

"So I'm not the only half-breed Cherokee you know," he remarked a little later, when she finally seemed to have relaxed.

"No, I work with one. Micah Parish . . . I told you."

He lifted his head a little and leaned closer, so that his mouth was right beside her ear. When he sighed, she shivered in response. "I hope he hasn't given you a bad opinion of breeds."

"I'm a breed myself."

He gave a quiet laugh, a soft puff of air that tickled her ear and made her shiver again. "Being a quarter Indian is interesting, like having a cattle rustler somewhere in your family tree. It's safe and doesn't seem to bother anybody much."

"But being half-Indian does?"

"Believe it, lady. Believe it. Especially when it's stamped on your face like an old Indian-head nickel. I'll bet Micah Parish would tell you the same thing."

"Maybe he would. He's one of those silent types, though. Never says much—well, these days he talks more often, ever since he got married. You should see him with his wife."

"Why?"

"She's such a little bit of a thing, hardly much over five feet, and he's huge, taller than you, I think. And she's one of those fairy-tale blondes, with hair so light it's almost white, and these really blue eyes. . . ."

He slipped his hand a little higher and let his lips brush lightly against the shell of her ear. "Don't tell me you want to be a fairy-tale blonde, Sara. Do you really think hair or eye color makes a difference?"

"Men seem to think so." And she was too aware of the man who held her to realize how much she had just revealed.

"*Boys* think so. Men know better." He let another warm puff of air pass from his lips into her ear and felt the minute, almost undetectable movement of her hips in response. For an instant he had to hold himself tense, so that he didn't respond as he wanted to, by rubbing his rapidly growing arousal right against that soft little rump. He'd known he was going to get hot and bothered, but he hadn't expected to ache quite this badly.

And he still had a mission to accomplish.

"So he married an Anglo," he remarked casually. His tongue swept across her earlobe. She shivered delectably.

"Mmm...it's not a dirty word, Gideon. And Faith loves Micah so much. Anybody can see it. She makes him smile a whole lot more, and he's so proud of the baby...."

"Baby?" He lifted his head a little. The investigator hadn't mentioned that when he'd said Micah had married in December. And wasn't it too soon?

"Well, it's not really Micah's baby. Everyone knows that. But it doesn't seem to make any difference to Micah."

This was a story he *had* to hear. "Do you know how weird what you just said sounds?"

She hesitated a moment, and then a soft laugh escaped her. "I guess it does. Okay, Faith's former husband was abusive, and she came up here to her father's ranch to escape him after he nearly killed her. They were divorced already.... Are you following?"

"So far."

"Anyhow, the guy followed her up here, and Micah and Gage Dalton barely managed to rescue her from him. Micah married her a couple of weeks later, and it never seemed to bother him that she was already six months along with her ex-husband's child."

"That's unusual." Damn, he couldn't imagine doing that.

"Micah's an unusual man," Sara said. "I think...I think he's known some pretty hard times, but he has this inner strength, a kind of inward serenity—oh, I don't know how to describe it. You just know, somehow, that he's made peace with himself and life."

As his grandfather finally had, Gideon thought, recognizing her description as one that would have fit the old Cherokee medicine man who had forced him to wake up and take responsibility for himself. As he would like someday to do himself, if he ever figured out how. The older he got, the more he ached to find whatever it was that had put that look in his grandfather's eye. Sometimes, in the morning silence, he almost thought he touched upon it, but then it slipped away, elusive as a wraith.

"I think I'd like to meet him," Gideon said.

"Well, sure. I'll introduce you." She was having trouble hanging on to her thoughts, and she suddenly couldn't remember why they were discussing Micah Parish, anyway. Gideon's hand had wandered higher, finding the valley between her breasts, where it lay in perfect innocence, as if he wasn't even aware of where he was touching her.

And why should he be? she asked herself. She was overreacting, like the inexperienced woman she was. Her sexuality hadn't had the opportunity to grow or change very much since high school, but this man was long past high school. He probably didn't find anything at all erotic in the way he was holding her, and if he wanted erotic he wouldn't hesitate to touch her intimately. He was no uncertain boy in the back of his dad's pickup.

Besides, she didn't want to be touched intimately, so she was a fool to let it affect her at all. Nothing good could possibly come of losing her head over a man like Gideon Ironheart. The most she could ever be for a man like him was an amusing back-country diversion before he moved on. She couldn't survive that kind of humiliation a second time.

But before she could stiffen her resolve, Gideon's lips found an exquisitely sensitive spot behind her ear. A shudder of sheer sexual delight ran through her, and she caught her breath.

Oh, yeah, he thought, forgetting purposes and mixed motives and guilt. *Oh yeah!* She smelled so good, like baby shampoo and woman. Her hair was as soft as silk against his cheek, and he wished she hadn't braided it. The skin behind her ear was as smooth as a baby's, and fragrant, and the sound of her caught breath when he kissed her there was an aphrodisiac for a hungry soul.

And he was hungry. Oh, God, he was miles hungry, years hungry, lifelong hungry, for things he had never had and never admitted he wanted. All the things he'd been running from were trying to catch up, and he needed to find a warm, soft sanctuary.

Gently, knowing he shouldn't but needing to, anyway, he tugged her shoulder. There was no hesitation when she rolled onto her back, her head resting on his arm, and looked up at him. Her eyes were dark, catching a touch of flickering orange and yellow from the fire. Her bottom lip was caught between her teeth.

She wanted this, too, he realized. She wanted *him*. But she was afraid of her feelings and afraid of him, with good reason. He leaned over her on his elbows, taking care not to let his arousal brush against her.

"I'm a traveling man, Mouse," he said softly. "I ride the wind from one place to another, like a tumbleweed. No roots, no baggage. I've got nothing to give you but a few moments out of a lifetime. But you've got something I want very badly."

Her gaze had grown almost sad as he spoke, and now, surprising him, she reached up and lightly touched his cheeks with her fingers. "What's that, Gideon?"

"A kiss, baby. Just a kiss." Just a warm, soft kiss to put in his soul to keep the dying fire there alive. Just a touch of lips and tongue given freely to tell him he was still a man, and that a woman could still want him. Just a small, soft reminder of an innocence he'd never really had. Just something *good* in a life that had known so little.

She lifted her chin a little, reaching for him in consent, and he lowered his head until their lips barely touched.

Warm, thought Sara at the first touch of his mouth. Warm and soft, surprising in a man who looked to be essentially hard and cold. Gentle, unexpectedly gentle, as he touched, retreated, then touched again. His tongue, warm and rough, found her lower lip and traced it, causing another shiver of growing awareness to shudder through her. Instinctively, she tipped her head, reaching for a stronger pressure and a deeper touch.

She hadn't expected this seduction of her mouth. Dimly, she realized that the long-ago kisses she remembered had never been kisses at all. *This* was a kiss, this cautious touch and retreat, this exciting sweep of tongue over highly sensitive lips.

"Open for me, Mouse. Let me in."

The gruffly whispered command was as thrilling as anything in her life. On a softly whispered moan, she opened for him and felt her heart stop as his tongue found hers. He moaned then, as if he liked it every bit as much as she did, and she felt, for the first time in her life, the weight of a man's chest on her aching breasts.

He was forgetting, and he tried to call himself back, but he couldn't, just couldn't, draw back yet. Her mouth was sweet and fresh and shy, and that shyness was maddening him. He'd never kissed an inexperienced woman; he had never imagined that shyness could be so damn arousing. He had taken practiced gestures for the real thing for so long that he was stunned to realize they were mere parodies.

This was the real thing, he realized. This, a woman awakening to her own needs and not quite certain of them or herself. He had never realized what a turn-on it could be to have a woman get genuinely turned on by him. He'd had women who gave because it was expected, and women who gave because they needed it, and for any of them he could have been anyone at all. Sara wasn't making him feel that way. Oh, no. Sara was discovering her passion because of him, because *he* turned her on enough to make her forget whatever it was that had her hiding behind a facade of toughness.

The realization terrified him.

He was kissing her with unabashed eroticism, thrusting his tongue into her rhythmically, and she was responding as if...damn it, as if she was going to find satisfaction from his kiss alone. He felt the minute movements of her body as she lay half-beneath him, and they told him how close she was to the pinnacle and how easy it would be to take her right this instant. She wouldn't even whimper a protest. So hot. So fast.

Oh, God!

With more strength than he would have believed he had in him, he broke the kiss and rolled onto his back, separating them. After a few moments, when the chilly night air had cooled his head a little, he reached for her and pulled her close.

"I'm sorry," he said roughly. "That damned well got out of hand."

"That—that's all right." She didn't know what she was going to do with all these wild feelings he'd awakened in her, with the hard ache between her legs that needed something he wasn't giving. She wondered if it would go away, or if she was going to feel like this forever.

"No, damn it, it's not okay," he said angrily. "I made you miserable!"

A few minutes passed in silence, but finally he seemed to relax. "I'm sorry," he said again. "I ought to be shot. First I get you all wound up, and then I shout at you. Damn!"

Suddenly Sara sat up. "Let's put out the fire and go."

Gideon sat up, too. "Wait a minute. Sara, don't..." Don't what? Don't get mad at him? Don't feel hurt and rejected? Damn it, Ironheart, you're an ass! And that made him furious.

"Damn it, woman!" He was on his feet in an instant and took her by the shoulders so she couldn't escape. "What do you want me to do? Throw you on the ground and have my way with you? Do you really want a fantastic one-night stand? I could give you one, baby, but would you be able to look yourself in the eye tomorrow morning?"

At first she had glared up at him, every bit as mad as he was, but when he asked that final, damning question, she averted her face, and a tremulous sigh escaped her.

He heard that sigh, and his anger fled. "I'm sorry, Mouse," he said quietly. "I wanted you so badly that for a minute I forgot and let things go too far."

No woman on the planet could stay mad when faced with an excuse like that, she thought as she darted an uncertain look his way. He'd wanted her so badly that he forgot? Any normal, red-blooded woman would be glad to hear a confession like that, especially from a man like Gideon Ironheart, who looked as if he didn't forget much and could have his pick of women. But she wasn't a normal woman, and she knew better than to believe any man could want her that much, least of all Ironheart.

He caught her chin with his index finger and turned her face toward him. "Forgive me?" he asked.

It was like watching a mask slip over her face. The shy, uncertain woman who had come on this picnic with him vanished. In her place was the tough deputy he had met the first night. With a sick sense of his own iniquity, Gideon realized that he had driven her back into hiding.

"Sure," she said briskly. "No problem. Look, I need to get back. I've got to be on duty at 7:00 a.m."

With the fading of her anger had come humiliation. There was no one to blame for this but herself, Sara thought. She'd broken every promise she'd ever made to herself and tangled with a man. Of course she felt like a fool. He had coaxed her into revealing things—needs, desires, yearnings—that could only be embarrassing when exposed. And then, having exposed her vulnerability, naturally he pulled away. A man had done that once before. Fool me once, shame on you. Fool me twice...

Grimly, she helped Gideon pack up the picnic. At least he didn't give her any more hassles about forgiving him.

It was small consolation with tears of humiliation burning in her eyes and throat, and her heart aching for what could never be. Sara Yates now knew, beyond any shadow of a doubt, that she was a failure as a woman.

Chapter 5

It was nearly ten o'clock when they pulled up beside the house. Afraid that Gideon might speak, Sara hurried to open the truck door. "Thanks," she managed to say. "It was fun. See you tomorrow." She wished she never had to see him again.

"Sara—"

She slid quickly out and turned to give him a brittle smile. "Good night."

"Sara, wait!"

But she turned again and headed toward the house. She couldn't stand another minute, she thought. It was too humiliating.

And then she froze, staring at the back door of the house. Her heart seemed to stop.

"Sara." Gideon reached her side. "Let me go in first."

He'd seen it, too, she realized. The way the back door was crooked on its hinges and not quite closed. "Nonsense," she said tensely. "I'm the cop."

"But I've got the only weapon."

She turned and looked at him. In his work-gloved hand was a two-foot-long steel bar with pointed ends. It looked deadly.

"I know how to use it, too. I'll go first."

This time she didn't argue, and when he handed her a long wrench with a handle that tapered to another point, she hefted its weight gratefully. These must be his connecting tools, she thought. Her weapons were locked in the Blazer, and the keys were upstairs in her bedroom. But who the hell carried a sidearm on a date in Conard County? she asked herself almost wildly.

She was scared, she realized. Terrified of what she was going to find. Her grandfather— She couldn't even stand to wonder about it. He had to be all right. He *had* to be.

Gideon touched her arm briefly. "If anyone is in there, they know we're here," he warned her.

Of course. They would have heard the truck drive up. She nodded without looking at him. "I know." She stared at the house, forcing herself to think, despite her nearly paralyzing fear for her grandfather. "We go in together. It might allow them to get away, but they won't be able to overwhelm us as easily."

He nodded and spared her a long, intense look. Tough, he thought. Despite the fact that she was scared to death. Admiration flickered in him again.

"But I go first," she said, stepping forward. "I'm trained—"

His hand closed on her upper arm, almost painful in its grip. "I'm trained, too. Marines." So what if it had been a long time ago? He'd had plenty of opportunity to keep in practice in holes like Happy's Bar the other night.

Relief touched Sara like a gentle breeze. She was glad to know he had some training. Glad for both of them. Glad for her grandfather. Glad that they could back each other up.

Angled as it was, the screen door would no longer swing open. Sara stood to one side as Gideon lifted the sagging end and moved the door out of the way. The interior door was open a couple of inches. They stood on opposite sides of it, their backs to the wall, as Gideon reached out with his connecting rod and shoved it open.

After a heart-stopping moment of apprehension, Sara leaned to the side and peered into the kitchen. Seeing nothing in the shadows, she reached slowly around the door frame and felt for the light switch. The fluorescent bulb hummed, flickered and sprang to blinding life.

Nothing.

Gideon slipped past her into the room, and after a quick look around headed immediately for the dining room beyond. Sara's heart lodged in her throat, but she was right behind him, giving him just enough lead space so that they wouldn't walk into a trap together.

The dining room was a mess, the chairs knocked aside from the table as if someone had run through here too fast to avoid obstacles. The sight caused her heart to skip a beat, and the absence of any normal sounds filled her with dread. Her grandfather...

"Sara?" Gideon's voice came from around the corner of the living room. "Sara, Zeke's hurt. Come watch over him while I check out the upstairs."

Sara nearly ran around the corner, then halted in horror at the sight of her grandfather lying in a pool of blood. "Oh my God..." she said in a whisper.

"He's breathing okay," Gideon said softly. "Sara, he's alive, just unconscious. The bleeding has stopped, so it's been a while and they're probably gone, but I need to check...."

Sara nodded and came swiftly to kneel beside her grandfather. This was no time for horror or any other feeling. Right now there were things that needed to be done. She had to draw a couple of deep breaths to steady herself, but she managed to find a core of internal calm. "Okay."

Gideon gripped her shoulder briefly, then started up the stairs. Sara's gaze followed his prowling movements until he disappeared. Then she looked down at her grandfather and started praying.

Gideon was back in under three minutes. "They were up there," he said, "but they're gone now. What's faster? Calling for help or driving Zeke to the hospital?"

Sara looked up bleakly, measuring minutes in her mind. "Call the sheriff's office and tell them we need the medevac flight. Then we'll need to position my Blazer to illuminate a landing pad and guide the chopper in."

The nearest patrolling sheriff's unit arrived in the yard in under ten minutes. Gideon went out to the porch to greet the deputy and found himself face-to-face with Micah Parish.

Damn, thought Gideon, the man was even bigger than he'd realized, at least two inches taller than Gideon, and built of solid muscle. And Parish's eyes were familiar, so familiar that Gideon felt his stomach knot.

"You must be Ironheart," Micah said. "Where's Sara?"

Gideon stepped aside, letting the deputy see Sara kneeling beside her grandfather. "He's hurt pretty badly, from what I can tell."

Micah nodded and brushed past, going to Sara's side, where he squatted and gripped her shoulder. "The chopper'll be here in just a couple of minutes, Sara," he said. "Yuma said to tell you that old Huey is going to break speed records."

Sara tilted her head and gave Micah a wan smile. "Thanks, Micah."

"Ironheart and I are going to position the Blazers so they can see where to set down. Where are your keys?"

"Top drawer of my dresser."

"I'll get them," Gideon said.

Sara glanced up at him. "Thanks."

Micah and Gideon parked the Blazers facing each other with the wide expanse of hard-packed yard between them, providing a flat, lighted area for the helicopter to set down on. They turned on the flashers of both vehicles so the pilot could use them as a guide.

"Who's Yuma?" Gideon asked Micah as the two of them listened for the *whop-whop* that would signal the Huey's approach. What he really wanted to ask was how Micah had known who *he* was. Had Sara mentioned him? Or had Micah heard that Gideon was asking about him around town?

"The best damn chopper pilot this side of the Mekong," Parish said.

Gideon had heard that kind of remark before from men and was easily able to fill in all the unspeakable blanks that arose from Vietnam.

Suddenly Parish's dark eyes riveted him. "You a vet?"

"Marines."

"Nam?"

"I was there during the evacuation."

For a moment Micah's black-as-night eyes seemed to impale him. "I missed that," he said finally. "Damn filthy duty."

So filthy it had given Gideon an unalterable distaste for military life, but all he said was, "Yeah. Filthy."

The distinctive whopping of the Huey drew their attention to the east and the approaching helicopter. With navigation and landing lights on, the Huey was highly visible against the star-strewn sky.

Yuma set the Huey down as gently as a feather. Two medics piled out of the side bay doors, carrying a back board between them as Micah pointed to the front door.

Yuma climbed out, too, and crossed the dirt toward Micah. He was a moderately tall, lean man who walked with a limp and had a face that looked as if it had been ravaged by nightmares. Deep lines scored it, and hell looked out of his eyes, Gideon thought. He'd seen that look before. Some nightmares never ended.

"I spotted two more units on the road headed this way," Yuma told Micah. "They'll be here within five minutes."

Micah nodded approval. "Good."

"How's Sara?"

Micah shook his head. "Stunned. She'll go with you."

"Of course. I've got room." He gave a nod to Gideon, then limped back to the helicopter to be ready to take off as soon as the patient was loaded.

Micah looked at Gideon. "I want you to stay here. You can help us check things out."

Reluctantly, Gideon nodded. His impulse was to go with Sara, to be there if she needed anything, but he understood the deputy's concern. Someone had to be here to show the cops around and to answer questions.

He watched them carry Zeke carefully out and load him into the helicopter. Sara didn't even glance toward Gideon. Of course not. She had room for only one thing on her mind right now.

He watched the helicopter lift off with a roar of its engines and stared after it as it shrank into the distance. And he realized, quite suddenly, just how much an old Shoshone Indian had come to mean to him.

"Let's go," said Micah in the sudden silence left behind by the chopper. "Show me what you saw and walk me through exactly what you and Sara did. Start at the beginning."

So he started at the beginning.

Sara shivered and drew her denim jacket closer around her. It wasn't really chilly in the waiting room, but the early hour made her feel cold.

In the past several hours she had experienced a whole gamut of emotions and had finally reached a plateau of relative calm resulting mainly from weariness. Now she waited only to hear whether they needed to send her grandfather to a larger hospital where he could receive more specialized care. Zeke hadn't come to yet, and a neurologist from Laramie was consulting over the phone with Dr. MacArdle, trying to determine the seriousness of Zeke's injuries.

Her hands knotted into fists deep within her pockets, and she closed her eyes against the sting of tears. She really didn't know how she would stand it if her grandfather didn't recover. She simply couldn't imagine life without Zeke's warm humor and steady support. The ache that image brought was nearly intolerable.

"Sara?"

She looked up through a blur of tears and saw Gideon standing uncertainly in the doorway. Her throat was too tight to speak, and she could only make a small, almost helpless gesture to acknowledge him.

It was enough. He closed the distance between them in two long strides, then sat beside her and gathered her into his arms. "Oh, baby," he said softly. "Oh, baby..." He pressed her cheek to his chest and rocked her gently, listening to her swallow again and again as she fought her tears.

Even through her worry and grief, Sara felt a dim sense of astonishment at how ready Gideon was to hold her comfortingly. The men she worked with would have offered an awkward pat to the shoulder and a few gruff words of concern. And that was all she would have expected.

He didn't offer any false hopes or assurances. Not once did he say it was okay or would be all right. Because both of them knew it wasn't okay and might never be all right.

She drew a few shaky breaths and managed finally to subdue the urge to cry. The weary calm returned, a muffling blanket.

"What do they say?" Gideon asked presently.

"They don't know for sure. Zeke is stable but unconscious, and Dr. MacArdle is consulting by phone with a neurologist. They may have to move him to a bigger hospital."

Gideon nodded, forgetting that she couldn't see the gesture with her cheek pressed to his chest. Stable but unconscious, and seventy-plus years old. Zeke was in great shape, and probably as tough as old shoe leather, but he was also getting on in years. How much could he stand?

It would have been impossible, Gideon thought, for minutes to move any more slowly without time coming to a complete halt. It had been like this the night his own grandfather had died, he remembered. His uncle had called him to tell him the old man wouldn't make it through the night. Seven hours and three connecting flights later, Gideon had sat in a room something like this and waited as the minutes dragged by.

His grandfather, he thought now, should never have been in the hospital. It hadn't been the place for a man who had devoted the better part of his adult life to healing through the old ways. Yet Adam Lightfoot had never mocked the white men's medicine, he remembered.

"You can't heal the body unless you heal the spirit, too," the old man had told him. "Anglo medicine heals the body, and heals it well, but the people keep getting sick because the spirit is forgotten."

Another one of those things that Gideon hadn't really heard until it was too late. *The spirit is forgotten.* He felt as if his own had not only been forgotten, but lost somewhere, as well.

Sara sat in her corner of the couch, folding into herself with her shoulders hunched and her hands tucked up under her jacket. She looked so small and lost right now, nothing like the deputy who'd saved his butt from that gang of rednecks.

"How about some coffee?" he suggested, and glanced at his watch. A little after three. No place would be open right now, so it would have to be the vending machine. "I'll get it," he said, when she didn't answer. "Be right back."

The machine was only a short way down the hall. He leaned against it, resting his forehead against his fist as he watched the stream of coffee pour into the disposable cup. When it was done, he moved it to one side and shoved his hand into his jeans pocket, looking for a couple more quarters.

"Here," said a deep, gravelly voice behind him, and quarters were slipped into the slot. "You must be Ironheart."

Gideon straightened slowly and turned to face a ruddy, stocky man of maybe forty-five. He wore ordinary jeans, a zipped-up nylon jacket and a battered straw cowboy hat. "That's my name," he agreed, thinking he had seen this man somewhere from a distance.

"I'm Nate Tate," the man said. "Sheriff Nate Tate."

Ah! thought Gideon. At last the inquisition. "Pleased to meet you."

"I've been hearing about you here and there," Tate said noncommittally. "You planning on staying awhile?"

"Awhile. At least until Zeke is better. Sara doesn't seem to have a whole lot of help."

Tate's unwinking gaze raked him from head to foot. "Sara's never had a lot of help, not since her ma died. And she doesn't need any more trouble than she's got."

"I'm not planning on making any."

After a moment Tate nodded. "She's here, I imagine."

"In the waiting room."

"Well, get the coffee, son, and let's go."

Feeling that he had passed the first hurdle with the sheriff, Gideon followed him into the waiting room.

"Nate!" As soon as she saw him, Sara rose to her feet. And then she hesitated, clearly uncertain whether he was here as her boss or her friend.

Nate settled it. "I'm sorry, Sara. I just heard." Closing the distance between them, he wrapped his arm around her shoulders. "How's he doing?"

"We don't really know yet. He's stable, but he won't... wake up." Her voice trembled a little and then recovered.

Nate gave her a little squeeze and let her go. Gideon offered her one of the cups of coffee, and she accepted it with a wan smile of thanks before returning her attention to Nate. "What have you found?"

"Not a whole hell of a lot, I'm afraid. Micah says it looks as if nothing was stolen, but very definitely as if they were looking for something. Something big, because they didn't bother opening any drawers, but they checked out all the rooms in your house, the bunkhouse and the barn. Maybe the most suspicious thing is that they left the valuables alone."

"I don't have any valuables."

"Ironheart here does," Nate said. When Sara plopped back down onto the couch, Nate sat in a chair across from her. "According to Micah, they passed on a Zuni belt buckle that's worth a small fortune and a few other things of that kind."

Gideon shifted uneasily, not sure he liked the way that sounded. "A lot of people don't have any notion of the value of Zuni jewelry. Or of Indian jewelry as a whole."

Nate nodded. "I realize that. It's still funny. Micah said something about a dirt biker you saw earlier?"

"I didn't exactly see him. I saw sun glint off metal or glass, and when I headed up toward the trees to investigate, he took off. It sounded like a dirt bike, or a small motorcycle."

"There might not be any connection," Nate said after a moment. He looked at Sara. "Anyhow, I need you to go through the house in the morning with one of the other deputies and tell me if anything is missing. You're the only one who can do that, Sara."

She drew a long breath and nodded. "Okay. Unless something happens with my grandfather."

"And you," Nate said, turning to Gideon. "I want you to show us exactly where that biker was. There has to be a reason Zeke Jackson is lying in a hospital bed right now, and no stone is going to be left unturned."

That might almost be a threat, Gideon found himself thinking. If a man wanted to take it that way. "No problem," he said. "I can show you right where it's at. And what's more, unless one of your deputies poked around up there, it hasn't been disturbed, because Zeke and I didn't even bother to check it out once the biker was gone."

Nate nodded approval. "Good."

"Sara?" Dr. MacArdle entered the room looking rumpled, tired and concerned. Giving Nate and Gideon only the barest of nods, he went to sit beside Sara. "Your grandfather's condition hasn't changed at all. No, wait," he said when she opened her mouth. "Actually, that's a good sign at this point. If he'd suffered any kind of serious neurological injury, say a blood clot in the brain, we'd expect a deterioration of his neurological signs. That's not happening. Dr. Brandeis and I have decided to keep him here in intensive care for a while longer, unless something changes. In the meantime, why don't you get some sleep? We'll call you if anything changes."

"You can stay with Marge and me," Nate said as MacArdle left the room. "We've got an extra bunk in Janet's room, now that Cindy's in college."

Sara shook her head, thinking that the last thing she could tolerate right now was the well-meaning concern of friends. She would much rather just stay here and wait. "Thanks, Nate, but really, I'd rather not."

"Holler if you change your mind." The sheriff rose, patted her shoulder and left.

"I could get a room for you at the motel," Gideon said. "And I packed some of your clothes, in case. They're out in my truck. You can go get some sleep, and I'll sit right here and wait, and I'll call you the minute anything happens." He leaned over and touched her arm. "Mouse, that old man is going to wake up, probably in just a few hours, and it's not going to make him very happy to see you looking like this."

Her eyes were blurring again, with tears and fatigue, and she didn't even argue when he drew her against his side and tucked her face to his shoulder.

"Okay," he said. "Okay. You sleep right here, then. Sleep, baby. You won't miss a damn thing, I swear."

All her life, Sara had had to comfort others. Her father when her mother died, her brother when their father died. Friends who had lost loved ones. Survivors of accidents. The injured and battered innocents of the world. Looking back, she couldn't remember one time in her adult life when anyone at all had simply held her as Gideon Ironheart did through the endless predawn hours.

She didn't see why he should do it. He had only entered her life a few short days ago, yet he seemed somehow to have taken root. Zeke really liked him, that was obvious. Something had clicked between the two men, almost as if they had been friends from another time.

She could imagine them in another time, too, the old warrior and the younger one, dressed in buckskin, surveying the plains and mountains, riding free. . . .

She sighed and snuggled closer to Gideon. He was so warm, so hard, so big, so comforting. He made her feel safe, and Sara honestly couldn't remember the last time she had felt safe. It was an illusion, of course. He was a tumbleweed, he'd said, moving on when the whim took him. But for right now he made her feel safe, and Sara was reluctant to fight a feeling she'd known so rarely.

This afternoon, sitting in the kitchen when Zeke had mentioned the vision quest, she'd had the strangest feeling that her grandfather had a greater purpose than simply helping Gideon find a vision to guide him. Almost as if...as if he had wanted to pass something on to the younger man.

What a crazy idea, she thought drowsily. What could possibly be passed on? An idea? A dream? A vision of...what? The future? She was aware that her grandfather had a mystical side to his nature, but it was something he kept closely private, because it was so intensely personal. Why had he mentioned such things to Gideon, whom he hardly knew?

But then, Gideon was different. It didn't take a genius to feel his...difference, for lack of a better word. It wasn't exactly charisma, it wasn't exactly...anything. Just this sense of power, of invisible whirlwinds around him, of silent lightning and thunder. Things beyond normal ken.

When she'd first met him, she had labeled him an "Indian with an attitude." But that wasn't it. Whatever it was that made a man face down ten other men rather than leave a place, whatever it was that made him take a stand rather than yield to overwhelming odds, was not an attitude. It might be foolish, it might even be suicidal, but it was also admirable.

Her grandfather must have sensed these things, she thought, unconsciously snuggling closer, enjoying the way Gideon shifted to accommodate her, the way his arm tightened around her shoulders. His heartbeat beneath her ear was steady, comforting, and his breathing was slow and regular. Soothing.

The gentle rise and fall of his chest was as relaxing as being rocked, and little by little she slipped into sleep.

"Sara? Sara, Zeke is awake."

She was never sure afterward whether Gideon or Dr. MacArdle had roused her, but it really didn't matter. What *did* matter was that fifteen seconds later she was standing beside her grandfather's bed in intensive care, and he was smiling at her.

That was when, for the first time, she realized just how old and frail Zeke really was. He was always so active, always so firm, that she hadn't really noticed, but now she did. He had aged considerably in the nine years since he had come to help her and Joey, and he was an old man now. She should be caring for him, not the other way around.

"I'm fine, child, just fine," he said in answer to her question. "Just a little headache is all. You go on home and get some rest. Is Gideon with you?"

"Yes, he's been here most of the night. I was so worried...."

"Sh-sh-sh," he said, and brushed away her tears with his fingertip. "My time has not yet come, child."

Sara looked away, biting her upper lip and blinking rapidly. Little by little the tightness around her throat loosened, and breathing became easier. Finally she found her voice.

"Do you remember what happened, Grandfather?"

"No. Dr. MacArdle already questioned me about that. He told me what happened."

"But you don't remember?"

Zeke shook his head slightly. "The last thing I remember is stepping outside to watch the sunset."

* * *

"He doesn't remember a thing," Sara was telling Nate only a short time later. The sheriff's office was gearing up for the day, a steadily rising level of activity apparent as they talked. Gideon stood over by the front window, waiting patiently. "Dr. MacArdle says that's normal, but that he might never remember what happened."

"That's probably best for Zeke," Nate rumbled, "but it sure as hell handicaps the investigation. At this moment, hon, we don't have a damn thing to go on."

Sara nodded, glancing toward the windows and the sun-drenched square beyond. Marigolds in the courthouse flower beds bobbed gaily in the gentle morning breeze, and old Bill Haldersen and Al Loomis were already out there reading the morning paper. Those benches ought to have their names on them, she thought vaguely.

"Maybe," she said after a moment, "I'll notice something when I get back up there. I'm the best person to know what's out of place."

"That's what I'm hoping," Nate agreed. "Micah will meet you up there a little later this morning. He especially wants to check out the area where the biker was spotted."

"But he worked swing shifts last night," Sara argued automatically, which meant he shouldn't work today at all.

"Yeah, but he figures this is his case. Hours don't mean a thing to Micah when he gets on something."

Sara nodded, remembering other times. "I'll need a few days off."

Nate half smiled. "You never needed to ask. You're off the schedule already. You can make up for it when Ed's wife has the baby."

Sara almost chuckled at that. Ed Dewhurst had been the first deputy in Conard County history to request paternity leave. Nate had granted it without a moment's hesitation, but the subject had been hotly debated in the Bible Study Group, over coffee at Maude's Diner, and probably in most of the bars. Opinion was pretty evenly divided, and not along lines of gender.

"I'd better go up and tell Joey about Grandfather," she said after a moment.

"He's still not talking," Nate warned her. "Sullenest so-and-so I've ever seen."

"Well, that's just too damn bad," Sara said, her ordinarily quiescent temper snapping. "He doesn't have to talk, but, by God, he's going to listen!"

Nate and Gideon watched her stalk up the stairs toward the jail, which was in an armored room on the second floor.

"That girl," Nate remarked, "was always a damn sight too patient with that boy. She should have kicked his butt out of the house at least two years ago."

He looked at Gideon. "Just so you know, I did a priors check on you."

Gideon nodded, undisturbed. Given the circumstances, Nate Tate would have been a lousy sheriff if he hadn't checked up on the stranger who was involved.

"One felony when you were sixteen and a couple of misdemeanors for barroom brawling don't make me nervous, Ironheart," Tate continued. "I've got people in this county who did a whole lot worse in their youth and lived to become upstanding citizens."

Gideon gave a brief nod, waiting, sensing more.

"But you make me nervous, anyway, son," the sheriff continued. "Something about you is ringing my bells like mad, and I get the definite feeling you're not just vacationing here. So I'm going to keep an eye on you."

Well, he'd been anticipating that all along, ever since he arrived and started asking questions about Micah. Conard County was so thinly populated that a stranger was bound to draw attention. "Fine with me, Sheriff," he said easily.

Nate studied him a moment longer, then turned away to greet Velma Jansen, the department's dispatcher, as she walked in the door.

Gideon turned to face the window, staring out over the courthouse lawn and flower beds, his mind wandering over the events of last night. There didn't seem to be any rhyme or reason to it, he thought. Unless somebody out there just got their kicks terrifying people or beating up old men.

And Micah Parish. The man was calm, assured and silent. Enigmatic. Not an easy man to know. But a man Gideon nevertheless wanted to know.

Last fall, on the seventieth story of the job he had mentioned to Zeke, there had been an accident. He and his partner, Barney Witt, had shinnied up opposing columns and waited for the derrick, resting on plank flooring thirty feet below, to swing a beam toward them. Connectors needed to have an almost telepathic understanding of their partners, needed to know them well enough to anticipate every move, needed to feel absolutely comfortable with them. Barney and Gideon were such a pair, and they *always* worked together.

As close as brothers, Gideon thought now. Facing the sunlit square, he forced himself to remember.

The beam had swung into place slowly, cautiously, guided by a tag line held by a man below. It was his job to keep the beam from swinging wildly or spinning out of control. To guide it into the right place. Below them, he braced his feet and leaned backward so far his shoulders were only a foot above the plank flooring as he kept that beam steady.

Gideon and Barney, clinging to their opposite columns, watched it come closer. Barney's end arrived a little sooner, and he reached out, grabbing a corner to help guide it toward his column. Gideon got ready to grab his end.

The tag line snapped suddenly. Without warning. The beam, released abruptly from the guiding pressure of the tag line, swung the other way and caught Barney Witt right in the chest and flung him from his precarious perch. Then it swung back, but Gideon had had just enough time, barely enough time, to slide downward on his column and get out of its way. He was safe even before Barney hit the ground.

Gideon broke into a cold sweat every time he thought of it. Every time he remembered clinging to his column with one hand and watching that beam spin and swing until he got dizzy. Every time he remembered hanging there while his heart stopped beating and his soul quieted. While everything inside him froze with the knowledge that Barney was falling. Barney was dying.

And then the instant Barney died. He hadn't seen it. Hadn't heard it. But he had felt it. A black, roiling wave had crashed through him suddenly, and he had known Barney was dead. Only then did his heart start beating again. Only then did his body move, his brain think. Only then.

But he would never, ever, walk the iron again.

He had lost a brother that day. The only brother he had ever really had. He had gone home to his uncle's ranch, and his uncle, as always, had given him a sanctuary. Gideon worked with the horses, mucked out their stalls, performed all the mindless labor he could manage, trying to silence his grief and loss and nightmares with bone-deep fatigue.

And then he had learned of the existence of Micah Parish.

His *real* brother.

Joey wouldn't even look at her. Sara stood outside the cell, fighting for patience and strength, and got madder and madder at her brother. He was sixteen, handsome as sin, with just enough of his grandfather's looks to make him exotically attractive. Up until two years ago she had always imagined a bright future for him. Girls flocked like bees to honey around him. Teachers had always praised his intelligence and creativity. He'd seemed only normally rebellious, normally difficult, for his age.

All that had changed. Not all at once, but rapidly enough. What had at first been called a phase by teachers, other parents and the minister, had finally become a serious problem. Detention and expulsion from school had only seemed to make it worse. He'd run up against the law any number of times, and time and again some deputy let him go with a warning. Sara heard about it all, of course. Her fellow deputies felt she needed to know what was going on. She hadn't been able to prevent it, though.

Now this. Grand theft auto and jail. A felony record. And no sign that he was going to turn around.

He still wouldn't look at her. She glanced at her watch and realized that she'd been standing there for five minutes, waiting for that sullen brat to look at her so she could tell him what had happened. She had stood there for five minutes, trying to rein in her rising temper. Why the hell should she?

"Okay," she said, not caring that her voice vibrated with anger. "Okay, don't look at me. I'm going to tell you this, and I'm only going to say it once. Somebody broke into the house last night and beat Grandfather badly. He's in the hospital with a fractured skull and some broken ribs. Right now he's in intensive care, but they think he's going to be all right."

No response. Nothing. Except that she thought, just maybe, he had stiffened a little. She couldn't be sure.

"Joey." With difficulty, she kept her voice level. "You wouldn't have any idea why anyone would break into the house, would you?"

Again there was no answer. Sara stood there for another moment, feeling as close to despair as she had ever come. And as close to violence. Her hands knotted, and she turned away, mentally washing her hands. That was it, she thought. No more. He could just sit there and rot.

Her hand was on the heavy steel door when he called her. "Sara."

His voice sounded rusty from disuse, and something in her ached for the boy he had been and the man he might never be now. For her baby brother. She hesitated only a moment, then turned to look back.

"Sara, tell him . . . tell Grandfather I love him."

"I will." Torn, she stood there, wondering what to do now. Go back to him? Try to talk some more? And then she decided not to push it. "I'll tell him," she repeated. "We love you, too, Joey." Then, before he could reject her again, she hurried away.

* * *

Sara, Gideon thought as he watched her cross the room toward him, had just about reached her limit for now. Her eyes were red-rimmed with fatigue and unshed tears. The corners of her mouth were drooping, and she was trembling. At her limit or not, though, she walked with her head up and her gaze steady.

She didn't say anything as they stepped outside and he opened the door of his truck to help her in. She didn't say a word as he backed out and headed out of town. She didn't say anything until Conard City was well behind them and the truck's engine strained a little harder as they began to climb gently toward the mountains. The early morning air was crisp; the sun was warm and bright.

"Gideon?"

"Ma'am?"

"Will you...can you..." Her voice trailed away, and she sighed.

"I sure can," he answered. "I plan on sticking around at least until Zeke can manage. Somebody's got to look after those dang mustangs of his, and I kind of promised I would."

"But you're on vacation."

"I don't like to be idle. Besides, I'm in no hurry to get anywhere."

"But..." Again her voice trailed away.

This was not like Sara, he thought. He might only have known her for a few days, but she wasn't one to tiptoe around things. And then he realized what might be troubling her.

"Last night?" he said. "Is that worrying you? Forget it, Mouse. I'm not going to jump your bones without an invitation, and I honestly don't expect to get one. Relax."

She averted her face, aware that worry and lack of sleep were making her stupid, fogging her brain and scrambling her words. If she were feeling anything like normal, she never would have brought the subject up, but she wasn't feeling normal. Her whole world had managed to get turned upside down in just a few hours, and strange things were going on inside her. Things that compelled her to pursue a subject she should have dropped like a hot potato as soon as it crossed her mind.

"No," she said, leaning her cheek against the chilly glass of the window. "I mean the way I acted. I'm sorry I blew everything out of proportion. I acted like ... like ..."

"A frustrated woman?" Gideon suggested, and a warm, teasing chuckle escaped him. "Hell, Mouse, I'm feeling like a bear with a sore paw myself. Self-control is miserable, isn't it?"

Slowly Sara turned her head and looked at him. He was so incredibly frank, she thought. No hidden agendas with him. A woman would always know where she stood with him, and to Sara that was an incredibly attractive attribute. "Don't you have any shame, Ironheart?" she heard herself say, surprised to hear the uncharacteristic teasing note in her voice.

He glanced at her and smiled. "Shame about what? I don't see why I should be ashamed of being a normal, healthy male, or why I should try to pretend that you didn't get me all hot and bothered last night. You're dynamite, Sara Yates, and I'm not at all ashamed that I reacted to you." He paused as he downshifted and turned into her driveway. "I don't see why people are so afraid to admit that."

Sara might be groggy, but her brain hadn't completely failed. "They're afraid of being manipulated."

They had reached the yard before he responded to that. "I guess," he said, as he braked and switched off the engine. "Fear is a terrible thing, isn't it? Messes up things that ought to be perfectly natural and perfectly easy." Like telling a man you're his brother. What the hell would Parish do, anyway? The worst he could do was tell him to get lost. He turned and looked at Sara and realized he had let things get serious. He flashed her a smile. "You're welcome to manipulate me anytime, Mouse."

His meaning was clear, and wild color blossomed in Sara's cheeks. He didn't wait for her answer but climbed out, chuckling, and came around to open the door for her. His laughter had faded by the time he handed her down, though.

"You go in and catch a nap," he said. "I'll take care of the animals and keep an eye out for Parish."

"But you haven't had any sleep yourself!"

He shrugged. "I feel okay. Second wind. Go on. I'll wake you if anything comes up."

He watched that nicely rounded bottom of hers sway as she walked toward the house, and he wondered if he was losing his mind. He had come to Conard County to learn something about the brother he had never known, not to get tangled up in the personal problems of the Yates family.

But here he was, anyway, promising to stick it out until Zeke could manage again, worrying about Sara and how she was going to handle Zeke's temporary disability and Joey's attitude.

And wondering who the hell would want to beat up a harmless old man.

Chapter 6

Mucking out stalls was filthy, backbreaking work, and Gideon threw himself into it with a will. In addition to the mustangs, which were wild, Sara kept three horses for riding. Zeke had brought them in last night, and this morning they were eager to escape their stalls. He put them all, plus Columbine's foal, into the fenced east pasture and stood for a few minutes watching them gambol.

They were sure feeling frisky this morning. He smiled and leaned against the rail, giving himself a few minutes to soak up the warm sun, the dry air, the pristine beauty of the mountains, trees and grasses. There was something about this place that had a quieting effect on his soul. Despite everything that had happened, everything that was worrying him, despite even his concern for Zeke and Sara, something deep inside him was opening, expanding, trying to flower in response to the sunlight and beauty of the mountains.

He was forty-one years old. In those years he'd experienced an awful lot, some of it things that other people would never experience. He'd had good times, he'd had bad times, and he'd seen hell more than once. He'd laughed with friends and had plenty of fun when he had a few extra bucks in his pocket.

But he'd never once been happy.

Right now something inside him said he *could* be happy. That all he had to do was let it happen.

"Ah, hell," he muttered, and turned from the pasture toward the barn. Stalls needed cleaning, a mustang needed some attention, and happiness was a mental Shangri-la, a delusion, a place people kept trying to reach and never did.

He was just spreading straw in the last stall when Micah Parish found him. Gideon straightened, tensing inwardly as he faced the man. His brother.

Damn. Micah's eyes were the eyes of their grandfather, not just in shape and color, but in their quiet intensity. Shaman's eyes. Eyes that could see past facades, into the soul.

Tell him. But the words wouldn't come. He wasn't ready. He had to deal with his own tangled feelings about this before he would be ready to deal with Micah's reaction, whatever it might be. Leaning on the pitchfork, Gideon studied his brother and said nothing. Today, he realized suddenly, Micah wasn't in uniform. It was the first time Gideon had seen him in anything but khaki, but jeans and a red shirt didn't make Micah any less intimidating.

Micah tipped back the brim of his straw hat and then leaned against the stall gate. "Morning, Ironheart."

"Parish." Feeling wary, Gideon waited.

"Is Sara around?"

"She was going to take a nap."

"Good." Micah's eyes flicked over him, missing nothing, coming to rest finally on the hand that held the pitchfork handle in a white-knuckled grip. "Zeke's doing pretty good this morning, I hear. I called the hospital before I came up here."

"That's good."

Micah's gaze returned to his face, and eyes like obsidian impaled him. "What are you doing mucking out stalls in

Conard County, Wyoming, when you could be building a skyscraper in Dallas or Atlanta?''

Gideon's breath caught deep inside for just a split second. This man didn't pull his punches. And suddenly Gideon didn't give a damn who knew the truth. A punch for a punch, he thought. "My partner fell from the seventieth story last fall. I don't walk iron anymore."

Micah was very still and very silent for a moment. When he spoke again, there was a slightly different note in his voice. "Things like that can play hell with a man. You got a minute to show me where you saw that biker?"

"Sure." A feeling close to relief settled over him. He set the pitchfork aside and led the way. "Out behind the bunkhouse, up in the trees."

"What were you doing when you saw him?"

This time, Gideon realized, the accusing tone was missing. Somehow his answer about Barney's accident had settled doubts in Micah's mind. "I was washing up at the spigot in the back."

"And Zeke?"

"He and Chester Elk Horn were at the corral there." He pointed. "I guess Chester was just getting ready to leave. I went around to wash up, and just as I was finishing—shaking the water off my arms—I looked up and saw the glint from the trees."

They reached the back of the bunkhouse, and Gideon pointed. "I knew right away it wasn't a piece of glass lying on the ground, because it flickered and winked. Had to be moving to do that. So I started up that way to investigate. Zeke and Sara don't mind hikers, but they hate ATVs and dirt bikers."

Micah nodded. "I feel the same myself. Some of those folks seem to think that just because they *can* go off the road, they have a right to go anywhere, including private property."

Halfway across the grassy pasture to the trees, Gideon paused. "Right here is where I was when the guy took off. It sounded as if he went up and to the left."

"Toward the county road, probably three miles as the crow flies."

Gidcon nodded. "About that far. Zeke caught up with me here right then. Said to ignore it, that it was only one biker and not much we could do." With his thumb, he shoved his hat farther back on his head and looked up into the trees. "I was kind of mad," he admitted. "Anyhow, we went back to the house and had coffee."

"So nobody's been up there?"

"Not as far as I know."

Micah nodded and began to stride upward toward the trees. The pasture was on a gentle slope, not particularly taxing, but Gideon hadn't fully adjusted yet to the altitude here, though he was better adapted than a week ago. He got a little winded by the time they reached the line of trees, but Micah wasn't even breathing deeply.

Micah gestured for him to stay back a little, and Gideon complied, understanding that the deputy didn't want any tracks or other signs disturbed. Micah moved in slowly, crouching often to study what appeared to be only a blade of grass or a twig.

Watching him, Gideon realized that his brother had training in tracking that far exceeded the ordinary. "LRRP?" he asked suddenly, pronouncing it "lurp."

Micah never even glanced up. "Special Operations Branch. Twenty-one years."

Special Operations Branch said more than Special Forces. Special Operations covered a lot of things the public never heard about, and included the most elite units. Gideon looked at Micah with new eyes. "That's a long time."

"Seemed like it upon occasion." Micah eased forward again, checking out some more blades of grass.

Ten, maybe fifteen minutes passed while Micah studied the area. Gideon, left with nothing to do but hook his thumbs in his belt loops, tipped his head back and watched a couple of fluffy clouds grow slowly in the deep blue sky. Maybe they would get some rain later. They sure could use it. The pasture was beginning to look a little dry, and the dust was getting thick in the yard.

"He was here for a while," Micah said abruptly. Straightening, he came back to Gideon.

"He?"

Micah nodded. "Size-eleven shoe, maybe 180 or 190 pounds, probably between five foot ten and six feet. Lots of prints, tramped back and forth for some time. Long enough to smoke half a pack of butts." He held out his hand, showing Gideon the filter tip of a popular brand of cigarettes. "He kicked dirt over it, but not carefully enough."

"Not just a dirt biker, then."

Micah shook his head. "Somebody was watching this place. Looking for someone or something, or looking for someone to leave."

Together they walked back to the house. Micah spoke again.

"I'll have to go check along the road and see if I can tell where he came out of the woods."

"That'll take forever."

Micah glanced at him. "Probably not. I doubt he was being as careful out there as he was up in those trees. If Sara's not awake yet, I'll go out and look into that first. No point getting her up unless I have to."

But Sara was already up. She had heard Micah's vehicle pull into the yard and now was waiting for them in the kitchen with a fresh pot of coffee.

She looked a lot fresher, Gideon thought. A few hours of sleep had done wonders, bringing the color back to her cheeks and the sparkle back to her warm brown eyes. She wore a denim skirt and white blouse. Gideon, who had never seen her in a skirt, couldn't help taking an eyeful of slender calves, delicate ankles and pink-tipped toes peeking from her sandals.

God, he thought, looking away, she was some woman. An armful. No twiggy model with legs so thin they were practically sticks. No, Sara was curvy. Curvy calves that led right up to thighs that would be soft and... He sighed and forced himself to pay attention to business.

"How are Faith and the baby?" Sara asked as she filled three mugs with coffee and joined the men at the table.

"Doing great," Micah replied. "Sally's just about the happiest baby ever born. Takes after her mother, I reckon."

Gideon thought about that for a minute, taking in Micah's obvious pride and pleasure in both his wife and child, and decided that even if the baby wasn't Micah's, it didn't matter to Micah. Unexpectedly, he thought of his uncle, William Lightfoot, and how delighted he would be to learn there was a baby girl in the family. He wouldn't have a problem with the baby's paternity, either. He would welcome the child as readily and warmly as he had long ago welcomed Gideon.

"I've got some chores to finish up," he said abruptly, rising from the table. "You let me know when you want to go through the bunkhouse, Parish."

He climbed the fence into the corral with the mustang and then stood still, giving a coaxing little cluck. The stallion's ears pricked and he took a tentative step toward the man.

Ironheart. He'd taken the name shortly after his eighteenth birthday. The judge who granted the request had been bored with the proceeding and had hardly glanced at the boy. Gideon had taken it with purpose, refusing any longer to bear the name of the father who had abandoned him. At the time the name Ironheart had been a statement of the man he intended to be. Now look at him, getting all bent out of shape over Sara and her grandfather, over the brother he had just met, and the child his brother hadn't sired but was fathering. He swore under his breath.

It wasn't that he wanted to be hard so much as it was that he didn't trust all those soft feelings. They were fleeting, fanciful, and all they did was weaken a man, make him vulnerable to some shaft or other. They were aberrations, not to be relied on. People said they loved someone, and the next thing you knew they were moving on without a backward glance. How many times had he seen it?

So it was just best not to let yourself be deluded by the momentary soft feelings.

He clucked again, and the mustang pranced a little closer. A game, he realized suddenly. That damn stallion was teasing him.

Gideon grinned then, suddenly feeling pretty good, forgetting all his musings about the unreliability of gentler feelings. "You better look out, boy," he told the horse. "I'll ride you yet."

Sara went to town to visit her grandfather right after Micah finished up and left. She invited Gideon to join her, but he told her he didn't want to leave the place unattended.

"There's no reason why they should come back," she argued. "They know we haven't got whatever they wanted."

He shrugged. "Say hi to Zeke. Tell him I'm thinking about the vision quest, but I'm going to need some convincing."

She took two steps toward her Blazer, then turned again to face him. "I don't feel easy about you being here alone. If they come back—"

She bit the word off as if she wished she could take it back, but Gideon had heard her, anyway, and the fact that she was concerned about him touched some long-locked place in him. He ignored the warm, syrupy feeling that tried to bring itself to his attention.

"If they come back, I'll hold 'em for questioning," he told her teasingly. "Go on, Sara. I'll be okay."

She looked at him standing there in the bright afternoon sunlight, his hands on his rakishly cocked hips, and realized that she had come to care for him. Foolishly, stupidly, she cared. She wanted, she realized with a sad, desperate ache, to always see him standing in the sun like this with his hips cocked and his hard, harsh face shadowed by the brim of his hat. She wanted to know that he was going to be there tomorrow and tomorrow.

And he had already told her that he wouldn't be.

"Sara?" His hands fell from his hips, and he stepped toward her. "Sara? What's wrong?"

She caught her lips between her teeth and shook her head. "Nothing. Really. I'll see you later."

Too late, she thought as she tooled the Blazer down the rutted driveway. Too late. She had been sabotaged by all the years that she had refused to have anything personal to do with men. The one man who had refused to be put off by her barriers had managed to slip beneath her guard because she hadn't been prepared. She'd had no defenses against a man who wouldn't take no for an answer. A man who could tease her out of her fear of him simply by being outrageous.

Well, she promised herself shakily, she wouldn't let him know she cared. And if she didn't let him know, didn't let anyone know, he could hardly make a fool of her, could he?

Gideon's image seemed to dance before her all the way to town, and all she could think was that all that raw masculinity ought to come with some kind of warning. *She* sure as hell didn't know how to handle it.

The clouds that had started out as a few white puffs in late morning had, by late afternoon, turned into the dark gray steel of thunderheads. Gauging them, Gideon decided to stable the saddle horses. The mustangs would manage on their own. Even the stallion would do better, so he let the horse out of the corral. The mustang hesitated only a moment before trumpeting his approach to the mares and then taking off across the pasture toward the woods.

That horse would have gone crazy if he were trapped during a bad storm, Gideon thought as he watched the roan disappear into the trees. He was a wild creature, more terrified of confinement than the elements. The saddle horses, used to stabling, would feel safer indoors.

Thunder rumbled hollowly, bouncing back and forth on the mountains and out of ravines higher up. The wind picked up a little, blowing a cold gust or two right off the snowfields above the ranch. He had to reach up to hang on to his hat and then decided to ditch it in the bunkhouse and get his slicker out. It would be a far sight more useful if those clouds dumped.

He had no sooner finished securing the barn and the bunkhouse when it hit. Hail fell, stones the size of marbles pelting the yard and denting his truck as he watched from the porch of the house. The roar of falling stones and rolling thunder was almost deafening, and he hoped to God it didn't panic the mustangs too much to take shelter beneath trees.

As suddenly as it had started, the hailstorm stopped. The hush was almost unreal after the racket, and only the rumble of thunder kept Gideon from thinking he'd gone deaf. The sky was leaden from horizon to horizon, and clouds seemed to scud along the very treetops. The temperature must have dropped fifteen degrees, he thought, feeling chilled and damp.

Well, he would go in and close up Sara's house completely before it started to rain, and then he'd settle in for the night. Little else could be done today.

The phone rang just as he was walking through the kitchen. Reaching out, he snagged the receiver and leaned against the wall. "Double Y Ranch," he said.

"Gideon, it's Sara. I'm at the hospital with Grandfather."

"How is he?"

"He's doing really well. They're going to move him into a regular room tomorrow morning. But that isn't why I called. One of the nurses just told me the weather service has issued a stockmen's advisory and a storm warning."

"Hardly surprising. We just had five minutes of marble-sized hail. I don't think my truck is ever going to look the same again."

"Oh, Gideon . . ."

He laughed. "Hey, Mouse, if that's the worst that ever happens . . . ! The saddle horses are safe in the barn, and I assume the mustangs are safe under the trees. I was just going upstairs to check the bedroom windows before the rain hits. The temperature must have dropped fifteen degrees. You're going to wish you'd worn a jacket."

She gave a small laugh. "The Blazer has a good heater. I'm going to be down here a couple more hours, I guess. I forgot to tell you that there's a pot of stew in the refrigerator for dinner, and some homemade bread in the bread box. And ice cream. Just help yourself to whatever looks good."

She'd thought of him, he realized a few moments later as he hung up the phone. She'd thought of him and worried about what he would do for dinner. That warm, syrupy feeling returned, and this time he didn't find it quite so easy to dismiss. With all she had on her mind right now, the woman had still worried about *him*. That was pretty damn special, and for once he didn't argue with himself about it.

Upstairs, he walked from room to room, closing windows and securing the latches. In Sara's room, he found a loose latch. It wasn't much to worry about on the second story, but he pulled a screwdriver out of his back pocket and went to work on it, anyway. He didn't like leaving things undone, and it gave him a sense of satisfaction to fix what was broken and mend what needed mending. He always had a screwdriver in one hip pocket and a tape measure in the other, and as often as not a small wrench tucked somewhere.

Beyond the window, heavy dark clouds moved slowly, looking almost low enough to touch. Above the pasture, the pines had turned almost black in the gray light, and beneath them shadows loomed mysteriously.

It was beautiful, he thought, pausing. Beautiful. Wild. Thunder boomed hollowly, lightning forked dazzlingly in the distance, and thunder cracked again. A fat raindrop hit the window with a splat, and moments later another joined it.

Something—a sense of unease—made him look toward the spot under the trees where the biker had hidden. There was no one there now, he was sure, but he reached for the shade anyway and lowered it. He didn't want Sara walking in here after dark and flipping on the light, becoming visible to anyone who might care to watch. He knew she would just cross the room and draw the shade—from the porch of the bunkhouse he'd watched her do it every night—but he didn't want anyone else to watch her. See her. Know that this was her room.

The feeling was rooted in some deep, dark instinct, and he didn't analyze it. Once the shade was closed, he was done, and he left her room without another glance, without in any way trespassing on her privacy.

He checked all the downstairs windows, too, and found a couple of other loose latches. He fixed them, then drew the blinds everywhere except the kitchen. She would be here alone, he thought, and he damn well didn't want anyone else to know that.

And maybe, he found himself thinking, he shouldn't stay in the bunkhouse tonight. Maybe he should sleep on the couch or get his sleeping bag and curl up on the porch.

Damn it, he didn't like this at all. If something valuable had been taken, he could at least feel easy about the motive for the break-in and be at least reasonably certain that the creep wouldn't return.

On the kitchen porch, he took the screen door down so he could work on the bent hinges. Thunder rolled down the hillside, bringing another gust of frosty air from the snowfields. Occasional big drops of rain continued to fall, one or two at a time, making little craters in the mud of the yard between the slowly melting hailstones.

The hinges were only a little bent, he saw, but the screws had been stripped out of the wood door. He would need some glue and sawdust, and both were in the barn. Grabbing the hinges, he shoved them into his pocket and snatched up his slicker. While he was there he could check on the horses and straighten the hinges, too.

The barn was still warm, redolent of horses, hay and manure. In the workshop beside the tack room, in the golden light from the overhead fixtures, he forgot the storm, forgot his worries for Sara and Zeke, and lost track of time. Once the hinges were fixed, he didn't stop. There was a broken kitchen chair, solid oak, that needed mending, an old dresser that needed new drawer bottoms, and a dozen or more other things, big and small, that needed fixing.

He lost himself in the smell of the sawdust, the solid feel of the wood, the pleasure of holding and using tools. Thunder rolled, rain hammered loudly on the roof, and the horses whickered softly. They were good sounds, a soothing background to his satisfaction in working with his hands again.

Sara found him there. It was after nine, dark, windy, cold and wet outside, and she had arrived home to find no sign that Gideon had even eaten his supper. She waited for a while, sure that he must have heard her Blazer pull into the yard and would come over to ask about Zeke, but he didn't show. Finally, concerned that he might have gotten hurt somehow, she went looking. The bunkhouse was empty, his bed untouched. That left the barn, she thought.

Lightning zigzagged through the dark, illuminating the puddled ground briefly as she hurried that way, guided as much by instinct as the little bit of light from the house. The lights were off in the barn, so she saw the yellow glow from the workshop immediately. Flipping the switch just inside the side door, she checked the horses quickly, noting they'd all settled for the night. Columbine snorted a little when the light came on, but other than that, all four animals ignored her.

On the threshold of the shop, she stopped in amazement. Gideon had his back to her, and he was singing quietly, in a deep, resonant voice, some country ballad of lost love. He wore her father's old safety goggles, he was covered head to foot in sawdust, and he had repaired two chairs, a table and her grandmother's old cupboard, by the looks of it. And now he appeared to be building drawers for the old dresser.

He'd taken the leather thong from around his forehead and used it to tie his hair back loosely at the nape of his neck. Something about that made Sara quiver deep inside with an almost urgent desire to pull that piece of leather free and sink her hands into that long, black-as-night hair. God, what fool had ever thought men were less masculine with long hair? There was nothing at all unmanly about that warrior's mane, or the man who wore it. As he moved, muscles flexed beneath his plain white shirt, muscles developed by moving mountains of steel and building the cities that were the hubs of this country.

He'd rolled back his sleeves, and as he reached for the planer and used it to smooth the edge of a piece of wood, she watched his powerful hands and forearms flex and bulge. She could have watched him for hours, she realized. Could have simply stood there and soaked up the sheer magnificence of Gideon Ironheart with her eyes until some empty spot in her was filled with it.

But she was concerned that he hadn't had his supper, and before she started heating food for herself, she needed to know if he was going to join her. She rapped on the doorframe, a quiet knock.

He broke off singing and glanced her way. A smile creased his dark, dusty face. "Hi. How's Zeke?"

That smile curled her toes in her sandals. "He's doing really well. He asked if you might come in tomorrow and see him, once they get him moved out of ICU."

"Sure. I'd like that." He tugged the goggles off and tossed them onto the workbench. "I'm sorry. I meant to be out front when you got home. I didn't like the idea of you coming home to an empty house."

"It looks like you've been busy."

He smiled, an almost sheepish expression that touched her deep inside. "I forget myself when I get tools in my hands."

"At the rate you're going, things that haven't been fixed in years are going to be fixed in no time at all." Lord, how she wanted to reach out and touch him. Was it only last night that she had lain in his arms before the campfire and felt long-dead urges awaken? How had he become such a craving? "I was going to make some supper. You haven't eaten, have you?"

"Nope."

"Then join me. It'll be ready in fifteen or twenty minutes." She turned before she could betray herself somehow, remembering her promise that nobody would ever know that she had come to care about this man. As a friend, she reminded herself. She cared for him as a friend and nothing more. He was, after all, going to move on.

"I need to shower," he called after her.

"Fine," she called back. "I'll make it thirty minutes."

That sounded casual enough, she thought with satisfaction, although at the thought of him standing naked beneath a shower, her heart had climbed into her throat and begun to beat like a pagan drum. Gideon Ironheart naked was bound to be even more magnificent and a hell of a lot sexier than Gideon Ironheart dressed. Too bad she couldn't peek.

Gideon left his muddy boots by the back door and stepped into a kitchen filled with rich aromas of stew and coffee. Sara had already set the table and was placing the stew pot on it when he entered.

"Grab a seat," she said, pointing. "Just let me get the bread out of the oven and we'll be ready."

She was still wearing that denim skirt. It wasn't a sexy skirt, but a perfectly plain little A-line that had obviously seen a few washings. It didn't have a flounce or a ruffle or anything else to enhance it, and it was just about the sexiest thing he'd ever seen.

Because *she* was wearing it, he realized. Because it was curving over her sweet little rump and her rounded hips and brushing against her soft knees and exposing her gently rounded calves. She had pretty knees, he noticed now. Very pretty knees. Not bony, not pointy, but nicely shaped with a little dimple on either side. He had a wild urge to kiss those dimples.

With effort, he dragged his attention away from her legs and focused on the plate in front of him. She joined him and passed him a basket of hot, buttered bread.

"Boy, does this smell good," he told her.

"Do you often forget to eat?"

He looked at her and saw a teasing gleam in her warm brown eyes. She had, he realized with relief, forgiven him for last night. All day long, though he had tried not to think about it, he had been worried about that. "No," he said in answer to her question, "I almost never forget to eat. Do I look undernourished?"

Actually, Sara thought, he looked *perfectly* nourished. But tired though she was, she had sense enough not to say so out loud.

"I don't think I should sleep in the bunkhouse tonight," he said, startling her out of her preoccupation with her attraction to him.

"What?" Confused, she stared at him. "Why not? Is something wrong?"

He shook his head. "I just don't like the idea of you sleeping here alone. I know you have a gun, and I know you know how to use it. I know you're a deputy and all that, but—" He shook his head. "But you're still only one person. Two of us even the odds better if something happens, but I wouldn't be much help all the way out in the bunkhouse. Short of utter mayhem, I'd never know anything was happening over here. So I'll sleep on the couch. Or the porch, if you don't want me inside."

An honest-to-goodness Galahad, Sara thought, not quite certain what to say. She had been raised among chivalrous men and had worked daily with some of the best for the last nine years. She was accustomed to seeing their courtliness to their wives and girlfriends, but not since Jeff Cumberland had offered to date her after George fled had anyone been so gallant on her behalf.

No, she thought suddenly. Not true. Gideon Ironheart had, in his own way, been gallant toward her from the start. He might not have been courtly in his manner, but it was pure chivalry that had refused to let her walk alone into those bars, gun or no gun, badge or no badge.

"On the porch?" she repeated. "You've got to be kidding. You'll freeze." Spring nights were chilly in the

Wyoming mountains, but the cold front that had brought the storm had made it chillier than usual. There would probably even be some fresh snow higher up come morning.

"I've got a good sleeping bag." Satisfied, he rose and carried his dishes to the sink where he began to wash them as naturally as if this was his kitchen and he did it every day. "I won't freeze. Look, Sara, I don't want to press you and I don't want to make you uneasy by forcing myself on you, but I'd feel a whole lot better if those guys had stolen something. The fact that they hurt Zeke and then didn't take anything leaves a really bad taste in my mouth. I don't want you facing them alone."

Sara was never sure why she said what she said then. Later, thinking it over, she decided it had more to do with her feelings about Gideon Ironheart than any fears for her safety. It sure didn't have anything to do with some female desire to put a man on an ego trip, though. *That* was definitely the last thing on her mind. "I'll be glad to have you here. You look like you could handle just about anything."

Gideon, with his back to her, stiffened visibly and for an endless moment didn't respond. Sara stared at his back, growing acutely embarrassed as she realized how that might have sounded. What it might have revealed. But before she could turn completely crimson, or embarrass herself further by trying to explain her remark, he turned from the sink, tossed aside the towel he'd been using to dry his hands and faced her.

Leaning back against the counter, he folded his arms across his broad chest and smiled. Grinned, actually. There was no mistaking the sudden teasing gleam in his steel-gray eyes. "Thank God you noticed. I'm getting tired of sucking in my gut to impress you."

Inevitably, instantly, her eyes were drawn to his incredibly flat stomach. "What gut?" she asked, realizing he'd done it again. He'd said something so outrageous that all the embarrassment was gone as if it had never been. He was good at saying things no one else on earth would have the nerve to say, saying things that lightened the atmosphere.

That troubled her a little, she realized suddenly. He was good at evading uncomfortable feelings, good at diverting attention. How had he learned to do that? And why?

And then she realized she was doing it again, drawing his attention to the fact that she was noticing such things. And now, worst of all, she was simply staring at a belly that probably looked like a washboard, and was inevitably noticing the male bulge lower down, a bulge thrust into prominence by the way he was leaning back against the counter.

Oh, Lord, she thought almost weakly, he was such a fine-looking man. Just looking at him made her intensely aware that she was a woman, made her intensely aware of her body in ways she hadn't felt in a decade.

God, thought Gideon, she was stirring him up into a roaring blaze just by looking at him. It was the *way* she was looking that got to him. He was used to being noticed by women, used to speculative looks, used to outright sexual invitation. Sara's look was different. In it there was no speculation, no blatant, knowing curiosity. In her face was simple yearning, and it ripped his soul, unleashing a torrent of needs and wants he had never acknowledged before and didn't even know how to name.

"C'mere," he said, his voice a rough whisper, a breath of sound barely forced past a dry throat. He was burning. Burning. "C'mere, Mouse." She had to come to him, he thought. Had to. He didn't want to ever wonder whether she really wanted to be in his arms. He didn't want to wonder later if he'd somehow . . .

The thought was never completed. Licking her dry lips in an unconsciously sensual way, Sara rose on shaky legs. She stood there, looking at him with huge brown eyes, yearning so plainly written there that his heart throbbed in response.

"C'mere," he whispered again. "Closer. . . ."

She moved toward him. It wasn't even a full step but more of a tentative edging his way.

"Oh, God, Sara," he said hoarsely. "Closer, baby...."
He unfolded his arms, widened his stance, aching for her...
aching.... "Sara..."

Just the way he whispered to that damn mustang, she
thought dazedly, edging closer...closer.... Except that there
was something so sexy, so sensual, about the grittiness of his
voice just now that everything inside her clenched in response.

And then, with a little sob, she was there in his arms,
wrapped in him, surrounded by him, and it felt good, so
good, to be held....

"Oh, God, baby..." The words escaped him on a ragged sigh of relief as he bowed his head and buried his face
in her hair. He couldn't remember the last time he had
wanted so badly to hold a woman, to feel her softness
pressed to him. Just to have her there, to hold her, to feel her
close, eased yearnings so deep he didn't have words for
them. Maybe he was losing his mind at long last, but for
now, right now, he didn't give a damn.

Sara's arms stole around his narrow waist and hugged him
back. He widened his stance a little more, drawing her
deeper into his embrace, and for a moment she didn't
breathe as she realized how intimately she was pressed to
him. Her breasts were crushed to a chest as hard as iron, and
nestled against her lower belly was that bulge that had earlier fascinated her. She could feel every hard, masculine line
of him, and all she wanted was to burrow deeper and deeper.

Easy, he told himself. Easy. This woman was the same one
who hid behind a deputy's uniform and mirrored sunglasses, who talked tough and pretended to be one of the
guys. Here at the ranch she softened up, as if here she felt
safe, and she had softened up considerably with him. He
didn't want to ruin that by hurrying her or pushing her. For
whatever reason, she was as shy as that mustang.

His hands ran slowly down her back, a soothing, gen-
tling touch, halting at her waist and then returning slowly
upward. Her hair was caught in a ponytail again, and without a word he snapped the rubber band and freed it.

"You have beautiful hair," he murmured against her temple. "Soft and silky." Gently, he combed his fingers through it. "So soft."

"You have nice hair, too," she said, feeling terribly, painfully shy, wanting whatever he might give her so badly that she could hardly stand it, and sure that he couldn't really want to give her very much. She was such a plain Jane after all, so dull and ordinary and unappealing. The kind of woman men fled from.

Reaching up with one hand, Gideon released the leather thong that tied his hair back and dropped it on the counter. Somehow that was, she thought as her insides twisted pleasurably, one of the most shatteringly intimate things a man had ever done in her presence.

It was also a silent invitation, as was the way he tugged one of her small hands up until her fingers were in his hair. "Touch me," he whispered, the slightest tremor in his breath. "Don't be shy, Mouse."

But she was, miserably so, and it was there in her soft brown eyes as she tilted her head back and looked up at him. But there also was the yearning, the longing, the need. Seeing it, he bent his head and touched her petal-soft lips with his.

"Sweet," he murmured. "So sweet." She *was* absolutely the sweetest thing he'd held in so very many years. Gently, so, so gently, he brushed his mouth back and forth across hers, coaxing and teasing. And little by little her hands slipped into his hair, stroking and finally gently pulling him closer.

Another ragged sigh escaped him, each of her tentative touches detonating along his nerve endings like dynamite. He opened his mouth over hers and ran his tongue along her lips, along the exquisitely sensitive seam between them. He needed to be inside her, needed the taste of her and the heat of her.

She gave it to him. With a soft little moan she opened to him and eagerly accepted the thrust of his hot, rough tongue. She knew now the kind of pleasure his kiss could give her, the way the stroking of his tongue seemed to reach every nerve in her body and cause a twisting, clenching thrill to run through her, making her ache for more and more.

She clutched handfuls of his hair, of his soft, silky, sexy-as-sin hair, and pulled him nearer still. The tug didn't hurt him, but it electrified him, causing his arms to tighten almost painfully around her as he heard all that she was unconsciously telling him.

She wanted him. Oh, God, she wanted him. He felt it in her clutching, tugging hands, in the way she molded herself against him, and the way her head sagged back beneath the onslaught of his mouth.

She wanted him as he'd never been wanted before, with a passion flaming every bit as hotly as his own, with a passion for *him*. He knew it in his very bones. Sara Yates was reaching for Gideon Ironheart and no one else. If he'd been anybody else, she wouldn't have wanted him. And that was the most seductive thing he'd ever known.

For a moment his passion flared even hotter. With a tug he yanked her blouse free of her skirt and sent his hand foraging beneath, across soft, satiny skin until he found the beckoning hill of her breast. Soft, simple cotton encased it, without even a trim of lace. As plain and everyday as Sara Yates herself. Finding the bra clasp between her breasts, he twisted it and freed her. She gasped and tore her mouth from his, but her head fell back in surrender as he covered her soft, small, aching breast with his large, warm hand.

"Gideon . . ." His name escaped her on a tremulous sigh, at once a plea and a sound of pleasure. Her breasts were small, just another one of the things that made her feel inadequate, but Gideon's touch almost made her forget such concerns.

"You feel so damn good, Sara," he muttered roughly. "I'll bet your breast is every bit as pretty as it feels. Do you like that?" He tugged gently on a small, hard nipple.

A rippling shiver passed through her and escaped her as a soft moan. The sound of her desire sent a shudder of pleasure racing through him, making him even harder and heavier than he already was.

He wanted her...wanted her...wanted her. The need was a drumbeat in his blood. And she wanted him. Just him.

And that was why he didn't give in to himself or her. The conviction that she wouldn't be responding this way to anyone else, the belief that she wanted *only* him, was the very reason he couldn't take her. She didn't offer herself cheaply, so he couldn't take her that way. It was just that simple.

For a long moment he held her, his hand on her breast, feeling his brain try to kick into gear through the muzzy red haze of his hunger. With just a single, ruthless effort he could have silenced reason, but he didn't. Sara had touched some place deep inside him, and concern for her overrode his hammering hunger. He couldn't hurt her. Wouldn't hurt her.

Gently, carefully, he withdrew his hand and pulled her snugly against his chest. Wrapping his arms around her, he hugged her tightly and rocked her tenderly, giving her time to return to reality and wake from the daze of passion.

Oh man, he thought, now she was really going to hate him. He was showing himself for a real fool. Getting carried away was an excuse that sounded pretty damn lame the second time.

But Sara didn't get mad. Leaning against him, soaking up the comfort of being held, she acknowledged that his withdrawal had been the result of his concern for her. Even now she could feel his tension and his arousal, and she'd listened to enough men talk over the years to know that an aroused man didn't call a halt because he didn't feel like proceeding.

"I'm sorry, Sara," Gideon said finally, still holding her and rocking her. "I did it again, didn't I? Damn it, woman, you turn me on like a switch. It's as embarrassing as hell at my age, but around you I seem to have about as much control as a sixteen-year-old."

NO COST! NO OBLIGATION TO BUY! NO PURCHASE NECESSARY!

PLAY "LUCKY 7" AND GET AS MANY AS FIVE FREE GIFTS...

HOW TO PLAY:

1. With a coin, carefully scratch off the silver box at the right. This makes you eligible to receive two or more free books, and possibly another gift, depending on what is revealed beneath the scratch-off area.

2. Send back this card and you'll receive brand-new Silhouette Intimate Moments® novels. These books have a cover price of $3.39 each, but they are yours to keep absolutely free.

3. There's no catch. You're under no obligation to buy anything. We charge nothing—ZERO—for your first shipment. And you don't have to make any minimum number of purchases—not even one!

4. The fact is thousands of readers enjoy receiving books by mail from the Silhouette Reader Service™ months before they're available in stores. They like the convenience of home delivery and they love our discount prices!

5. We hope that after receiving your free books you'll want to remain a subscriber. But the choice is yours—to continue or cancel, anytime at all! So why not take us up on our invitation, with no risk of any kind. You'll be glad you did!

NOT ACTUAL SIZE

You'll look like a million dollars when you wear this lovely necklace! Its cobra-link chain is a generous 18" long, and the multi-faceted Austrian crystal sparkles like a diamond!

PLAY "LUCKY 7"

**Just scratch off the silver box with a coin.
Then check below to see which gifts you get.**

YES! I have scratched off the silver box. Please send me all the gifts for which I qualify. I understand I am under no obligation to purchase any books, as explained on the back and on the opposite page.

245 CIS AJDR
(U-SIL-IM-05/93)

NAME

ADDRESS   APT

CITY   STATE   ZIP

7 7 7	**WORTH FOUR FREE BOOKS PLUS A FREE CRYSTAL PENDANT NECKLACE**
🍒 🍒 🍒	**WORTH THREE FREE BOOKS PLUS A FREE CRYSTAL PENDANT NECKLACE**
● ● ●	**WORTH THREE FREE BOOKS**
🔔 🔔 🍒	**WORTH TWO FREE BOOKS**

THE SILHOUETTE READER SERVICE™:HERE'S HOW IT WORKS

Accepting free books puts you under no obligation to buy anything. You may keep the books and gift and return the shipping statement marked "cancel." If you do not cancel, about a month later we will send you 6 additional novels, and bill you just $2.71 each plus 25¢ delivery and applicable sales tax, if any.* That's the complete price, and—compared to cover prices of $3.39 each—quite a bargain! You may cancel at any time, but if you choose to continue, every month we'll send you 6 more books, which you may either purchase at the discount price . . . or return at our expense and cancel your subscription.

* Terms and prices subject to change without notice. Sales tax applicable in N.Y.

If offer card is missing, write to: Silhouette Reader Service, 3010 Walden Ave., P.O. Box 1867, Buffalo, NY 14269-1867

BUSINESS REPLY MAIL
FIRST CLASS MAIL   PERMIT NO.717   BUFFALO, NY

POSTAGE WILL BE PAID BY ADDRESSEE

SILHOUETTE READER SERVICE
3010 WALDEN AVE
PO BOX 1867
BUFFALO NY 14240-9952

NO POSTAGE
NECESSARY
IF MAILED
IN THE
UNITED STATES

She still ached, and she still yearned, but common sense told her that she was going to be very glad later that Gideon had as much self-control as he did. More, apparently, than she could claim for herself. It wasn't as if she hadn't been an eager and willing participant. "That's okay," she managed to say.

"Is it? Is it really?" He caught her chin and urged it up so he could read her face. "You're not furious?"

"I think I'm flattered," she said, and blushed. "I mean ... well, I never thought of myself as being ..." How had she gotten into this? There was nothing she could say that wouldn't embarrass her.

"Irresistible?" he supplied. A smile began to dawn on his dark face, and a twinkle came into his dark gray eyes. "A femme fatale? A sex object?"

"Gideon ... !" Squirming, blushing wildly, she tried to break free.

"A siren," he said relentlessly. "Yeah, that's what you are. Something about you is an irresistible lure. It might be those legs of yours. You've got great legs, Mouse. Or maybe it's those warm brown eyes. A man gets an urge to drown in them. Beautiful."

"Gideon, please!"

Laughing softly, he pressed her hot cheek to his shoulder and let it alone.

Later, much later, he lay on the living room floor, his sleeping bag wrapped around him. The storms outside had moved on, leaving the night utterly silent. He could almost feel the emptiness around him, feel the vast spaces outside this house where not another human soul breathed for miles. Closing his eyes, he tried to reach within for the silence in himself, the place that gave him strength and what little peace he'd ever known.

But he couldn't find it. Every time he looked inside himself, he found memories of Sara. Remembered how she had felt in his arms. The woman was easy to hold. Too easy.

A man might forget himself and start building castles in the air with a woman like that in his arms. He might forget that it was all just illusory, and that love was a meaningless word.

He might find himself standing in quicksand with no way out—if he were a deluded fool.

But Gideon Ironheart was nobody's fool.

Chapter 7

The wind blew down off the high snowfields and rippled the grasses of the pasture with its chilly breath. Storm clouds were brewing over the peaks again, promising late afternoon rain.

"Need a jacket?" Gideon asked Zeke. More than a week had passed, and Zeke was getting around pretty well now, except that his ribs pained him if he moved the wrong way. Gideon was still doing all the chores, steadfastly refusing Zeke's help and insisting that the older man take it easy.

"I'm fine, boy," Zeke answered. "It'll take a little more than a breeze to chill me." He still didn't remember what had happened the night he was beaten, but other than that, he insisted he was just fine.

Gideon smothered a smile. "You're just a damn tough old bird, Zeke. And about as hardheaded as they come." He glanced toward the tree line, waiting. They waited every afternoon at this time for the mustangs to make their appearance. He would feel their approach first, through the earth beneath his feet. They always came into the meadow at a dead run, their hooves making thunder on the ground. And it always caused his heart to race and his spirits to soar in some primitive way.

"Have you thought any more about a vision quest?" Zeke said suddenly.

Gideon hesitated, reluctant to admit that he *had* been thinking about it. Simple fact was, the longer he stayed here, the less he wanted to move on. Even his primary purpose in being here, getting to know Micah Parish, had somehow become less pressing. "Why is it so important to you, old man?"

Zeke raised a hand, resting it on the top rail of the corral. He stared past Gideon, beyond even the trees and mountains to someplace only he could see. "You were meant to be *wichasha wakan,* a holy man."

Gideon felt his scalp prickle, as if a chilly wind had touched him. His grandfather had told him the very same thing.

"A holy man is not necessarily a good man," Zeke said presently. "He doesn't have any rules to follow or a certain way he must live. He is an ordinary man living an ordinary life."

"Then why—"

Zeke shook his head. "Listen. A holy man is special only because he has power in him. You have power. I can feel it in the air around you. I'm sure others have told you the same."

Gideon couldn't deny it, but this conversation was making him distinctly uneasy. What *power?* He had never understood what was meant by that.

"You see the grass, how it grows? You see the trees that stand so tall? Each thing must be itself. Must fulfill itself. You have not fulfilled yourself, Ironheart. And you don't need me to tell you that."

No, he didn't need to hear it from Zeke, Gideon thought uncomfortably. But a vision quest?

Before he needed to say anything, he felt the hammering of approaching hooves through his feet. "They're coming," he told Zeke.

The eight horses emerged from the trees at a full, thundering gallop. Reaching the center of the unfenced portion of the meadow, they turned abruptly, circling before coming to a halt.

God, Gideon thought, they were beautiful. Sleek coats, losing some of the winter's protective thickness, glistened in the sun as the seven mares tossed their heads and waited for their stallion to take off again.

Gideon clucked softly, and the roan's ears pricked forward. The game again. Man and horse appeared to enjoy it equally. This time, though, Gideon changed the rules a little. Instead of waiting for the mustang to edge closer, he left the corral fence and walked out into the grassy meadow.

The stallion snorted and reared a little, warning. Gideon halted, then clucked again, softly. "Come on, boy. You know I'm not going to hurt you. Come on...."

Whispering, murmuring, he called the horse to him. Behind him, he heard the sound of Sara's Blazer coming into the yard. She was off duty early, he thought, but both he and the horse ignored the intrusion. They were too absorbed in one another to be distracted.

"Come on, boy. Come on." The meaningless liquid syllables, learned so long ago, tripped over his tongue as he willed the mustang to approach. And little by little the roan pranced nearer, pausing often to snort and visibly hesitate.

But the man, it seemed, was an irresistible lure to the horse. Finally, minutes later, the stallion stood with lowered head right before Gideon and accepted the affectionate touch of the man's hands along his neck and shoulder.

Something swelled in Gideon, a golden bubble of feeling so warm that it was like internal sunlight. The horse trusted him. For an instant he closed his eyes against the emotion and told himself the feeling would pass, that it was just fanciful, that the tightness in his throat was just...

Ah, hell, he thought, and drew a deep, shaky breath. He was having a lot of these feelings lately, feelings he'd never had before, and it was getting harder to tell himself it was a reaction to Barney's death. Parts of himself that had been walled off since childhood were breaking loose, and he was beginning to feel as if he were standing in the middle of shifting sands.

The horse nudged him gently, then laid his head over Gideon's shoulder, just as he often did with his mares. Just as if he felt the man's need.

A sudden, sharp, piercing whistle shattered the quiet. The stallion snorted, jerked away and ran into the trees with his mares hot on his heels.

Gideon swung around angrily, unable to believe that either Sara or Zeke would have done that, and looked into a pair of dark eyes that might have been his own twenty-five years ago.

"Joey!" Sara's horrified exclamation was ignored by her brother. The boy stood there, a black-leather-clad maternal nightmare, and looked at Gideon with all the resentment and anger only a sixteen-year-old boy could feel.

Gideon knew that look. He knew it in his heart and soul, knew his grandfather and uncle had faced it from him nearly every day for years. And he knew what lay behind it. Without a word he began walking toward the youth.

Only the slightest movement betrayed the boy's uneasiness as the tall, powerfully built man bore down on him. Gideon halted just two feet from the boy.

"Why'd you do that?" he asked, his voice deceptively soft.

Joey shrugged. "Hell, it looked like you were going to f—"

The word never escaped the boy's mouth. Before he finished his obscenity, Gideon had lifted him off his feet by the front of his leather jacket.

"Let's get something straight here, boy," Gideon said softly. "You're nothing but a little punk until you prove you're a man, and nobody around here is going to take any crap from a punk. You make your sister or your grandfather upset, and you and I will be talking out behind the barn. And while we're on the subject, clean up your language."

For an interminable moment he stared into the blazing hatred in the boy's eyes and saw the fright behind it. Then he set Joey on his feet.

"With that out of the way," Gideon said quietly, "I'm sure we'll get along just fine. I'm Gideon Ironheart." He held out his hand and waited.

For an endless time it seemed that Joey would ignore the gesture. Sara watched, torn between a feeling that Gideon had had no right to handle Joey that way and the realization that her brother had deserved it. More, that he had *needed* it. And now she could hardly breathe for fear that her brother would refuse to shake hands with Gideon. What then? If Joey made things too uncomfortable around here, Gideon might leave, and Sara honestly didn't think she could stand that.

But Joey reached out at last and shook Gideon's hand.

"My pleasure, son," Gideon said as if nothing at all had happened before the handshake. Then he touched the brim of his hat to Sara, nodded to Zeke and headed for his truck.

"I'll be out late," he tossed over his shoulder. "Don't wait dinner." He had to get out of here, he thought. Absolutely, positively had to get out of here. It was getting too easy to hang around, getting too comfortable to be here. Why should he give a damn about what was going on inside Joey Yates? Why should he feel any urge at all to straighten the boy out? The kid wasn't his problem.

And Sara. Sara *was* his problem. The woman was living, breathing temptation. Well, that was one ache he could ease in town.

If he could make himself sink that low.

Somewhere around two in the morning, Sara gave up all pretense of trying to sleep. She pulled on her jeans and a sweater, and tiptoed downstairs with her boots in hand. Thank goodness she didn't have to work in the morning.

Outside, clouds had buried the stars, leaving the night inky. Wind shifted restlessly, a lonesome sound in the dark.

The air smelled of pines and grass, and was soft with a promise of rain.

She pulled on her boots and wished there was moonlight so she could take a walk. Instead, she had to settle for standing in the yard and soaking up the scents and sounds of the night.

Gideon hadn't returned yet, and she guessed she wasn't going to sleep until he did. He'd walked off, leaving the evening chores for her and Joey to take care of, and that wasn't like him. The Gideon she had come to know these past couple of weeks was an extremely responsible man, not the kind to forget evening chores or assume someone else would do them. For all he claimed to be a tumbleweed, he never left a thing undone. Not a thing. He was a finisher, not a quitter.

Something had been troubling him, and she didn't think it was Joey, obnoxious as he had been. Gideon had been mad, not shocked by the boy. And whatever was bothering him, she suspected, had been coming on for some time. Any number of times in the past week she'd caught him staring pensively at nothing in particular, and once or twice she'd seen him grab on to something and just stand there for several minutes, as if he was in some kind of pain. And then he would straighten and carry on as if nothing had happened.

She wished—oh, how she wished!—there was something she could do for him. And wished he would touch her again, kiss her again, hold her again. She wanted to be in his arms so badly that she ached nearly every moment of every day. Ached so badly that sometimes she was even able to convince herself that it didn't matter that he'd eventually leave if only she could have him right now.

Which made her a fool again, she thought with a sigh, whether anybody else knew it or not. And why should he want her, anyway? George had been so chilled by the prospect of bedding her that he'd fled all the way to Denver. So scared of being stuck for life with her that he'd tried to hide. Maybe Gideon hadn't backed off out of some sense of nobility, after all. Maybe he, too, had found her in some way repulsive.

Hardly thinking about it, she walked to the bunkhouse and sat on the porch step, knowing that she wouldn't sleep until Gideon returned, so she might as well make sure he got back in one piece.

He'd probably be full of beer or whiskey and smelling of cheap perfume, she told herself. Nine years as a deputy had taught her the uglier side of male pastimes. She knew every dive, every hooker and every easy woman in town. Sooner or later she'd had to deal with every single one of them. Even in a county this underpopulated, there was plenty of work for prostitutes. Cowboys in from the range made sure of that. Gideon would probably have to fight the women off. If he even wanted to.

That thought caused her a serious pang, but she shoved it aside. She knew men, and she wasn't going to let herself fall into some delusion that Gideon Ironheart was different. There was no reason why he should be. He wasn't married and didn't have kids to worry about, after all.

She heard his truck on the drive long before his lights punctured the darkness. There was plenty of time for her to escape, to run back to the house so he would never know she had waited for him, but something kept her where she was, holding her as surely as if she were nailed to the spot.

If he was drunk and reeking of some woman, she told herself, it would free her of this need she felt for him. She would be so disgusted that she would never want him to touch her again. Men in that condition always revolted her.

And if he wasn't . . . if he wasn't, she might be in serious trouble.

The truck pulled into the yard, and its headlights pinned her in their glare. Slowly Gideon pulled up and stopped. For a minute he let the engine run and stared at her sitting there on the bunkhouse porch. Waiting for him. Looking a little lost, a little sad and a whole lot frightened.

If he had a single ounce of common sense, he told himself, he would drive out of the yard right now and head back to town. But he evidently didn't have any common sense, because he switched off his lights and his engine and climbed out.

She didn't move. For a moment neither of them moved, waiting for their eyes to adapt to the darkness.

"Is something wrong?" he asked her finally.

She shook her head. "I just couldn't sleep." He didn't sound drunk, she thought with relief.

"Yeah." He hesitated a little longer, then came to sit beside her on the porch step. "I'm sorry I stomped off the way I did. I know I left you with all those damn chores."

"Joey helped. That's why he's back here, you know. He managed to convince Nate that he wanted to come home and help out because Grandfather was injured."

"And I was here. No wonder the kid was so mad. Maybe I should just move on." He'd been thinking about that all evening but couldn't quite convince himself to do it.

"No," said Sara, battling a wave of panic. "No. Not unless you want to. Nothing around here is going to get bent out of shape for Joey ever again. It's time he started learning to accommodate himself to other people."

Gideon nodded, granting her that. It was a lesson everyone had to learn sooner or later. "Well, I'm still sorry I tore out of here and left you to cope. I don't usually do that."

"I know you don't."

The quiet conviction in her voice caused him to turn his head and peer at her in the dark. Her confidence in him was like a warm touch. "Thank you," he said, meaning it.

"I've had nearly two weeks to learn a few things about you," she told him, brushing it aside. "You're honest, you're honorable, and you don't leave things undone."

"A regular Boy Scout, huh?"

She surprised him with a soft, rippling laugh. "Not quite."

"That's a relief. A man likes to think he's at least a little bit of a rogue." He wanted to reach out and catch a handful of her hair, reach out and pull her close until her mouth was under his and her small breasts were crushed against his chest. Three times tonight he'd sent an interested woman away because he just couldn't stir up any interest in anyone but Sara. He'd been thinking about that, too, when he thought about moving on. "Why are you sitting out here, Sara Yates?" He meant here on the bunkhouse steps instead of her own porch. She could ignore that distinction if she chose to.

She didn't choose to, maybe because it was the middle of the night and her mind wasn't as clear as it should have been. Maybe because deep inside she wanted him to know, wanted somehow to close the distance between them. "I was worried about you."

He wanted to dismiss her concern with some easy, flip remark, but the words wouldn't come. "Thanks," he said gruffly. "Thanks." God, nobody had worried about him in more years than he wanted to think about. Nobody had waited up for him; nobody had even wondered where he was. "Sometimes ... sometimes I just have to be by myself."

Sara bit her lip, afraid to press him, yet concerned enough to be unable to let it alone. Finally concern won out. "Sometimes...sometimes I get the feeling that you...hurt very badly."

Gideon's heart stopped. He didn't even draw a breath as an extraordinary stillness filled him. All his life, whenever he hurt, he had been expected to go off by himself and lick his own wounds in private. Nobody wanted to hear, nobody wanted to know. Even his uncle, forever understanding about such things, was silent about them. He gave Gideon the place and the privacy, but left it to him to manage his own pain. It was the way a man was supposed to do it.

Nobody ever, not once in his entire life, had wanted to hear about it. To share it. And he didn't know if he could even talk about it. Not really. Not in any meaningful way. "I, um ..."

Sara reached out and touched his forearm. "I know it's none of my business, Gideon. I just ... worry."

And suddenly the world was spinning again. Even though it was pitch-dark, he saw spiraling blue sky, saw the beam swinging and spinning, felt his grip on the steel slipping, felt as if he was falling....

"I felt him die."

The words seemed to be torn from Gideon's throat, and he bent over until his head was between his knees. Sara hesitated only a moment and then reached out instinctively to wrap her arm around his back. She felt the horrible tension in him, felt the subtle tremors of violent emotion suppressed.

"I keep feeling it," he said, his voice little more than a raw whisper as the pain erupted from the deep well in which he tried to hide it from everyone else. "Over and over and over."

For the longest time he stayed as he was, doubled over and silent, buffeted by waves of anguish. And then, almost as swiftly as he had been overcome, he overcame it. He straightened, looking out into the dark as if he could see something there. When he spoke, his voice was once again normal—or close to it.

"Sorry. I get these flashbacks and feel like I'm falling."

"You fell?" Sara asked tentatively, trying to understand what was happening, why he was so torn up.

For the space of several heartbeats he didn't answer, and Sara began to think he wasn't going to. And that was his right, she told herself. Absolutely his right.

"Connectors work in pairs," he said suddenly. "It's absolutely essential to be able to read your partner, to know what he's going to do, how he operates. You have to be able to trust him with your life. So when you find a good partner, you tend to stick together. Barney and I worked together on every job for the last thirteen years. We were... close. Really close." He drew a long breath. "Last October, Barney fell. Seventy stories."

"Oh, my God!" She reached out again, covering his hand with hers and holding on tight. "Oh, Gideon!"

"I felt him die, Sara. Maybe nobody will ever believe that," he said rawly, "but I felt him die. And there wasn't a damn thing I could do except hang on to the column and wait for it to be over. But I felt it, Sara. *I felt it*."

"I believe you. Oh, Gideon, I believe you."

He turned suddenly and gathered her to him, crushing her to his chest, hanging on as if she were a lifeline in a world gone mad. There just weren't words to tell anybody how it had felt to have Barney *gone*. There was a hole in him where Barney had been, and in the moment of his friend's death he had felt something ripped out of his soul by its roots, leaving nothing but a bleeding wound.

For thirteen years he and Barney had worked together, drunk together, fished together, hunted together. Brothers. Even Barney's marriage hadn't come between them. They'd simply packed Jolene up with the tent or the boat and taken her with them. Jolene had loved it. She had even loved moving from town to town, wherever the jobs took them.

"What happened to Jolene?" Sara asked softly.

Her question jarred him out of his memories, and back to the chilly Wyoming night and the restless sighing of the wind in the trees. Only when she spoke did he realize he'd been talking. Rambling. Spilling his guts about Barney. He started to pull away, but her arms tightened, clinging, and honest to God, he needed her touch. He stayed.

"She...uh...she told me she didn't want to see me again for a long time. Said I made her...think of Barney every time she set eyes on me."

Oh God, Sara thought, pain ripping her heart. Even then, the person who could have most shared his grief had left him on the outside. He'd been on the outside his entire life, never belonging, never fitting. Always looking in but never asked to come inside. Except for his grandfather and uncle, she amended. They'd asked him in, but she suspected he was so used to being on the outside that he didn't know any other way to be.

Squeezing her eyes shut against the ache in her heart, she had a sudden memory of Gideon Ironheart as she had first

seen him, standing at the center of a group of men who
wanted to beat him to a pulp. Refusing to give an inch.
Fighting for the right to stand at a damn bar and order a
sandwich. Refusing to be cast out because of his skin.

But he was already an emotional outcast, and he didn't
even know it. Didn't even realize that he had accepted that
he should always be on the outside looking in.

That was the moment when Sara realized that she had already invited him in. He was there, in her heart, as not even
George had been. But how could she tell him that? she
wondered miserably, aching for both of them. He would
rear up like that damn mustang and dash for the trees, believing himself to be a wild creature. He would shy away and
tell her that he was a tumbleweed, that he didn't believe in
love.

And he didn't. That was the really odd thing about him.
He didn't believe in it, but he practiced it with nearly every
breath he took. Look at the way he took care of Zeke. The
way he had fretted about her safety, the way he looked after the ranch when Zeke couldn't. The way he whispered to
that damn mustang. The way he called his uncle every few
days to check on the old man.

She couldn't tell him, she realized, tightening her hold on
him. But she could certainly show him.

When at length he eased away, she let him go. You
couldn't hold a wild thing, she reminded herself. It had to
want to be held.

The wind whispered of things lost, and the night yielded
no secrets. It was lonely out here, and empty. The vastness
of the Wyoming night was awesome.

"I'm sorry, Sara," he said after a bit. "I didn't mean to
dump all over you."

"That's what friends are for."

"You've got enough problems of your own. Joey's a real
handful, isn't he?"

She let him change the subject. "He can be."

"What exactly do you think is eating him?"

She sighed then and lifted her feet to a higher step so she could hug her knees. "I'm not sure. He was little when we lost our parents, but he was never a problem until just about two years ago. I keep thinking something must have happened, but I sure don't know what. I've tried talking to him. I've suggested counseling. I've begged his teachers for clues and patience and help, and nothing changes."

She wiggled her toes in her boots and shivered a little as the breeze snaked into the neck of her sweater. "Nate didn't really want to send him home," she said after a few minutes.

"Why not?"

"He doesn't believe Joey's really turning over a new leaf. He said Joey's just scared right now, but not scared enough to change."

Gideon thought about what little he'd seen of the boy during their confrontation this afternoon. "He's scared, all right. More than a little scared."

A small laugh escaped Sara. "Frankly, Gideon, I think anybody would be petrified to have you lift them right off their feet with one hand the way you did Joey. Lordy, I couldn't believe I was seeing it!"

He chuckled and raised his arm, making a muscle for her inspection. "These arms have moved more tons of steel than Schwarzenegger. Joey's a snap by comparison."

She reached out and touched the bulge of his biceps through the chambray of his shirt. "Hard," she said approvingly. Like steel. Like iron.

He let his arm relax beneath her hand, and the firm resilience of his flesh proved far more seductive than the bulge of taut muscle. She snatched her hand back as if burned, realizing that friendly play might turn into something else. Much as she wanted him, she wasn't yet convinced she should take that step.

"It's late," she said, telling herself that she really ought to go back to bed. She was still restless, but the excuse of wanting to be sure Gideon returned safely was no longer even an excuse. She had absolutely no business being out here with him like this. He was bound to be wondering about it, and what if he drew the wrong conclusion? Not that she was sure there was a wrong conclusion.

The crazy spiraling of her thoughts suddenly stopped dead when Gideon claimed her hand and held it between both of his. His touch was warm but innocent. She could have sworn he was hardly aware of what he was doing. But *she* was aware—acutely, exquisitely aware of the dry, callused heat of his palm against hers.

"Just a few more minutes," he said.

"All right."

"You never told me why you're hiding, Sara Yates."

She stiffened and tried to yank her hand away, but he held on tightly. The reminder of George was as good as a fall into an icy river. In an instant she was very much alert and very much wary.

"Come on, Mouse. I bared my soul. Now it's your turn."

She turned her head and looked straight at him, wishing she could see him better, could read his expression. It was so dark, though, that she could barely make out the deep-set hollows of his eyes. "Who said this was a trade?"

"Me. I've been wondering since I clapped eyes on you." Keeping his grip on her with one hand, he raised the other to touch her cheek. It was a touch so exquisitely tender that her throat tightened. "Someone hurt you," he said. "Someone wounded you, and now you talk tough and wear a badge and hide behind a shotgun and mirrored glasses."

"Gideon—"

"Hush, little mouse," he said softly. "Hush. I've been living here for twelve days, and the Sara Yates who lives at the Double Y is not the Sara Yates the rest of the world sees. You put on a shell when you leave here. Why?"

She licked her dry lips and tried not to lean into his fingers, which were now tracing the curve of her cheek. He was leaving, she reminded herself for the umpteenth time. At any moment he would get bored with ranch life and go back to building skyscrapers. "Why do you call me 'Mouse'?"

He chuckled softly. "Changing the subject, Mouse? I call you Mouse because you remind me of something very small, very soft and very warm." He hesitated, and then thought what the hell. Sara would understand. "When I was in the orphanage, there was this little brown mouse who used to come into our dormitory at night. It took a long time and an awful lot of bread crumbs, but he finally would climb onto my knee when I sat on the floor. And sometimes he would let me touch him. That little brown mouse is the only really good memory I have of those years."

Her hand was suddenly gripping his hand as tightly as he gripped hers. She *did* understand.

"So," he said quietly, "who hurt you, Mouse?"

He wasn't going to let it go, she realized. And maybe, she thought, it was only fair. It was just that it was so humiliating to remember, so humiliating to speak of. She kept telling herself she shouldn't feel that way, that she hadn't done anything wrong, and that it was George who should be embarrassed, but the fact was, rejection was humiliating. No two ways about it. And no woman wanted to admit that she'd sent her fiancé into panicked flight.

A sigh escaped her, and at the sound Gideon slipped his arm around her shoulder. "What happened?"

"Oh, it sounds so stupid," she said, her voice little more than a shaky whisper. "I dated this guy all the way through high school, you know?"

He squeezed her, letting her come at things in her own way.

"We went everywhere together, did everything together. It was just ... accepted, I guess, that we'd marry. Everyone thought so. His family. My family. All our friends. The date was set before we even graduated."

"Weren't you kind of young?"

Sara shrugged. "We're behind the times out here. People don't think it's unusual to marry out of high school. I mean, if all you're going to do is ranch, why wait? And there sure isn't any fast lane around here to dabble in."

"No, I guess not."

"It's changing, I guess. Not so many people marry right away now. A lot more of them go to college than even ten years ago."

She was changing the subject again, he realized. So he pulled her back. "What happened?"

"We set the date for my birthday, August third. His mother and father were still alive then, and they wanted a big bash. I think everybody in the county was invited, and an awful lot of people from Laramie and Cheyenne. They weren't going to be able to get everyone into the church, so a lot of people only got invited to the reception, which is unusual, I guess. It was to be a big barbecue at the Bar C, the Cumberland ranch."

Gideon tried to look down at her, but the dark defeated him. "We aren't talking about Jeff Cumberland, are we?"

She shook her head. "His younger brother. George Cumberland." Even the sound of his name made her stomach roil. "Things were out of my control right from the start. I remember feeling like a doll. I got pushed this way and pulled that way by Mrs. Cumberland. I didn't even get to say two words about my wedding dress. She dragged me to Laramie and picked it out herself. Sometimes I think—" She broke off.

"Think what, Mouse?" he prompted gently. "What do you think?"

"That maybe George wouldn't have gotten so scared if his mother hadn't taken over the way she did. I mean, I hardly even got to see him from graduation day until our wedding day. When I did, there were always a dozen other people there. It was like riding a runaway train."

"Didn't you get scared, too?"

"A little. I threw up my whole breakfast the morning of the wedding." She blushed and averted her face, forgetting he could barely see her in the dark, anyway. "I'm sorry. You didn't need to know that."

He gave a soft laugh. "It kind of completes the picture, Sara. My stomach is knotting in sympathy. Okay, here we are, the morning of your...eighteenth birthday, right?"

"Eighteen," she agreed. "That morning Dad gave me my mother's necklace, a gold chain with a tiny diamond pendant. I felt so grown-up when I put it on." She sighed again and unconsciously leaned against him. "To make a long story short, I dressed, I went to the church, everybody arrived, and people squeezed in until you could almost hear the place groan. And George never showed up."

"Never?" He let go and put his other arm around her, holding her tight. "What happened?"

"He chickened out. Only we didn't know that at first. At first we just waited. Then we got scared something had happened to him. I think I must have cried a couple of gallons of tears. Nate had the deputies searching high and low. Honest to God, Gideon, we expected to find a corpse."

"I imagine so." His heart squeezed for her, imagining the hell she must have gone through.

Sara drew a deep breath and plunged ahead, needing now to finish it. "He finally called around midnight and told Jeff that he was in Denver and he was never coming back, that he wouldn't marry me if I were the last woman on earth...."

"Jeff told you that?" Gideon wanted to sock the rancher right in the jaw.

"No, oh no. We were all sitting in Jeff's study by that time. Mr. and Mrs. Cumberland, Jeff, my father, Reverend Fromberg. Waiting to hear from the sheriff. When George called, Jeff put it on the speaker. When George started talking like that, Jeff switched off the speaker, but not before I heard—" Not before she heard. Not before the scar had been hacked even wider and deeper by George's tongue. "I was mortified," she whispered. "I wanted to die. And everyone was so nice, so sweet. Jeff offered to date me.... I think he'd have married me on the spot if I'd wanted it. And his parents were wonderful. But...conversations came to a dead halt whenever I entered a room for months afterwards. And I felt . . . I felt . . .''

"Violated? Wounded? Emotionally raped?" Gideon would have liked to wring George Cumberland's neck.

Somehow her head had come to rest in the hollow of his shoulder, and now both his arms cradled her gently. "All of that and a few other things besides," she admitted. "I hid out here on the ranch for a long time, but then Dad died, and I really needed to go to work if I was going to hang on to this place. Nate hired me, and the rest, as they say, is history."

Well, that sure explained it, Gideon thought. She had been publicly humiliated, so, naturally, for the last ten years she'd put on a tough facade that told everyone she didn't care and couldn't be hurt.

Some tender little place in him, some private little corner that hadn't been blighted by all the abandonments in his own life, ached for her. He wanted so badly to soothe her pain, to wipe away her embarrassment, but he didn't know how. Her rejection by George had left a deep wound, a wound made all the deeper by the fact that he had blamed his defection on her.

"The bastard didn't know what he was throwing away," he said gruffly.

Sara almost smiled into his shoulder. "You're sweet."

"Sweet? Me? Hell, no."

He sounded so uncomfortable with the idea that Sara chuckled softly and let it go. Telling him about George, crazily enough, seemed to have lifted some kind of load from her shoulders. Somehow she no longer felt quite as humiliated.

The wind rustled in the treetops and blew a chilly breath across her cheeks. "It's late. I really ought to get to bed." She started to pull away from him, wishing like mad she could stay, knowing such a wish was in vain. He'd made it clear enough over the last week that he wanted to avoid involvement with her. Since the night in the kitchen, he'd tried very hard not to even brush against her by accident.

"No," he said, surprising her by tightening his arms around her and preventing her escape. He'd been holding this woman for the last half hour, and now his throbbing, aching, hungry body was doing the talking. "No. Stay with me, Sara. Please."

Chapter 8

At the instant he spoke, the wind ceased and the world grew hushed. In the silence, he heard her sharply indrawn breath.

Oh, God, he thought, wishing he could take back the words. How could he have said it so baldly? How could he have asked such a thing of her without even a kiss to sweeten the words? Why had he said it at all? She deserved a lot more than he could offer, and he had no right to ask this of her.

But he *had* asked, and the words lay between them in a world that seemed to be holding its breath. Sara didn't move, didn't try to pull away, but she, too, seemed to be holding her breath, waiting for something more.

He had little experience of women like Sara. She was a cut above him in so many ways, aeons removed from the easy women he'd met in bars when the need got too great to ignore. They had been lonely, too, and hungry, and looking for a night of forgetfulness. Sara wasn't like them.

So what now, Ironheart? he asked himself as the whole night seemed to wait with bated breath. If she stays, will I be able to please her? If she stays, will she hate me tomorrow?

It would be better, he told himself, if he just laughed and told her he'd been teasing. Except that he'd waited too long to laugh now. The significance of his words grew with each passing moment.

Stay with me, Sara. Please. The words echoed in her mind, resounded in the hollow emptiness of her heart. A moment ago she had been wishing she didn't have to leave, and now he had asked her to stay. Wisdom dictated that she flee. Years of avoiding the pain and humiliation urged her to run as if all the hounds of hell were in pursuit. Her heart, empty for so long, begged her to stay. And her body... her body was on fire from little more than the roughly murmured plea to stay.

If she stayed, she would eventually hurt, because Gideon would eventually leave. She was honest enough, even as longing drizzled through her to the most private of places, to admit that she didn't know if she would be able to endure being a spurned lover. The pain of losing Gideon, she suspected, was going to be far worse than the pain of losing George, even if they never made love.

Yet if she turned away now, she would probably spend the rest of her life regretting it. Lately it had been occurring to her off and on that the last ten years had been a wasteland. Someday she was going to run out of future, and it would be awful to look back and see nothing but missed opportunities.

But even that didn't sway her as much as her need. Every cell in her body yearned toward Gideon. Her heart reached out to him; her soul recognized him. If heaven granted her only one night, it was a night for which she would be forever grateful.

And then, for one agonizing moment, it occurred to her that he might have been teasing her.

"Do you—" Her whisper fractured, then steadied. "Do you mean it?"

Now. Tell her it was a joke. Tell her that he'd momentarily lost his senses but was sane again. Tell her.

"With every cell in my body," he said roughly. "With every single aching inch of me. Damn it, Mouse, I'm on fire for you. Now get out of here before I do something about it."

She should have run. He was surprised when she didn't. He was stunned when she put her hand on his thigh. "Is this—is this where your little brown mouse perched?"

Sara's heart was in her throat, hammering so hard she could hear it. Resting her hand on his thigh was the most daring thing she'd ever done, more daring by far than breaking up a brawl or chasing a speeder. Dying, she thought, would be easier than exposing herself this way. George had fled, and perhaps Gideon just hadn't yet noticed whatever it was that made her so repulsive.

But the feel of denim and taut muscle beneath her palm was as exciting as anything she had ever felt, and she couldn't bring herself to be wise. Scared to death, hoping against hope, she waited.

Maybe she didn't understand what he meant. He had to give her one last chance, one last warning. "I won't stop."

"God, I hope not," she said shakily.

She understood, and he had run out of nobility, restraint and self-control. Rising, he pulled her to her feet and drew her toward the bunkhouse door. Toward his cave. Toward the dark warmth of a private place where he could claim her as men have claimed women since time immemorial.

He wanted a light. He wanted to be able to see her, but he ignored the wall switch as he tugged her into the bedroom, then ignored the lamp on the nightstand. He wanted nothing, absolutely nothing, to jar her and cause her to rethink her decision. He didn't want any harsh light of reality to pierce the darkly sensual mood that stretched between them.

What he most wanted right now was the feeling. The feeling of closeness and caring, of need and hunger. Later he could fill his eyes with her, but right now he wanted to fill his hands with her, his lungs, his mouth, and to fill her body with himself.

A shaky little sigh escaped her as he tugged the sweater over her head and discovered she wasn't wearing a bra. He growled softly with pleasure as he found her small breasts and covered them with his callused hands. Her hardening nipples pressed his palms, and recognition of her growing arousal zinged straight to his groin, making him throb.

"I'm...so small," she whispered apologetically.

That almost inaudible confession punched him in the gut. For an instant he froze, absorbing a truth about Sara Yates that he'd somehow managed to miss. Somehow he hadn't seen the fears and inadequacy she felt, hadn't realized that George Cumberland had done more than humiliate her. He had gutted her womanhood, leaving her frightened, uncertain and full of self-doubt.

"You're so exactly perfect," he corrected her gruffly. "You have no idea just how good you feel to me. Just take my word for it. You're exactly right for me. And I can't tell you..." Still cupping her breasts, he bent and pressed a kiss to her shoulder. "Oh, babe, I can't tell you what it means when you let me touch you like this. Especially when you're shy about it." And that was true. The fact that this was not a casual, easy thing for her to do aroused him as little had, piercing the armor plating around his heart.

She drew another shaky breath, and then a soft little moan spilled from her as he brushed his thumbs over her beading nipples. The sigh and the moan passed directly into his ear as he kissed her smooth shoulder, and his loins clenched with deepening need.

Pretty little breasts. He didn't need to see them to know that, and it didn't matter whether they were crowned in pink or brown. What mattered was that her nipples rose eagerly to his touch, and her body moved restlessly in response. What mattered was that she let him bend and draw her swollen nipple deep into his mouth, and then clutched wildly at him as the pleasure ripped through her.

"Oh, baby," he whispered raggedly when he tried to catch his breath. No woman had ever responded to him this way, so quickly, so hotly, so artlessly. Her hands tugged at his shoulders, and she whispered something. "Hmm? I didn't hear you, Mouse."

"Your hair," she whispered breathlessly.

"My hair?" He had once again tied it at the nape of his neck with the thong.

"Untie it," she demanded on a gasp. She wanted all of him, and that included his unbound hair. She couldn't have begun to express why that aroused her so much, except that it seemed like such an intimacy. Except that his hair was never completely free but was always tied back, or restrained by the thong around his forehead. Except when he was loving her.

Lifting a hand, Gideon yanked the leather from his hair and threw it across the room. Then he grabbed the snaps of his shirt and ripped them open. Sara's hands were there immediately, reaching out to help him pull the cloth from his shoulders. A violent shudder ripped through him as her breasts brushed the smooth skin of his chest.

"Sara..." Her name emerged on a deep groan as he gathered her closer.

She raised her arms and plowed her fingers into his long, dark hair, finding his scalp and then grabbing handfuls of his mane to tug his mouth down to hers. He liked it. Oh, God, he liked the way she demanded from him, liked the way she grabbed and pulled him closer. And now she was stretched against him, her breasts crushed to the hard wall of his chest. Roughly, almost urgently, his palms swept the long, silky length of her back and closed on her soft, full rump. With another groan he tightened his grip and lifted her against him.

Sara tore her mouth from his and threw back her head, arching against him, still clutching handfuls of his hair. A moan escaped her as for the first time in her life a man's body fitted intimately to hers. Two layers of denim were suddenly all that lay between her and fulfillment. Wanting more, so much more, she wrapped her legs around his narrow hips, settling the hard ridge of his arousal even more snugly against herself. And even that was not nearly enough.

If it were possible, his powerful arms tightened even more around her, pressing her so close now that she could barely breathe. The world spun wildly, and then she found herself lying on her back on the quilt of his bed. Her knees were still locked around his hips, and he knelt over her, bearing his weight on his elbows.

"Lord, Sara," he muttered, and began dropping hot little kisses over her cheek and neck. "You turn a man inside out."

Fear struck her, freezing passion in an instant. "Is that— is that bad?"

Her words stilled him. For what felt like an eternity, Gideon didn't move, didn't breathe. Finally he spoke harshly. "I'll kill him. If I ever lay eyes on that son of a bitch, I'll kill him."

"Who?" Sara asked, confused, afraid that she had somehow revolted him.

"George Cumberland, that's who. The man— Man? Hell, I won't even dignify him with that. The *creep* who made you feel something is wrong with you. There's not a damn thing wrong with you, Mouse. Not a one. As for being turned inside out, it's never happened to me before, but I'm loving every minute of it."

Except that now he was mad. Growling with frustration, he rose from the bed and stripped off the rest of his clothes—the boots, the socks, the jeans, the briefs. Sara couldn't see a thing but dark shadows flying this way and that, but she heard the thumps and muttered curses.

And then he was with her again. Reaching out, he pulled her against his naked body and settled one hand on her denim-clad bottom.

"Let's talk about this, Mouse," he said roughly.

"Talk about what?" Her voice was little more than a tentative whisper. He was mad, and she knew it was her fault, and something inside her squeezed painfully as she waited for Gideon to tell her what she had done wrong. To enumerate her failures. God, she was no good at being a woman. Hadn't George said that? How could she have forgotten?

"This. Cumberland. How you feel. How you make me feel. And whether you really want to do this."

"But—" He silenced her with a finger over her mouth before she could protest that she did, indeed, really want to do this. That she thought she would die if she didn't.

"Relax," he said softly. "I'm here, and I'm not going anywhere. Believe me, Mouse, you'll have to *throw* me out. But there are obviously a couple of things that need clearing up."

She wished she could see his face. Wished she could see him as he was now, completely nude. And was glad the darkness hid her from him. "Such as?"

"Such as how you make me feel. I've been wanting to make love with you since the night you rescued me from those rednecks. I kid you not. I was standing there, hating having to be rescued by a woman, and getting so turned on by your voice I was worried you'd notice."

"My voice?"

"Your voice is husky and sexy and enough to drive a man out of his mind. From the first word you spoke, I was having visions of being with you like this. Before I even noticed what a beautiful rear end you have. Before I realized that you've got the sexiest little sway when you walk. Before you wore that denim skirt and I got an eyeful of your legs. I've been wanting to kiss your knees for a solid week now. And as for your breasts..."

Sara gasped and arched as his mouth suddenly closed over the aching mound of her breast and his tongue teased her nipple into hardness.

"As for your breasts," he said huskily a short while later, "any more than a mouthful is wasted. I don't know what was the matter with George, Mouse, but there sure as hell isn't a problem with your sex appeal."

Shivering with longing and heat, Sara lay against him and hung on for dear life, waiting for the world to settle down again. He didn't give it much chance.

"Now, about turning me inside out," he continued, his voice deep and throaty as he reached for the snap of her jeans. "Babe, I love it. I love it when you grab me and pull me closer. I love it when you kiss me, when you touch me, and I hope to heaven you'll be making a lot more demands on me before this night is out. Get bossy. Tell me what you want and make me give you enough of it, because, sweet little mouse, there's no bigger turn-on in the world for me than knowing you want me, too."

His words were as arousing as any touch he had given her, and spirals of shimmering need swirled through her, reaching her core and leaving her damp. "Gideon," she whispered achingly. "Oh, Gideon . . ."

He tugged the snap on her jeans and released it. At the sound, her entire center seemed to clamp with an almost painful throb of need.

"Tell me now, Mouse," he said. "Tell me now. Another thirty seconds and nothing will stop me."

"Don't stop," she said hoarsely. "Don't ever stop."

The husky demand nearly pushed him right over the edge, but he caught himself before he acted on it. Liquid fire lapped at his loins, and his lungs strained for more air, and he hadn't yet even removed her jeans. God, had he ever gotten so hot so fast? So easily?

Her boots resisted his tugs, but only briefly. He peeled her jeans and panties down her legs without regard to modesty. It was dark, after all, so there was no reason why she should be embarrassed or shy.

And then they were pressed together, naked skin to naked skin. Sara drew a shuddering breath and dug her nails into his shoulders. "Oh, you feel so good. . . ."

And it was so unbelievably intimate to be pressed to him this way. She could feel every line of him, including his hard arousal and the thicket of hair from which it sprang. And almost as if it had a mind of its own, her hand slipped downward and closed around him. She had never touched a man so boldly, but the need to touch Gideon that way overwhelmed every inhibition. He was big. He was hard. He was built like a warrior, she thought dizzily.

Gideon sucked air through his teeth as her curious touch unleashed rivers of fire in his blood. Slowly, helplessly, he rocked his hips and rubbed himself against her palm.

Grasping the idea, her natural shyness warring with an equally natural desire to drive him out of his mind, Sara mimicked the motion with her hand. And smiled into the dark when Gideon groaned. "You like that?" she whispered. Even that much was hard to say when she felt so breathless, so hot, so excited.

He was in little better state. He answered in a whisper that sounded as if air was in short supply. "Oh, yeah!" Sara's hands were not a soft woman's hands. They were hard-working hands, callused and strong, but the roughness was just a new titillation, and for a few moments he let himself enjoy the sheer magic of her touch.

Pleasuring Gideon was the most powerful aphrodisiac Sara had ever experienced. A low, steady throbbing began in her, seeming to time itself to the motions of her hands and the slight, subtle movements of Gideon's hips as she touched him. Unconsciously, she clamped her legs together tighter and tighter, trying to ease the growing ache, trying to banish the increasing sense of emptiness. Unconsciously she began to rock her own hips, seeking more.

Then suddenly, almost before she knew it was happening, Gideon pushed her onto her back and captured her hands above her head. One of his long, powerful legs settled between hers and began to move slowly up and down, pressing, retreating. Sara caught her breath and clamped her legs together, catching Gideon between them.

He gave a soft, deep laugh. "Ah, she likes that." Before Sara could manage a response, he covered her mouth with his and stole her breath in a stunningly erotic kiss. His tongue and leg moved in matched rhythms, causing her womb to throb in response. Forgetting everything but what she was feeling, Sara arched, pressing herself to him. More. Harder. Deeper. She clutched at him with her legs, undulated against him and made little sounds deep in her throat.

And he loved it. Oh, damn, did he love it. With one hand he held her wrists above her head, using the other to prop himself above her. After a quick nip at her lower lip, he took his mouth from hers and moved lower, seeking those small, shy breasts. When his tongue found her, she arched as tightly as a drawn bow and moaned his name.

The sound was like liquid heat pouring into his ears and running to the farthest, darkest reaches of his body. Of his soul. The sounds of this woman's pleasure affected him as no other's had. The feel of her silky skin beneath his palm was warmer, smoother, than any he had ever touched. Each slender, graceful line of her seemed precious, perfect.

He wanted her...wanted her...wanted her. The desire was like a drumbeat in his hot blood, hammering at him, driving him. Not sure he could wait much longer, he slipped his hand downward, heading toward her womanhood, needing to feel her heat. Needing to measure her readiness.

She stiffened at the first touch of his fingers, stiffened and grew utterly still. He was past stopping now, though. Well past. He found slick folds and pressed further, drawing a gasp from her as he slipped a finger into her. Just a little way. Just enough to feel her wetness.

She panted. Once. Twice. Again. Then he drew his now wet finger upward until he found that tiny knot of nerves, that one place that could push her to the brink. Gently, carefully, he stroked her.

"Do it for me, Mouse," he whispered huskily. "Do it for me."

She had no idea what he meant, but she was in no condition to care. Each touch of his fingers sent ribbons of electricity through her and built the growing ache at her center. When he released her hands, she reached for him, needing him closer. Needing to be filled by him, crushed by him. Needing him ... needing him ... needing him ...

"Gideon ... oh, Gideon, please ... please ..."

Her broken whispers and pleas, her clutching hands, snapped his last thread of control. With fumbling fingers he grabbed the protection he had stashed in the night table a week ago when it began to seem he might lose his head over this woman.

"Gideon . . ."

"Just a second, Mouse. Just a—" There. Ready now, he eased her legs apart and knelt between them. She stilled, and a moment of perfect clarity settled over him. For an instant he rose above the swamping haze of passion, moved away from the throbbing of his own body. This was, he recognized, no simple act of passion gone out of control. Like a crystal note, the understanding resounded in his soul. This was special.

But his body's demands surged again, muddying thought and bringing him back to the elemental level of a man loving a woman. Leaning forward, he pressed the heel of his palm to Sara's mound and rubbed gently until her hips were arching, reaching for him, and she was whispering his name brokenly, again and again.

"That's it, Mouse," he whispered encouragingly. "That's it." Leaning forward, he found her moist opening with the tip of his shaft. Pleasure swept through him like an electric shock as he leaned into her. Pressed into her. Sought relief and release in her hot, slick depths.

And then he swore.

Sara felt the light like twin knives in her eyes. Confused, startled, she blinked and tried to see the face of the man who hovered over her, the man whose body was partially embedded in hers. Why had he sworn? Why had he switched on the light? "Gideon?"

Eyes closed, he muttered a string of imprecations that turned the air blue and made Sara's cheeks rosy. She'd heard plenty on the job, but Gideon knew all of the worst ones.

"Gideon?"

His eyes snapped open, and dark gray steel bore down into her. "Why the hell didn't you tell me you'd never done this before?"

"Why the hell did you think I had?" she demanded, frustration fueling her normally somnolent temper.

"Because... because you almost got married!"

"So? Nice girls don't—"

He caught her face between his hands and shook her. Just a little. With incredible gentleness, considering he looked mad enough to kill. "Nice girls don't?" he repeated roughly. "Then what the hell are you doing in bed with a naked half-breed savage?"

"Good God!" Sara stared at him in complete astonishment. "Who called you that?"

He went utterly still, shocked by what he had just revealed. Briefly he closed his eyes, seeking internal stability before he continued with the issue at hand. Then he glared down at her. "Quit changing the subject."

"I didn't change the subject. You said something horrible, and I want to know who called you that."

"Just answer the question, damn it!"

"What am I doing here?" Loving you, she wanted to say, loving you with my whole heart. "Making love with you. Or I thought I was."

"But nice girls don't," he reminded her.

"So? So maybe I'm not so nice anymore," she said hotly, her temper flaring again. "Maybe I don't want to die a nice virgin. Maybe I want to find out what it's all about. Maybe you just turn me on so damn much that all I can think about is—" She broke off. "Gideon Ironheart, if you stop now, I'm going to get my .45 and... and..."

A little trickle of amusement ran down his spine. Just a tiny trickle, but it washed the anger right out of him. She was as mad as a wet kitten, he thought, studying her flushed face and sparkling eyes. Mad and frustrated, and who the hell was he to argue if she wanted to get rid of her virginity? It was her decision, not his. And he was still hot for her, still heavy and hard.

"And what, Mouse?" he asked, one corner of his mouth hitching up. "Force me at gunpoint? Damn, that's kinky. I think I could learn to like it, though. With *you*."

She caught her breath, and all the harshness of anger slipped out of her face, leaving her looking soft. In an instant she was throbbing from head to toe again, acutely aware of the tip of him just barely inside her.

"You should have told me, Sara," he said huskily. "I don't want to hurt you. I might have, by going too fast."

"You're killing me by not going fast enough," she said raggedly. "Damn you, Gideon, don't do this to me."

"Tell me you're sure." Even as he spoke, he pressed just a little deeper into her. Impulses were zinging through his body, every one of them zeroing in on his hips, trying to drive him into making one great thrust. "Tell me."

"I'm sure. Damn it, I'm sure."

"Why, Mouse? Why?"

"I want you." She was almost sobbing. Reaching up, she grabbed his hair and tugged. "Every time I look at you I ache. I need so badly for you to touch me, fill me, take me...."

And he needed so badly to know it. He took her then, with one long, smooth thrust that transformed her, and he never once took his eyes from hers. He saw the flash of pain and felt it in his heart. He heard her caught breath and felt it in his soul. And he saw pain slowly transformed into revived passion as he moved again, just a little. In and out.

And then her hands slipped down and grabbed his hips, pulling him closer, urging his pace to quicken. Reassured, he gave her all he had and moments later listened to her keening cry as she crested the peak. An instant later, in an explosion so violent he heard it in his brain, he followed her over.

She didn't want to let go of him, so he took care of necessary matters with one hand and then pulled her over him like a warm, soft blanket. The light was still on, and he debated a moment whether to turn it off and let them both fall asleep, or to wait a little and make sure that Sara was all right. He'd never made love to a virgin before, but he suspected this was a momentous event for her that she wouldn't want to let pass without a little talk.

Nor did he, he realized. He wanted to hear her sexy, husky voice, wanted to see her smile and wanted to look into her warm brown eyes to be sure she wasn't regretting this. Man, how he hoped she didn't regret this.

"Mmm…" Sighing, she stretched a little, rubbing against him as if she thoroughly enjoyed the sensation.

"Feel good?" he asked her huskily.

"Mmm." She lifted her head and smiled down at him, a lazy contented smile. "I feel fabulous." Then the shadow of doubt flickered across her face. "You?"

He spared a moment to imagine kicking George Cumberland's butt, then reached up to sweep Sara's tousled hair back from her face. "I feel like somebody just made me king. I feel … special. Very, very special."

"You *are* special." Bending, she kissed his chest. "I wouldn't be here otherwise."

His throat tightened, and he found himself wondering why it seemed that she was reassuring him, when he should be reassuring her. When he should be telling her just how special she was.

"And I should be getting back," she said shyly, not wanting to put him in an awkward position. Now that they'd made love, he probably didn't want her hanging around. "You need your sleep, and I—"

He silenced her with a deep, almost savage kiss. "You're not going anywhere. I want you right here. I want to wrap myself around you while you sleep in my arms. I want to open my eyes at dawn and find you right beside me."

A soft, warm glow came to her face, telling him how good he had just made her feel. And he was sure in trouble now, because he'd never wanted a woman to spend the night in his bed. In fact, he always went to *their* beds so he could leave when he was ready.

But Sara was different, he admitted. Very different. Sooner or later she would want more than he could give, and that would be the end of it. But for now, right now, he wanted everything *she* could give, and he wanted to give her anything he had to offer in return.

Reaching down, he tugged her legs to one side and then sat up with her still on his chest.

Sara drew her head back and stared at him. "I don't believe you just did that."

"Just a sit-up."

"With about a hundred pounds of me on your chest."

"Stomach muscles," he said with a shrug.

She looked down and saw that he did indeed have a washboard belly. And farther down... Quickly she snapped her gaze to his face. He was grinning, damn him. "All this from connecting?"

"Yep." In one easy movement he stood with her in his arms. "You don't weigh anything compared to a beam or a header, babe." He headed down the hall toward the bathroom, liking the way she looped her arms around his neck and pressed her face to his shoulder.

"You smell good," she said, sighing.

"You too." Reaching the bathroom, he set her gently on her feet and bent to turn on the water in the tub.

"What's this?" she asked.

He smiled over his shoulder at her. "A warm, soothing shower. I get to wash you, and you get to wash me."

That was when she saw the blood on him. Her blood. Just a little. And when she looked down at herself, she closed her eyes. "Oh my!" Her voice sounded thin.

"Now, don't be embarrassed, Mouse," he said, tugging her under the spray with him. "It's just one of those things that can't be avoided the first time. Besides, you're supposed to be proud of it, not ashamed."

Her eyes snapped open. "Next you'll want to hang the sheets over the balcony."

He tipped back his head and laughed, then shook his head. "Oh, no," he said lowering his voice. "That's our special secret."

Then he put the soap in her hand and, taking her by the wrist, guided her hand all over him, making it clear that there were no more barriers between them, no more boundaries that couldn't be crossed. That she was free to explore, touch and look however she wanted.

She wanted. Oh, how she wanted. When his hand fell from her wrist finally, she never noticed. She was too absorbed in the incredible male beauty of Gideon Ironheart. His chest was broad and smooth, powerful with muscle, sleek without hair. The twin points of his dark nipples fascinated her, drew her like magnets. When at last she licked one with her tongue, he shuddered and groaned softly.

He liked that, she realized, recognizing other changes in his body as well. Standing back a little, she looked down. Oh my, but he was magnificent!

Gideon chuckled at the way she smiled. He recognized female satisfaction when he saw it. "See what you do to me?" he asked. It was important for her to know that. She needed to know it, and he didn't mind at all that she did.

He would have loved to let her continue, but he figured the hot water couldn't last forever. Taking the soap from her, he treated her to the same slick caresses and exploration she had given him.

Nor did he spare her modesty. While she had washed him, she had forgotten herself, but now she grew painfully aware of her nakedness and her every imagined flaw. Gideon hushed her broken protests and brushed aside her whispered apologies. He touched her everywhere and did it with his eyes wide open. He told her how she excited him, how pretty she was, how sleek, how slender, how perfect....

Until with a growl he shut off the water and grabbed a towel. She could barely stand on her own legs, but he didn't mind. Excitement had made her weak, but it had made him strong.

And that was exactly how it was supposed to be.

* * *

The first pink fingers of dawn found their way through a crack in the curtains of Gideon's east-facing bedroom window. They trailed across Sara, who was awake, and Gideon, who slept soundly.

Her head propped on her hand, Sara watched him slumber. Sometime during the night he had kicked the quilt away, and now he sprawled in magnificent nakedness. He was, she thought, beautiful.

She ought to leave, to spare herself and him any morning-after awkwardness. She didn't know the protocol, after all—what to say, what to do. What if he opened his eyes and she saw regret?

And if she slipped away now, no one would know she had been here. But as soon as she thought that, she knew better. Joey wouldn't know, because Joey never stirred until someone made him. Zeke would know, though, because Zeke somehow knew everything. She sometimes thought the wind whispered tales in his ear.

She stayed, facing the possible awkwardness that would come with Gideon's awakening, because she couldn't bear to leave before she absolutely had to. Because she hoped, wildly, that he would draw her to him one more time. Because she needed another kiss, another touch, another smile.

God, she had it bad. She was like a thirsty woman faced with water. Her eyes drank him in, and she felt that she would never get enough. And if he ever suspected such a thing, he would be gone before she could say "scat."

A naked half-breed savage. Someone must have called him that at one time or another. Those weren't words most people would apply to themselves. Nor were they words Gideon would have taken to heart if they had been hurled at him by some drunk in a bar. No, he probably heard crap like that all the time from idiots who'd had one too many.

Someone else had spoken those words, had made them so hurtful that they had come out of him in a moment of intimacy and anger. Just the memory of them made her want to cry for all the hurts he must have suffered. Why, she wondered for the umpteenth time, were people so cruel to one another?

Almost unconsciously, she reached out and rested her hand on his chest. She was so pale against the beautiful copper of his skin. Her father's Irish heritage had run true in her, giving her a fair, milky color with an undertone of roses, a smattering of freckles everywhere and a sensitivity to the sun that kept her in broad-brimmed cowboy hats and long-sleeved shirts most of the summer.

Why, she wondered, would anyone object to a skin as beautiful as Gideon's? To hair so black and beautiful? How could anyone call a man who was more civilized than most a savage?

Oh, yes, she really had it bad.

Suddenly a prickle of awareness penetrated her preoccupation. Looking up, she found Gideon watching her study him. She felt her cheeks heat as she realized he had caught her gawking like a star-struck kid.

"You're beautiful in the morning," he said roughly. "Beautiful."

Before she could do more than register his words, he tugged her gently toward him and kissed her deeply. Relief caught her and then gave way to sheer erotic bliss, to a warm feeling of being wanted, being needed. To the deep satisfaction of Gideon's arms around her, holding her tightly.

"Ah, babe, don't do that," he whispered when her hands began to roam. "Don't, Mouse. It's too soon for you...."

Understanding poured through her like warm, golden honey. He had kept her with him because he had wanted her there, not because he expected to make love again this morning. Slowly she lifted her head and looked him right in the eye.

"Gideon Ironheart," she said huskily, "you are one in a billion."

For an instant, just an instant, he looked embarrassed. Then his face stiffened and he said, "You don't want to start thinking that way, Mouse. I'm just another one of a billion tumbleweeds, is all."

"Right," she said. Right, she thought as she let her cheek come to rest on his smooth, powerful shoulder. Absolutely. "I hear you." She did, too.

But damned if she could make herself believe it.

Chapter 9

Zeke was in the kitchen pouring coffee when Sara entered. The early morning light filled the room with the clarity of a day just beginning and seemed to etch the moment in glass. Her grandfather looked at her, intently, she thought. She had the uneasy feeling that he could read every thought in her head. Then, giving a small, almost imperceptible nod, he turned and reached for another mug.

"It's going to be a beautiful day," he remarked.

"Yes. Yes, it is."

He handed her the freshly filled mug. "Take it up with you while you change."

Well, Sara thought, he'd said all he was going to say on the subject, and she didn't know whether to be surprised or not. Zeke had always been extremely protective of her. But he had also allowed her to grow up and take risks that many grandfathers or fathers would certainly have objected to. He had let her become a deputy, after all, without a word of argument.

"You do what you must, Sarey," he had told her. He had told her essentially the same thing just now.

Dressed in fresh clothes, still too high to feel the lack of sleep, she knocked on Joey's door and told him to hop to. "We're late getting the garden in," she called through the door. "Come on. I want it done today."

A muffled curse answered her, but she ignored it and headed downstairs. Joey had just started tilling the acre on which she raised vegetables before he'd had to go to jail. If they delayed planting much longer, they would run out of growing season for some of the things she liked most.

Downstairs, she found the kitchen empty. Beyond the windows, she saw Zeke and Gideon standing in the yard, talking, and almost in spite of herself she stopped and watched them. They talked a lot, those two, each of them seeming to have found in the other a good friend. It pleased her to see them together, to know that there was genuine liking there.

That was when she remembered that Gideon had wanted to meet Micah Parish, another Cherokee half-breed. They might have a lot in common, Sara thought, watching the way the sunlight seemed to disappear in the absolute black of Gideon's hair. Micah's work on Zeke's assault case had brought the two of them together, but not in the kind of capacity that would allow them to become friends. And that, Sara thought now, was probably what Gideon would have liked. And if he had friends around here, perhaps he wouldn't be so quick to leave.

Well, it would be easy enough to ask Micah and his wife and daughter to dinner. She'd entertained them once before, just after Micah's marriage, and had really liked Faith. And perhaps she should ask Gage and Emma Dalton, too.

A little chill touched her heart as she realized what she was doing, that she was in fact going to present this man to her friends in the hopes that they would like him. She was setting herself up to be played for a fool again.

But almost as soon as she had the thought, she dismissed it. No, she was doing this because Gideon had asked her to, no more, no less. As for asking her dear friend Emma and her new husband, well, that was just because more people would make the situation less awkward. Because Micah and Gage appeared to be good friends. Because she thought Gideon would like Gage, too.

Certainly not because she wanted her friends to like him. Certainly not.

Joey came down and ate his breakfast in a silence so sullen that Sara's palm itched with the wish to turn him over her knee.

"I'll come help with the tilling," she said.

That got his attention. "No."

Sara stared down at him, torn between wanting to shake him and begging him to tell her what she had done wrong. Finally, aching, she turned her back. "Fine. Do it by yourself. But get it done, or the vegetables I have to buy are going to come out of your paycheck."

Unable to stand another minute in the same room with the boy without losing her temper, she went outside to join Zeke and Gideon.

"You have to send a sacred pipe and tobacco," Zeke was saying to Gideon. "That's the proper way to ask a holy man to perform a ritual for you."

"But if the vision quest is done alone, why do I need the holy man?"

"You need to purify yourself first. He'll hold a sweat for you, cleanse you. Then you're ready."

"And the pipe? Where do you get a sacred pipe?"

"You carve it yourself."

Sara looked at Gideon, wishing she could touch him, but not certain how he might react. "You're going to seek a vision?"

Gideon shook his head. "I don't know. Not yet. I was just asking about it. Like most kids, I never listened to my grandfather when I had the chance. Now I'm bugging Zeke about it."

"It is different from tribe to tribe," Zeke said. "The way of your people may be different."

"Well, I don't know a whole hell of a lot about it," Gideon said. "One way is as good as another from where I stand. I never listened and never participated in anything my grandfather did. I wasted a lot."

They all turned as the kitchen door slammed and Joey came out of the house. The boy said nothing, merely scuffing his way across the yard to the barn. A few minutes later he returned, pushing the tiller ahead of him. When he reached the battered 1963 pickup, Gideon went over to him.

"Let me help with that, Joe."

Joey didn't answer immediately. He fiddled a moment with the gas cap and tightened down a screw with his thumbnail. At last, though, he nodded. "Thanks," he said.

Sara almost stopped breathing as man and boy hoisted the tiller onto the pickup bed. Then, as if they had reached some kind of agreement, Gideon simply walked around and climbed into the passenger seat. Joey hesitated only a moment and then got behind the wheel.

The field Sara always planted was only a couple of hundred yards from the house, but she had chosen to plant there because the groundwater level was higher and the land dipped a little into a hollow that reduced the wind's drying effects. It was, however, visible from the house, and she watched in amazement as boy and man climbed out and set to work together.

"I don't believe that," she said.

"That Ironheart is a unique man," Zeke said from beside her. "Joey feels it, too." He glanced at Sara, and suddenly his dark eyes were twinkling. "Of course, it helps that they settled who was boss."

Sara felt herself smiling back. "I suppose it does," she agreed, and then laughed, because this was, after all, one of the best days of her life.

Sunset in these mountains happened in stages. After dinner that night, Gideon watched the last stage, when the twilight that had blanketed the world for several hours was suddenly shot through by streamers of pink-and-orange clouds as the sun, long hidden behind the mountains, really set. It was a strange effect, he thought, sitting in the near dark while sunset blazed in the sky above his head. Beautiful. Unforgettable.

He wondered if Sara would come by tonight. He had tried to let her know she would be welcome, but between Zeke and Joey, they hadn't had a private moment all day. And now Sara was on duty and wouldn't be home until after midnight. No, she would probably go on up to the house. Sara wasn't the kind to impose, and she'd probably figure that she would be if she came without invitation.

Hell, he thought, and sighed. That was for the best, wasn't it? He didn't want to hurt the woman, and from the way she looked at him sometimes, he figured tough Sara Yates would be remarkably easy to wound.

A sound snagged his attention, and he looked around, spying Joey standing in the yard. The boy looked lost, Gideon thought. Probably the same way he had looked at that age, pretending to be tough and uncaring to hide the hurt.

They had worked together well enough throughout the day, tilling the field and planting the vegetables. And Joey had, without being asked, helped with the other chores this evening. Not a bad kid at heart, it seemed. Just a troubled one. A worried one.

A frightened one.

Gideon wasn't sure how he knew that, or even that he was right about it, but several times today he had gotten the feeling that Joey Yates was scared to death and didn't know what to do about it. That he was in worse trouble than violating his probation. But nobody could help Joey if Joey didn't talk, and Joey had no intention of talking.

Sighing again, Gideon almost let it go. Then, feeling a twinge of conscience, he called out, "Nice evening."

A moment of silence preceded Joey's answer. "Yeah."

Well, that was hopeful, Gideon thought. At least it could pass for courteous. Anything more, though, would have to come from Joey. And then he decided to make one more stab at it, anyway. "Jail is the pits, isn't it?"

That caught the boy's interest. Joey tensed a little and looked at him, although he didn't come any closer. "You been there?"

"Six months, when I was sixteen."

"What for?"

"I stole an expensive belt buckle. They gave me probation right off, but I blew that, too, so I spent six months in a cell." He hesitated, then volunteered a little more. "I swore I'd never again do anything to get myself locked up like that. I can't stand being caged."

Joey's answer was a long time coming. Just about the time Gideon was ready to give up, he said, "It's awful."

And whether he knew it or not, Joey was edging closer. Just a shuffling step here and there, but he was closing the distance. From the corner of his eye Gideon watched and remembered a brown mouse long ago. Suddenly he smiled into the night. Two little mice in one family. Must be genetic.

There was an old refrigerator in the bunkhouse, one so old it more closely resembled an icebox, and in it were soft drinks. When Joey edged up to the end of the porch, Gideon asked him if he'd like one.

"Uh, yeah. Thanks."

That response had come more easily, Gideon thought. "Cola, orange or ginger ale?" he asked the boy.

"Cola, please."

When Gideon returned with the soft drinks, he found Joey sitting on the opposite end of the porch step from where Gideon had been sitting. Offering no comment, he simply handed the boy the aluminum can and returned to his own seat.

For a long time the only sound was the sighing of the wind in the pines and the occasional whinny of a horse. It was soothing. Peaceful. A man could easily get addicted to it, if he let himself. He could grow used to the quiet, the lack of human ruckus, the nose-tickling scent of pine on the air.

Joey spoke suddenly, startling him. "You like my sister?"

Gideon turned his head and tried to read the boy in the fading light. No such luck. "I like your sister," he agreed. "I like her a whole lot."

"She tell you what George Cumberland did to her?"

"She did." Gideon waited, wondering if he should halt this conversation right now. Sara sure as hell wouldn't like knowing they had discussed her. On the other hand, for once Joey was talking instead of glaring sullenly, and shutting him up might be a big mistake.

"She needs someone to be good to her," Joey said after a moment.

"I couldn't agree more." Nor could his conscience, which was pricking him right now. "She's also old enough to make her own decisions."

"Yeah." Joey sipped his drink and didn't say any more for a while. Then he asked, "So you're Cherokee?"

"Half of me is." He suddenly wondered why he always qualified it. *Half-breed*.

"Gramps is Shoshone. But you know that."

"Yeah."

"He says because he was raised in that orphanage he knows more about being Sioux than about being Shoshone. Shoshone aren't one of the Seven Council Fires of the Sioux."

"I didn't realize that." Interested, he leaned back against the porch pillar and turned to look at Joey.

"There are really seven bands," Joey said. "Grandfather knows the ways of the Oglala mostly because of Chester Elk Horn. I think Chester sort of adopted him." Even in the dark, Gideon saw the flash of Joey's smile, quickly appearing and just as quickly gone.

"Well, he sure knows more about being Oglala than I know about being Cherokee. I was a hardheaded kid, I'm afraid."

"Like me," Joey said.

"Worse, believe me."

"I went to a Sun Dance the summer before last with Chester's grandson," Joey said after a little while. "Over at

Pine Ridge. I thought it was a little...commercial. Tourists and things. But I hear they do it more privately on the Rosebud Reservation. The real thing, for religious reasons."

"Hmm."

"Chester's grandson wants me to go with him this summer. Maybe dance this time."

Gideon sat up a little straighter. He *did* know a little something about the Sun Dance. "That's...rough."

"It kind of scares me a little," Joey admitted.

"I imagine so." He hesitated, wishing his familiarity with the subject were a whole lot greater. "Why would you want to do it? I, uh, understand that it has great religious significance."

"That's the point." He looked at Gideon. "It's meaningful. More meaningful than going to school and making money."

Gideon stared at him hard and then gave a quiet laugh. "Joe, you smartened up about twenty-five years younger than me. So you're going to do it?"

"I don't think I can. I'm on probation, and they won't let me go anywhere." He looked away.

A couple of minutes passed. Gideon listened to the sorrowful murmur of the wind and wondered how this boy had gotten so messed up. "Why'd you do it, Joe? Why'd you steal the car?"

"I was dumb!" Shouting the words, the boy stood up and hurled his can across the yard. "You look bad and everybody believes it! Even your own family believes it!"

Gideon watched him tear off into the darkness and wondered what the hell he had meant.

Clouds were scudding across the moon when Sara pulled into the yard after midnight. More rain, she thought, tasting it on the breeze. The mountainous part of the county always got more rain than the eastern sections, but even so, they were having considerably more than usual. But the whole year had been that way, she reminded herself.

All evening long she had thought about Gideon, wishing she could go to him when she got home, and knowing she couldn't. He'd gotten what he wanted last night, and men seldom wanted more than that, judging by what she had seen. They certainly didn't want to feel things were getting sticky, and it would probably feel very sticky if she showed up on his porch. No, she had to let him know that she wasn't going to pressure him or demand anything.

And then she caught sight of movement at the edge of the beam of her headlights. Looking, she saw Gideon walking across the yard toward her. He was still up, as if he had been waiting for her. And he was walking like a man with a purpose.

He opened the door of the Blazer and reached in to switch off her lights. Then he looked at her, simply looked, with a hunger that seemed to reach out and touch her.

Everything inside her went into instant meltdown. She could feel herself softening, dissolving, liquefying, and somehow she was leaning against him, wrapped in his arms and cuddled to his chest.

"Oh, babe," he whispered. "Oh, babe." He lifted her down and waited patiently while she locked the Blazer. Then, as easily as if she were a wisp of the night air, he lifted her from her feet and carried her toward the bunkhouse. He'd figured she would want a shower and something to eat, and he had it ready for her, but the way she had softened against him and wrapped herself around him told him the shower and food might well have to wait.

He needed her. As the hours of the endless evening had ticked by, the need had grown, a need for more than the warmth of her body. He'd never felt this way before and didn't like it at all, but, like a man driven, he'd waited and hungered, every cell in his body focused on the moment of her return. The Wyoming night spun away, and nothing existed for him now except Sara, warm and willing in his arms.

The sound of his huskily whispered "Oh, babe" in her ear caused shivers of longing to pour through her. He'd waited up for her. He wanted her. It was more than she had dared hope for, and all she had been able to think of for hours.

She had been so afraid that she might have allowed herself to be used like some disposable tissue. So afraid that once had been enough, that in some essential way she had failed to give him anything that he would want again. Now here he was holding her and carrying her as if she were infinitely precious.

The bedside lamp was already on, and the bed was already turned down. When Gideon set her carefully on her feet, Sara looked from the bed to him and felt her chest tighten with emotion. He had taken a risk she would never have had the courage to take herself, she realized. He had come to her risking rejection, and now he'd brought her in here and let her see that he had indeed been waiting for her. She would have done anything to avoid exposing herself that way.

Aching, yearning, needing, fighting back tears of emotion, she leaned into him and wrapped her arms around his narrow waist. He was so hard, so solid, so strong. So warm, so alive. So real. She couldn't imagine why he should want her at all, but she wanted him with a depth and breadth that was terrifying. He drove away a loneliness that she hadn't even been aware of until he had completed her. She couldn't bear, absolutely couldn't bear, to think how empty she would feel when he moved on.

"Sweet Mouse," he murmured in a voice so passion-roughened that it was as sensual as a caress. "Sweet, sweet Sara." He hugged her tightly for an instant and then set her back a little so he could undress her.

First there was the gun belt. Never in a million years would Gideon have imagined himself removing a gun belt from a woman so that he could make love to her. Unexpected humor tugged the corners of his mouth, giving him a cockeyed smile.

"What's so funny?" Sara asked.

"Me taking this gun off you," he replied, and gave her a teasing look. "Not quite *High Noon,* is it?" He set the heavy belt and gun on the battered wooden dresser.

"Does it bother you?"

He faced her, taking her gently by the shoulders. She was feeling inadequate again, he saw. Worried that she was somehow wrong. "No, it doesn't bother me," he said softly. "I was just amused, because it suddenly struck me that out of all the fantasies I've ever had about taking something off a woman, I never imagined a gun belt."

He reached for the buttons of her khaki uniform shirt. "Now, a shirt was on my list," he said, his voice dropping huskily. "And slacks and jeans and even boots, but not a .45. Just goes to show you that life can always rustle up a little surprise." He pushed the shirt from her shoulders and let it flutter to the floor, and saw her small breasts cupped in the plain cotton bra—the same bra he had discovered the first time he had touched her breast, that night in the kitchen.

"No lace," he said. "Not a smidgeon. Damn it, Mouse, it's the sexiest darn thing I've ever seen."

Startled, she looked down at herself, unable to imagine that he would find such a utilitarian garment appealing. Only this afternoon she'd considered stopping in at Freitag's Mercantile to see if they had something prettier. "Sexy?"

"Yeah." Reaching out, he ran his finger along the top edge, causing sparks deep inside her. "It's not playing any games. It's doing its job without pretenses. Like you, Mouse. Just like you." With a twist he undid the front clasp and released her small breasts. "You're the sexiest woman I've ever seen."

He meant it, too, as he slipped the bra from her shoulders and then bent to flick each pink nipple with his tongue. She gasped and grabbed his shoulders in response.

She was absolutely the sexiest woman he'd ever known, and he suspected that had a lot to do with the fact that, for her, sex was most definitely *not* a game. And he'd played games for too many years.

Lifting his head, he looked into her slumbrous eyes and nearly smiled with delight when he saw the glowing coals of passion there. "You've had a long day," he said roughly, even though he hated like hell to say it. "You must want a shower and something to eat."

Sara's eyes widened. She couldn't believe it. Her damp nipples felt chilled from the air and cheated by the absence of his mouth, her lower half was aching in a steady, clenching throb for the feel of him on her and in her, and he was talking about food and a shower?

Tonight he wore the leather strip around his forehead. Sara reached up and pulled it off, tossing it away. "The only thing I'm interested in right now is *your* gun."

He laughed. A low, throaty sound, it spilled from him as he tumbled them both to the bed. Springs creaked, slats groaned, and Sara's giggles joined his.

"God, you're a handful, Sara Yates," Gideon said, his dark eyes smiling down at her. So different, so special, so unique, he thought, lowering his head so he could find her mouth with his. Special....

Heat flared swiftly; licking flames danced along nerve endings as passion spread. So right, Sara thought as she tugged at Gideon's clothes. So right. This was how she was meant to be, who she was meant to be. He had opened the self-made coffin in which she had been hiding and breathed new life into her with his hands, his mouth, his body.

She had been made for this man. The certainty filled her as surely as the coming of dawn. She had existed and endured until now just so that she could be here at this place and this time to become part of the man who now held her.

Gideon groaned deeply as he slid down the bed, trailing kisses from her small, sweet breasts to her tummy. Hot. He was so damn hot for this woman. Years of experience had taught him to expect waning passion with familiarity, to know that he would want less the second time than the first. That wasn't true this time. Not at all.

It had been many years since he had wanted a woman more than once. Not since his one ill-starred love affair in the green days of his youth had he felt this degree of longing and need, this constant, unremitting desire for a particular woman. He'd given up hope of ever rediscovering this clawing hunger, this sharp thrill of excitement. This groaning, wrenching, aching need.

His exploring mouth ran into her belt buckle, and he gave a low groan of frustration. Propping himself on his elbows, he tugged at the buckle, at the button and zipper of her khaki slacks. Then he reared up on his knees and impatiently tugged slacks and panties down.

Sara caught her breath as she watched him. So big, so dark, so hard, so wild-looking. His shirt hung open, one tail pulled out by her hungry hands. He straddled her, worn denim cupping his aroused masculinity, molding to his powerful thighs, revealing each muscular flex as he struggled with her clothes. His long black hair spilled forward, making him look as if he came from another time.

His impatience with the obstruction of her clothing excited her even more. Never had she felt so wanted, so prized, so special.

He muttered an oath as he dealt with her stubborn cowboy boots and then dragged her pants off her. At last she lay completely naked for him, sprawled wantonly on the bed, her soft brown eyes never leaving him. And then, damned if she didn't lift her arms and whisper, "Hurry."

He hurried. He cast off his clothes and lowered himself to the bed between her legs. He heard her gasp as he propped himself on his elbows and cupped her soft rump, lifting her to his mouth.

"Gideon . . ." She sounded shocked, excited, only faintly protesting.

"Let me, Mouse," he said hoarsely. "Let me give you this." This, something he had never given any woman. Something he had never wanted to give any woman until this one. How could he explain his absolutely overwhelming need to love her in every way possible, to leave the memory of him on every inch of her? Lowering his head, he claimed her.

He took her to a place where pleasure was so intense it was nearly pain. She writhed wildly, clutching the sheets, then clutching his head, afraid he would stop, afraid she would die if he didn't. She whimpered and twisted and suddenly drew taut, arching up from the bed as a sharp-edged wave of excruciating pleasure ripped through her and carried her over the edge.

Dimly, from the other side of oblivion, she felt Gideon slide up over her, felt him slowly, surely, fill her. And then he was lifting her yet again, carrying her away as if he were winged Pegasus heading for the stars.

"Now," she heard him say hoarsely. "Now!"

And in some fantastic, unbelievable way, she turned into a supernova in a burst of light, heat and joy that seared her very soul.

Cold roast beef sandwiches had never tasted so good. Having finished hers, Sara sat in Gideon's bed, wrapped in one of his flannel shirts, her hair still damp from her shower, and thought that dreams really could come true. Despite all that had happened between them, she still couldn't believe that this powerful, virile, attractive man, wearing nothing but unbuttoned jeans, was lying propped on an elbow beside her on his bed. That he had just loved her to the edge of sanity, and that now he was calmly pulling the stems from green grapes and popping the grapes one at a time into her mouth. Smiling each time he did so.

Impulsively, she reached out and touched the corner of his lips. Immediately he turned his head and drew her finger into his mouth. Feeling the rasp of his tongue on her sensitive flesh, she caught her breath. Remembering what that tongue had so recently done to other tender flesh, she stopped breathing entirely.

Gideon bit her finger gently and released it. Smiling, he popped another grape into her mouth. "Full yet?" he asked. Sara's appetite for food was as healthy as everything else about her.

"Getting there," she managed to say.

The corners of his eyes creased with a deepening smile as he gave her another grape. "Have y'all figured out anything about who attacked Zeke?"

Sara shook her head. "There isn't a whole lot to go on. No fingerprints. The yard was too hard to take a tire impression. About the only hope we have is that Zeke will remember."

"Those cigarette butts and boot prints Micah found weren't useful, then?"

Sara shook her head and declined another grape. "I'm stuffed. We'd probably never catch him even if we did have something more. Nate's pretty much convinced it was just some drifter looking for money, probably on drugs or something, and he got mean when he didn't find what he wanted."

"Since we haven't had any more trouble in a week, I guess he's right."

Sara shrugged. "What else could it be?"

"Nothing." He took the bowl of grapes from the bed between them and twisted to set it on the night table. Then he was looking at her again, head propped on his hand, a faint smile on his firm mouth. "You've enchanted me," he said unexpectedly.

For an instant everything inside Sara stilled to perfect quiet in a moment of exquisite awareness. Then she shook loose, reminding herself that this man was a tumbleweed, and that nothing he said mattered beyond the moment. "Must be those newt eyes and toadstools I threw in your lunch earlier."

"Must be." The corners of his eyes crinkled. "Or it could be I'm a sucker for little brown mice with warm eyes and a need to be stroked. I talked to Joey earlier this evening."

The swift change of subject distracted her, as he had intended. "Joey?" she repeated. "Has he done something?"

"No, nothing. We just got to talking. Some of the things he said ... Sara, I just can't figure how he went bad."

"Me, either," she admitted. "I never thought ... I never *saw* anything in him that made me think he was bad. But the way he's been acting..."

"He's mad. Something has really hurt him." Gideon paused, then added, "He was talking about doing the Sun Dance this summer."

"He was?" Sara was clearly astonished, but after a moment she looked thoughtful. "He went to the Pine Ridge Reservation two years ago for the annual powwow. Chester Elk Horn and his grandson took him."

"He told me."

"I remember he was irritated by all the tourists. Not so much that people were interested, I guess, but rather that they didn't understand the religious significance of the Sun Dance. He didn't feel it should be performed as a public spectacle. Grandfather reminded him that tourists attend religious ceremonies all over the world. Catholic Masses in missions around San Antonio. Processions in Mexico.... That kind of thing. I'm not sure it calmed him any. You know how passionate kids get about things at that age."

"About some things at *any* age," he said, and leaned over to kiss her wrist. He smiled when he felt her shiver faintly in response. "He mentioned Pine Ridge to me, too. He said he wants to participate in the Sun Dance that's held privately on the Rosebud Reservation. And he appears to think he won't be allowed to go because he's on probation."

"He's probably right. Unless Nate agreed to let me take him. He's Joey's probation officer now."

"Would you take him?"

Sara's gaze rose from her lap to his dark eyes. "I don't know," she said truthfully. "I was raised with a foot in two worlds, but mostly in the Anglo world, and so was Joey. Zeke has always spoken of these things, the way he does with you, but he has always recognized that this is a white man's world now, and Joey and I are more Anglo than not. I have to question why Joey wants to do this."

"Maybe he needs a sense of who he is that he hasn't discovered so far. Maybe he needs a purpose he hasn't found. Maybe he needs it to find his manhood."

Sara's head jerked a little, and she stared hard at him. "Gideon?" There was more in his words than a casually considered group of possible reasons for Joey's desire to participate in the grueling Sun Dance.

"Ah, hell." At the back of his mind, a flashback was trying to happen, a sense of splintering blue sky that kept dancing in the corners of his mind, a sensation of falling when he was lying perfectly still. "Ah, hell," he said again. He needed to talk. His whole life long, he'd never really talked to anybody. Even Barney, his best friend, had never been a confidant. "You're tired," he said, making one last attempt to keep from spilling his guts.

Somehow Sara knew. The impassioned speech about Joey finding himself had said an awful lot about Gideon Ironheart. Not so much in words that her ears had heard, but more in feelings that her heart had sensed. She lay down facing him, and before he could react in any way, she threw her long, bare leg over his denim-clad hips and wrapped her arm around his neck, drawing his head into the dark, warm hollow created by her shoulder and cheek. "I'm not too tired to listen."

"Ah, hell," he said roughly. "You don't want to hear this crap."

"I do," she murmured, tunneling her fingers into his long hair. "I want to hear anything you need to tell me. It's about Barney, isn't it? About his fall and your flashbacks."

"What are you? A mind reader?"

"Grandfather always taught me to see with my heart, not my eyes," Sara answered softly, while every cell in her body tensed for his inevitable rejection. She was pushing him, she knew, pushing him hard, and he would probably step down hard on her. But somewhere in her helpless, headlong tumble into love with this man, she had discovered a new kind of courage in herself, a courage to take emotional risks. For him she would expose herself to the reopening of the scar that had kept her in hiding for a decade.

To see with her heart. Slowly, slowly, Gideon relaxed against her, giving up the battle with himself. If she saw with her heart, then perhaps she could see through the pain that scoured him raw. Perhaps she could point the way to the other side of the spiritual chasm that yawned before him.

"I'm afraid," he said, his whisper husky. "It's not unusual for a man to be scared after a near miss. It happens to us all, and for a time we work on the ground, until we feel ready to go up again. Nobody thinks anything of it. It's normal. Natural."

Sara's hand never stopped moving, just kept combing soothingly through his hair. "I should think so," she murmured when it seemed he needed some kind of response. "Only a fool wouldn't have some kind of reaction."

"Yeah. Most of the time it only takes a week or two. But... I can't go up at all anymore. Hell, I even get vertigo in the barn loft. I'm not sure I could handle a drainage ditch, to tell you the truth."

None of this sounded so very terrible on the face of it, but, listening with her heart, Sara heard something else. Something more. She heard what had happened to his self-confidence, his self-image, his identity. In one fell swoop Gideon had lost his best friend, his career, his belief in himself, and an essential part of his manhood: his courage. Or what he believed to be his courage.

It was on the tip of her tongue to point out that going up to the top of those buildings to walk those narrow beams in the first place had displayed a kind of courage few people ever had. And that in losing that courage he had merely come down to the level of the rest of the world. But that was easy to say, and it wouldn't help Gideon at all. He had lost something of himself, something he'd once had, something that had been an integral part of him. The fact that it was something most people never had was hardly going to mitigate the loss.

Finally, she said the only thing she could. "I'm sorry. That must really hurt."

He nuzzled her shoulder, inhaling deeply of the scent of warm woman, the scent of Sara. Then, relaxing even more, he wrapped his own arms around her waist. After a while he spoke again.

"It's not that I want to be a connector again," he said slowly. "I'm too old, and there's no way on earth I'd do it even if I found a partner as good as Barney. I'd be a danger to him, because I'm slowing down. Barney and I would have had to quit soon. We both knew it. We were getting older, slower. Not enough to be dangerous yet, but enough that we couldn't pretend we weren't. We'd even begun to talk about working on the ground."

Sara made an encouraging sound and let her hand wander lower, to the smooth, warm skin of his back.

"It's just that..." He didn't know if there were even words to encompass all that he had lost along with Barney. "It's just that everything I ever knew, everything I ever believed about myself, turned out to be an illusion. All of a sudden, there I was with nothing. Absolutely nothing. As if everything I'd done with the first forty years of my life was absolutely pointless. Why am I telling you this?"

"Because you need to. Because I want to listen."

He tilted his head back and looked her right in the eye. He was suddenly angry with himself for spilling all this ridiculous tripe on her, but just as suddenly his anger died. Something in her soft brown eyes killed it. Something of understanding and caring and concern. In that instant, he knew he had words to say what he felt, and that she would understand them.

"Mouse," he said hoarsely, "I lost myself."

Her expression grew sad; the corners of her mouth turned down. Her hand lifted from his shoulder to touch his cheek gently, to trace the line of his strong jaw, then to cradle the back of his head and draw him closer.

"Let me hold you," she whispered. "Let me hold you, because I've only just found you."

Somehow that seemed to make perfect sense. He wrapped himself around her, wrapped her around him, and neither let go of the other until the night was over.

Chapter 10

"We're going to have guests for dinner tonight," Sara announced. Three masculine heads at the breakfast table lifted from plates full of ham and eggs and looked at her. "I'll do the cooking, Grandfather."

"Don't be silly, child. I've been cooking for this household since you started working. *I'll* cook, and you'll help."

Sara laughed at the twinkle in her grandfather's eye. "I invited Micah and Faith Parish over. I asked Emma and Gage, too, but they couldn't make it. Emma has to speak to some library meeting or other in Cheyenne, so they'll be gone for a few days."

"Well, just ask them for next week," Zeke said. "It's been a while since we had guests." He was always pleased whenever Sara invited any of her friends over, and always encouraged her to do it more often.

"I'll do that." She glanced at Joey and found her brother looking indifferent. Well, he would probably just vanish right after dinner, so it wouldn't make a whole lot of difference to him. Looking past him to Gideon, Sara said,

"You're invited, too, of course." In case he didn't realize that. "You said you wanted to meet Micah."

Gideon nodded briefly and fastened his attention on his plate. "Thanks," he managed to say. Moments later he shoved his chair back from the table and carried his half-eaten breakfast over to the sink. "I need to see to some stuff in town, Zeke. I took care of the livestock already, so there's nothing that can't wait until I get back." Snatching his hat from the peg, he stomped out of the kitchen.

"Well, what got into him?" Sara wondered aloud.

Zeke shrugged. "Time will tell, Sarey. Time will tell."

Muttering every oath he knew, Gideon drove down the rutted drive to the highway and wondered if he carried a personal curse of some kind. Maybe the fates were after him because he'd never listened to his grandfather, never lived up to the responsibility of the "power" people kept telling him he had.

All he knew, all he could remember, was holding Sara in his arms the night of their picnic, gently seducing her and himself, and asking about Micah. Silently encouraging her to offer to introduce him to Micah. He swore again and spun loose gravel out from beneath his tires. He didn't need to be a genius to know what Sara was going to think if she learned Micah was his brother.

But surely, he told himself, she would remember that he hadn't mentioned Micah again since that night almost two weeks ago. She *had* to realize by now that he wasn't making love to her because he wanted her to introduce him socially to Micah Parish. Surely.

Cursing again, he pulled off onto the road that led to Sara's favorite glade. Once there, he climbed out of the truck, walked through the thick wildflowers, yellow ones now joining the paintbrushes, and sat cross-legged on a rock beside the snow-fed stream. Farther up the slope, a water-fall provided a soothing rush of sound.

He needed to go into the silence, he thought. It had been days since he had taken the time for his morning meditation, and he was sorely feeling the lack. His center seemed to be escaping his grasp along with his identity and his manhood. He was losing his hold on everything. Everything.

So he closed his eyes and dove inward, seeking the deep, quiet pool of his innermost self, that place from which all the rest of him sprang. He was in desperate need of an anchor to hang on to, a piece of solid ground on which to stand. Without that, he couldn't even hope to begin rebuilding his life.

Gideon watched from the window of the bunkhouse as Micah Parish and his family arrived. Faith Parish was every bit as small and blond as Sara had said, so tiny beside her large husband that she looked like a sprite, almost insubstantial. And it was obvious from the way the big man hovered over her that she was the center of his world and the light of his life.

Gideon smiled in spite of himself and felt a painful yearning tug in the vicinity of his breastbone. He ignored it, wondering what he was going to do about Micah. The question had settled onto the back burner lately while he'd been busy working the ranch, worrying about Zeke and getting to know Sara. Now it couldn't be ignored any longer.

He had come to Conard County with the best of intentions, wanting only to learn something of the brother he had never known, never intending to disrupt any lives. He had convinced himself that if he said nothing, no one would be hurt.

With each passing day, however, his silence looked less like wisdom and grew closer to deception. At the beginning he had told himself that he only wanted to know a little about Micah, to see him for himself, but not to establish any kind of relationship with him. After all, if Micah or their father, Amory Parish, had ever had any interest in what had happened to Gideon, surely it would have showed by now.

He felt, he thought, something like a kid who'd been adopted, needing to know something about his real roots, but aware that his interest might be very unwelcome. Coming anonymously to Conard County and saying nothing to Micah had initially seemed like a matter of respecting Micah's privacy. It had also seemed like a way to protect his own. What if Micah had turned out to be a man he wouldn't want to know?

Gideon sighed, thinking his reasons sounded awfully flimsy now. And the closer he grew to Sara and Zeke, the worse it got.

His grandfather, he felt suddenly, would probably have had his hide for a stunt like this. For all his faults, the old Cherokee medicine man had been unfailingly honest with himself and all those with whom he dealt. Without a doubt, he would have told Gideon that nothing justified deception.

"Ah, hell." And he still hadn't decided whether to tell Micah the truth. All he knew was that the longer he waited, the tougher it was going to get.

"Hell," he said again, and turned from the window. Time to go up to the house before his tardiness became remarkable.

Everyone except Joey had gathered in the living room. For a moment Gideon stood unnoticed on the threshold between the dining room and living room, and he took the opportunity to study his new sister-in-law. She was every bit the fairy-tale princess Sara had said, tiny, blond and lovely. She watched Micah with adoring eyes when he spoke, and cradled her child close to her breast.

And again Gideon felt that strange pang of longing.

"Gideon!" Sara spied him and smiled. "We've been wondering where you were. You know Micah, of course, and this is his wife, Faith, and their daughter, Sally."

Micah rose to shake his hand. For an instant, a split second so brief it might almost never have happened, their eyes locked, and Gideon felt something pass between them. Something beyond words.

Then he was treated to the full effect of Faith Parish's shining blue eyes and brilliant smile. And, irresistibly, he was drawn to squat and bend over the baby. A pair of blue eyes stared back at him from a frame of pink blanket and fragile skin. A tiny rosebud mouth opened in a yawn.

"She's beautiful," he told Faith, and reached out to touch one tiny fist. "Three months?"

"Three and a half. How could you tell that? Most men aren't very interested in babies."

He glanced at Faith's smiling face and felt himself grinning back. "I have six cousins who have a slew of kids. Every time I go home to Oklahoma, I wind up baby-sitting, and so far there's always been an infant or two in the bunch."

"Wonderful," said Faith, and she leaned forward, depositing Sally in Gideon's surprised arms. "I'm not above taking advantage of you." She laughed and smiled winningly. "If you don't mind, of course."

"I don't mind." He looked down at the small bundle he now held and felt a stupid grin grow on his face. "She's a heartbreaker, all right. I'm already in love."

Conversation resumed and flowed around him, but he only half heard. He supposed it wasn't something most men would admit—or even feel—but he got a kick out of babies and kids. That was why he always wound up baby-sitting when he went home, and it was never a chore. His cousins' wives had swiftly learned that Gideon was a sucker for babies, and there was never a family gathering where his arms weren't full of one infant or another.

He was still holding Sally when they moved into the dining room for dinner, and he assured Faith that he was quite content to continue holding her. He felt Micah's eyes on him, but the man didn't say anything. Sara seemed equally fascinated by Gideon's fascination with Sally, and when he glanced her way, he saw a soft warmth in her brown eyes that made him ache in some indefinable way.

Conversation wandered around the weather, passed over the assault on Zeke, and finally settled on the plans being made for this year's Fourth of July celebration. There was to be a picnic down by Conard Creek, where the Cattlemen's Association was planning to barbecue beef ribs for all comers. The Jaycees were organizing a parade, and a memorial service would be held afterward in the Courthouse Square.

The only fly in the ointment appeared to be Micah himself. He was refusing to don his uniform, his green beret and all his medals, and give a speech.

"I don't give speeches," he said now.

"It's more than that," Faith said, utterly unintimidated by the dark look her husband sent her. "You'll never convince Micah he's any kind of hero, so he doesn't want to be treated like one."

Micah scowled and said, "Actually, I just don't want to cut my hair."

Gideon chuckled. "After twenty years of G.I. haircuts, I can understand it."

Micah flashed him a faint smile.

Sara spoke. "I really don't think anyone would expect you to cut your hair just for a couple of hours in uniform."

"I would," Micah answered.

Faith threw up her hands. "You see, Sara? He's impossible!"

Just as dessert was served, Sally decided she was hungry and began to holler for her mother. Faith immediately came to the rescue, taking her daughter into the living room to feed her. Gideon's arms felt empty without the baby.

"I miss her already," he said to Micah. "She's cute as a button."

Micah fixed him with a stare. "She could sure use an uncle."

Heat, then cold, washed through Gideon in waves as he stared into obsidian eyes. Shocked, he understood.

Micah already knew they were brothers.

Zeke refused all offers of help cleaning up the meal, insisting that he and Joey would take care of it. Sara and Faith he shooed into the living room with coffee. Then he looked at Micah and Gideon, seeming to know they had a secret they had not yet shared.

"You two need to take a walk. Go."

Micah and Gideon looked at one another, Micah impassive, Gideon uneasy, uncertain whether he was angry or relieved. As one, they turned toward the kitchen and the back door.

Outside, the spring night had already settled in, and a chilly breeze blew off the mountaintops. Micah wore a flannel shirt and seemed impervious. Gideon doubted he would ever feel any colder than he had felt in that moment of shock.

"Want to walk?" he asked. "Or go talk in the bunk-house?"

"Walk," Micah said. Then, "You know."

"Yeah, I know." And now he was feeling angry that Micah had known about him and done nothing. It was the rejection he had felt all his life long, and now it was being inflicted again.

"Did you know when you arrived here?" Micah asked.

"Yes." They headed down the driveway, each walking in a separate but parallel rut.

Micah shoved his thumbs into his front pockets, looking for all the world like a man out for a casual stroll. "Why didn't you say anything?"

For a minute Gideon didn't know how to react to that. In the depths of his hurt anger, he realized that Micah was asking him the question he wanted to ask Micah. And somehow he managed to shrug, as if none of this was as important as it suddenly felt. "None of it seems to make much sense right now. I wasn't sure you knew you had a brother. I wasn't sure that, even if you did, you would want to meet me. I wasn't sure I would want to know you. It just seemed more sensible at the time to wait and do a little reconnaissance before taking an irrevocable step."

"I can see that." For a while they walked on in silence; then Micah spoke again. "That doesn't explain why you stayed silent."

Gideon halted abruptly and faced him, old hurts suddenly fresh and sharp. Micah, too, stopped, and they stared at one another, separated by a gulf that neither was really sure he wanted to cross.

"Our mother," Gideon said tightly, "died when I was just over two. I was raised in an orphanage until the age of twelve, when one of the nuns managed to track down my uncle. From then until now, there was never any indication that our *father* gave a damn if I was alive or dead."

Micah nodded and tipped his head back, studying the stars. "I felt the same way about our mother."

Gideon was struck. Somehow he had never imagined that, and now he felt stupid because of it.

Micah continued his survey of the heavens. "I knew you existed, probably because I was older and had some kind of memory of you before our mother left with you. I asked Dad about it once when I was maybe seven or eight. He said they had agreed to each take one child rather than one of them having to lose us both."

Gideon yielded a long breath and let go of an old, old tension. It somehow didn't sound as bad when put that way. "But he didn't keep in touch?"

"He said he tried once but was told she was dead. I don't know if that's true or not." Micah lowered his gaze to Gideon. "Our father was not... Well, hell. Fact of it is, he wasn't much of a father. Oh, from time to time he got his father duds on and gave me a lecture about something. Once he even told me not to be ashamed of my ancestry, because on our mother's side I was descended from powerful medicine men."

"That's true."

Micah shrugged. "The point is, that was the extent of his fathering. He was a cold man, Ironheart. If you want the honest truth, he didn't have enough heart to make an attempt to keep after you or our mother. He would probably have been just as happy if she'd taken me, too, the way it felt at times. At best, I think he never forgave her for leaving. Anyhow, by the time I got old enough to ask any serious questions about you, he didn't remember anything useful, and then he died. And truthfully, it seemed like a lot of water over the dam at that point.''

Gideon nodded his understanding. Except for Barney's death, he never would have felt compelled to look for Micah. He started walking again, and Micah followed suit. What he had learned was hardly a blinding revelation, but it helped him understand.

"Our grandfather didn't help matters," Gideon said. "He declared our mother dead when she married our father. Maybe that explains why he only once attempted to get in touch with her."

"Could be. Did the old man ever come around?"

"By the time my uncle took me from the orphanage, he'd lived to regret banishing her."

Micah swore. "Never ceases to amaze me how people can mess things up. Things would just be so simple if folks would let them."

They walked on a little farther in silence, then Gideon asked, "How did you know who I was?"

"I heard there was a half-breed Cherokee named Gideon Ironheart in town. That got me wondering, because I knew I had a brother named Gideon. Then I saw you. Don't know if this will bother you or not, but you got our father's eyes. I'd've recognized 'em just about anywhere."

"You've known that long?"

"Yep." He glanced over at Gideon. "You weren't saying anything, though, and I wasn't sure you knew. Faith was sure, though. That's why she dumped Sally in your arms tonight. She's been fretting that Sally wouldn't have any relatives, and now she's bound and determined you're going to be the baby's uncle. And I'd better warn you—when Faith makes up her mind, there's no deterring her. I've tried."

Gideon couldn't help the chuckle that escaped him. The image of Micah being helpless before the determination of his tiny wife was inescapably amusing. "I'm being adopted?"

"Reckon so," Micah agreed.

Gideon tilted his head back, pretending to study the stars while he tried to cope with an unexpected tidal wave of feeling. His throat ached, and his chest felt almost too tight to breathe, as some ancient hurt began to let go. Then Micah astonished him by briefly clapping a hand to his shoulder.

"I told you," he said to Gideon, "life is really very simple. It's pointless to make it complicated. We're brothers. Whether that will become anything more than a word is something only time will tell."

Gideon managed at last to draw a long breath. He faced Micah. "Just play out the hand and see what happens?"

Micah nodded. "I spent my whole life telling myself I preferred to be alone. Faith convinced me I didn't really mean that. Reckon there's room for a couple more good folks, too."

Sara was right, Gideon found himself thinking. Micah Parish had made peace with himself. And Gideon felt a stab of painful envy. He forced it down. "Faith is quite a steamroller, huh?"

Micah laughed, a rare sound from the silent man. "You wouldn't believe one little moonbeam could throw her weight around the way she does. Take a word of advice, Ironheart. Don't even *think* of arguing with her about anything."

Sara's face was full of questions, but Gideon ignored them. After saying good-night, he turned and headed toward the meadow, thinking he would take a stroll and try to get his thoughts in order. He hadn't asked Sara to come to him tonight, so he was pretty sure she wouldn't. She didn't have enough self-confidence to push him. Another time that would have bothered him, but right now it was merely a relief. He had too many personal demons he needed to face tonight. He didn't have anything left over for anyone else.

On the far side of the meadow, well away from curious eyes, he settled onto a flat boulder at the base of a tall pine and leaned back, drawing one knee up to rest his elbow on it. Around him the pines whispered of things lost and found, of things to be learned and unlearned. An owl hooted eerily from somewhere above, and then the sense of something silent passing in the dark came to him.

The sense of anticlimax was inevitable, he supposed. His discussion with Micah had been fraught with little of the intensity he had expected. Instead, they had behaved like two civilized men discussing the antics of people they had never understood. And somehow, as a result, the bitterness he had carried with him for so many years suddenly felt childish, self-indulgent, foolish.

They would never know, now, what had driven their parents to behave as they did. Nor did it really matter. All of that was water over the dam, as Micah had said, and that was the realization that made Gideon feel foolish.

Sitting there in the dark with only the stars, the wind and an owl for company, he faced the fact that he had allowed his life to be ruled by a confluence of events that had occurred at a point so early in his childhood that he could not even remember the time. He had no memory of his mother, and his father had been an ogre built out of childish resentment and a terrible sense of rejection. He had for a time even hated those who had come to his rescue, who had taken him in and tried to make up for their mistakes.

For his entire life, he had worn his hatred, anger and bitterness like a shield to keep others away, to prevent anyone getting close enough to reject him again. The way he had once believed everyone had rejected him.

But his mother hadn't rejected him; she had died. And his father had not rejected him either; he had simply failed, through a variety of reasons, to be there. Nor had his grandfather or uncle rejected him. Just as soon as they had learned where he was, they had come to get him.

Ironheart. That was what he had wished for. He had buried his feelings in places so deep he could hardly find them anymore. He had skimmed the surface of every damn thing like some kind of water skate, until Barney's death had yanked him down into the depths of painful reality.

He hadn't lost himself because of Barney's death. No, he'd lost himself a long, long time ago. Barney's death had just made him aware of it.

He wasn't sure what alerted him. He was still sitting on his rock, doing some long-overdue thinking, when it was as if the atmospheric pressure changed. The wind was rustling in the treetops too loudly for any but the loudest sounds to reach him, but still he felt as if he had heard something.

Leaning forward intently, he strained every sense, convinced somehow that he was no longer alone out here. And the first thing, the very first thing, that occurred to him, was that Zeke's attacker had come back for some reason.

But why would he? Zeke and Sara had very little apart from their land. There wasn't a thing in that house worth stealing, as the perpetrator had evidently discovered his first time through. And if he had wanted anything of value, why hadn't he taken Gideon's Zuni belt buckle?

He strained his eyes, telling himself that it was late, that he had probably just dozed and dreamed without realizing it. But still he couldn't shake the conviction that someone else was out here.

All the lights below were out now, indicating that everyone was in bed. Glancing at his watch, tipping it this way and that, he finally managed to see that it was after midnight. Definitely too late for someone to be stirring.

Sara. Perhaps Sara had gone to the bunkhouse looking for him, after all. The thought brought him instantly to his feet. He was halfway across the meadow before a warning prickle caused him to stop and stare into the dark ahead of him. The starlight provided scant illumination, but enough to make the familiar shapes of the house and barn visible.

And then, against the light tan color of Sara's police Blazer, he saw a low, crouching shadow move.

There was no way on earth Sara would be skulking like that in her own yard. Moving as quietly as he could, counting on the rustling wind to cover any inadvertent sounds he made, Gideon hurried forward. Whoever was down there in the yard wouldn't be expecting anyone to come from this direction, and he was counting on that to keep him undiscovered until he got closer.

And it did. He made it to the rear of the bunkhouse without being spotted. Then, working his way carefully around, he looked into the yard. The shadow was still there, and he could swear it was checking out Sara's vehicle, looking for something.

Or tampering with something....

A flicker of light betrayed that the shadow was using a small flashlight. He was definitely looking around under the Blazer.

Gideon measured the distance between himself and the vehicle. Maybe twenty yards. If he alerted the guy to his presence right now, the man would probably get away. Gideon might be in great shape, but he was no world-class sprinter, and cowboy boots were the devil's own invention when it came to running. He spared an instant to wish he was wearing his work boots instead.

He eased out of the shadows around the bunkhouse and headed across the yard at a steady, quiet walk, figuring to get as close as he could before he was noticed. *Then* he'd charge.

Later, Gideon was to consider his own stupidity with disgust. At the time, though, he was merely amazed that he got as close as he did without the other man becoming aware of him.

But the other man *was* aware of him, and when Gideon was almost on him, he rose in a fast, blinding whirl and struck out, catching Gideon in the side of the head with something hard and heavy. Then he took off at a dead run down the driveway.

Gideon swore, battling a momentary confusion resulting from the unexpected blow. Then, damning his cowboy boots, he charged after the assailant.

For a hundred yards, two hundred, they ran down the rutted driveway, the other man managing to keep a good lead. And then Gideon began to gain on him. The other man was tiring, he thought, ignoring the fire that seared his own lungs as he struggled for added oxygen. Damned if that bastard was going to get away!

Just as he was almost close enough to make a leaping tackle, the guy swung around. Gideon had just enough time to throw up his left arm in front of his face to block the blow. Something as solid and heavy as a lead pipe connected with his forearm, and shock waves of pain shot up his entire arm. He glimpsed another swing coming his way and ducked, but as he did so, he stepped into a rut and went sprawling, getting a solid, crippling blow to his solar plexus when he hit the ground.

His assailant took off again, evidently not having murder on his mind. Gideon lay there, struggling to get his diaphragm to work, struggling to get air into his lungs, and wondered why he had ever been so stupid as to think he might be cut out to be a hero. He should have scared the guy off and gone in to call the cops. Or at least to get Sara to unlock her damn gun and go after him in a vehicle. That would have accomplished a hell of a lot more than chasing after him on foot in the dark. Idiot!

"Oh, God," he muttered as he dragged in the first few lungfuls of blessed air. "Oh, God." But now that he could breathe, his arm sent excruciating signals flashing to his brain. For a moment all he could do was roll onto his side and hold his arm like a baby while a long moan escaped him. Fighting ten guys in a parking lot had never hurt quite this badly.

Some damn hero!

At last he rolled to his knees and managed to get to his feet while cradling his arm. The damn thing was broken. Of that he had not the least doubt. Over the years he'd managed to break a bone or two, and he knew the sensation. Well, once it was set it wouldn't be much of a problem.

He was feeling a little ragged, he thought as he made his way back to the house. Not quite with-it. When he reached the yard, he considered going to bed and waiting until morning to ask someone to drive him to the hospital. But then he staggered to one side and realized he was feeling a little drunk. Maybe it wouldn't be smart to wait.

Just then the kitchen porch light flipped on and Sara stood there, .45 in hand, looking ready for anything, even in her terry-cloth bathrobe. Damn, she was one hell of a woman, Gideon thought groggily. If he'd known they grew them like her in Wyoming, he would have headed this way years ago.

"Gideon?" Sara stepped out onto the porch. "I heard something— Oh, my God! What happened to you?"

She was off the porch in a shot, and the next thing he knew, her arm was around his waist and she was guiding him up the steps, across the porch and into the kitchen.

"Sit down," she said, helping him ease onto a chair. "My God, your head...."

His head? He looked at her, wondering what she was talking about. "My arm's broken, I think."

"We'll take care of that if you don't bleed to death."

Bleed? That was when he realized his head was aching fit to burst. Turning a little, he looked at himself and saw that his entire right side was covered in blood. "Where'd that come from?" he said.

"Oh, my God," Sara said again, and this time she sounded as if she was going to cry. Taking a clean dish towel, she pressed it to the side of his scalp. "I've got to get you to the hospital. Can you hold this towel on your head while I wake up Joey?"

"Sure." Anything the lady wanted. "Don't drive your car," he said, wondering why his words seemed to be running together.

"What?" She leaned back and stared at him. "Why not?"

"Somebody... fooling with it."

"The person who hurt you?"

"Yeah." Then he set his broken arm on the table and reached up with his right hand to hold the towel. "I'll be okay, Sara," he said seriously.

"Oh, Gideon," Sara said, and leaned forward, kissing his cheek. "Of course you will," she whispered. "You have to be. I only just found you."

Then she turned swiftly and disappeared from the kitchen.

He never lost consciousness, although for a while he wasn't very far from losing it. He was aware of Sara calling the sheriff's department to report the incident while Joey went out to the bunkhouse to get Gideon's truck keys. He'd managed to get the point across that they needed to take his truck, not Sara's vehicle, which might have been tampered with. He was too far out of it to realize that his own might have been tampered with also.

Joey, however, wasn't. He took a flashlight out and went over Gideon's truck while Sara talked to a deputy on the phone and Zeke applied pressure to the wound on Gideon's head.

He was aware of a low-voice fight between Zeke and Sara.

"I don't want you staying here alone, Grandfather. Something is going on, and I don't want you hurt again."

"I'll lock the doors and get the gun, Sarey," Zeke told her. "I'll be just fine until the deputy gets here."

"But, Grandfather—"

"Look, Joey's ready. Just get Ironheart to the hospital."

By the time he'd been x-rayed, had his scalp stitched up and a cast put on his forearm, Gideon's head had pretty much cleared up. Doc Randall was agreeable to releasing him, so Gideon was able to pull on his blood-crusted shirt and skedaddle.

Joey was out in the waiting room, and he eyed Gideon doubtfully, shaking his head. "Man, you don't look so good."

"I'm better than I was a little while ago. My head still feels like somebody's beating on it, though. Where's Sara?"

"Ladies' room. She'll be right back. So your arm's broken? But not your head?"

"Not my head. I think it's almost as hard as yours."

That surprised a crack of laughter out of Joey, who grinned at him. No, thought Gideon, this boy wasn't bad at heart. So what was going on?

Sara smiled when she saw him, relief and concern apparent in her face and eyes. "How do you feel? Are you okay? What did Doc Randall say?"

"That my arm is broken, that my head is harder than steel, and that I'll live. We both agreed that guy must've been swinging a lead pipe, though."

Sara drew a sharp breath. "Do you want to tell me exactly what happened?"

Gideon looked down at her and thought of all the things he *wanted* to do, and none of them involved discussing the night's events. They were more like curling up in his bed with a naked Sara Yates beside him, with her soothing, enticing, wicked little hands doing soothing, arousing, devilish little things.

"Now?" he said. "Here?"

Her chin took on a mulish set, belying the worry in her eyes. She had her moments, Gideon thought. "Or at the office."

He sighed. "This is official, huh?"

Sara nodded. "You can talk to another officer, if you prefer." And if he did, she would kill him. This had happened on *her* property, after all, and had already involved her family.

"Why would I want to talk to anybody but you, Mouse?" he asked, ignoring Joey's interested look. "Okay. But can't we go someplace where we can sit and have some coffee?" Truth was, he was still feeling a little ragged, maybe from blood loss.

"Let's go over to the office, then. I can fill out the paperwork while we talk."

"Fair enough." Anything was better than hanging around in this lobby looking like an escapee from *Halloween*.

The coffeemaker at the Sheriff's office had been cleaned out and stood ready to brew. Sara asked Joey to make the pot while she and Gideon settled down at the front desk. Sara found a yellow pad in the bottom drawer and pulled it out, and from a cup at the dispatcher's desk she retrieved a black felt-tip pen.

Gideon held up his injured arm and said with all the appeal of a small boy, "Will you sign my cast? Please?"

It was as if he had pulled a plug. All of a sudden the tension went out of Sara, and she looked at him with huge, luminous eyes. "I was so worried," she whispered. "So worried."

Gideon lowered his arm. "I'm sorry. I acted like a grade-A jackass, going after the guy, and I probably got less than I deserved. All I could think of was that somebody was tampering with your Blazer, maybe with intent to do harm, and I guess I saw red. Or something. I sure wasn't thinking clearly." He had in fact reacted instinctively to protect Sara. He wasn't sure thought had entered into it at all.

That wasn't like him. He had fast reflexes and swift responses to danger, developed by twenty years at the top, but as a rule, he didn't go leaping *into* danger without thinking things through first. No connector did, if he wanted to live long. But tonight he had. For Sara.

The awareness settled into him uneasily, but he was too damned tired to think about it now. Nor was he sure he wanted to think about it at all. He suspected the reasons behind his behavior were not going to make him happy.

"Tell me what happened," Sara said, drawing the pad closer. She was all business now. All deputy.

So he told her. From the moment he was hit in the side of the head, though, his memory of events had become fuzzy, and he could give her only the highlights of his ill-fated chase. One concern stuck forcibly in his mind, though.

"Has someone checked out your Blazer?"

"Not yet. It's too dark. They'll look it over in the morning. You don't remember anything at all about your assailant that might help us identify him?"

It had been dark—too dark, really—to get more than a blurred impression of anything. He shook his head slowly, only saying, "Just that he was big, maybe my height. Heavyset."

"Fat?" Sara queried.

Gideon hesitated, and shrugged as he looked at Joey, who was listening intently. "Not really. Broad, solid." He gave Sara a rueful smile. "Of course, my mental image of him may have been affected by the damage he did to me. The guy who beats you bloody is *always* bigger, by definition."

By the time they arrived back at the Double Y, Gideon felt as if he'd tangled with a gorilla. His arm ached fiercely, his head ached worse, and the bruise on his solar plexus was beginning to throb in time to his pulse. All he wanted to do was crawl into his bed and sleep off the worst of the pain.

In no mood to wrestle one-handed with his clothes, he simply lay down on his bed fully clothed and closed his eyes. It was nearly dawn, and he should have fallen asleep effortlessly, but his mind was in high gear and wouldn't slow down.

Fact: Little more than a week ago, Zeke had been brutally attacked, and the house and bunkhouse had been searched but nothing taken.

Fact: Tonight someone had been prowling around Sara's vehicle and possibly other vehicles in the dead of night.

Conclusion: Somebody was looking for something at the Double Y.

But what? Something that might be hidden in the undercarriage of a vehicle? Something small?

Hell, it could be just about anything, he supposed. The real question was what anybody on the Double Y might have that would arouse such interest. And why they had beaten Zeke so badly, yet tonight had come stealthily. Had they thought Zeke might tell them something? But Zeke seemed to have no earthly notion what anyone could be looking for.

"Gideon?" It was an almost soundless whisper.

Opening his eyes, he saw Sara standing hesitantly in the bedroom doorway, just visible in the first early glow of coming dawn. She was still fully dressed, and he suspected she wasn't sleeping any better than he was. Too much had happened that shouldn't have happened.

"I'm awake, Mouse. Come here."

Moments later she was curled up against his good side, her head tucked on his shoulder. Turning his head just a little, he could feel the silkiness of her beautiful hair and fill himself with her wonderful scent. Now, he thought, he could sleep.

An alarm sounded somewhere at the back of his mind, but sleep was already washing over him, muffling it, making it seem unimportant.

Sara was here, and now he could sleep. Nothing else mattered.

Chapter 11

Zeke and Chester were building a sweat lodge, and Gideon had the not quite comfortable feeling that he was going to be drafted into using it along with them. After last night's events, the two elderly men had evidently decided that some help was needed, and that started with *Inipi,* Chester explained. Purification. Then he and Zeke would ask for help in *Yuwipi,* a spirit-calling ceremony.

With his arm in a sling, there wasn't a whole lot Gideon could do except watch. Not that anyone would let him. Joey took care of the chores, and Zeke and Chester took care of the Stone-People-Lodge, as they called the sweat lodge. Together they cleared a circle of ground at the back of the meadow, and in it measured another circle, which was dug out to make a shallow bowl. Then they paced off ten steps to the east and dug another hole, this one deeper, in which they would heat the rocks for the sweat, they said. This was called the Fire of No End. By this time, both men were so busy they quit explaining, and anyway, Gideon was content to watch and offer his one good hand where he could.

"The lodge must always face east," Chester said as he and Zeke began erecting the willow saplings that would frame the building. "From there comes the light of knowledge."

Gideon helped hold one of the saplings in a bowed position while Zeke tied it to another. "Don't you need a holy man to do this?"

Zeke chuckled, and Chester regarded him with dark, twinkling eyes. "I *am* a holy man," Chester said. "I'm all we need. Offer me a pipe, Ironheart, so we can get you started on your quest."

Hell, thought Gideon, now Zeke even had Chester doing it. Disgruntled, he walked back to the house to get himself a glass of water. Just as he reached the porch, thinking about filling a water jug and taking it up the meadow to Chester and Zeke, Sara returned to the yard in her own Blazer. Early this morning it had been towed to town to be checked over, and apparently now had a clean bill of health.

"Did they find anything?" he asked Sara when she climbed out.

"Nope. Somebody looked, but he didn't mess with anything."

"No prints?"

"Nope."

He realized suddenly that he was watching her stiff back as she stalked toward the house. Something was wrong. This was not the woman who had smiled sleepily in his arms only a few hours ago and then proceeded to take his battered, aching body to heaven with nothing but the gentle touch of her hands and mouth. God, the mere memory of that zinged through him like wildfire!

But…she was disappearing stiffly into the house, and he had to find out what was wrong. She had her back to him when he entered the kitchen.

"Sara?"

She didn't turn to look at him. "Yes?"

"What's wrong?"

For an endless time it seemed she would not answer. When finally she did, she still wouldn't look at him. "I saw Faith Parish in town this morning."

His stomach sank to his boots, and he no longer had any doubt what was coming. Nor did he have any defense.

"She thought I knew you and Micah were brothers," Sara said tightly. "Do you have any idea how embarrassing it was that I didn't?" Even now she remembered the cold sensation of shock that had made her nearly dizzy as she realized that she knew nothing about this man to whom she had given her heart. As she realized that he was keeping secrets. That he was using her.

"Sara, I—" Oh, God!

She whirled suddenly and faced him, angry and hurt beyond belief. "Shut up, Ironheart! I don't want to hear your excuses. I felt a little better when I learned that you hadn't even told Micah, but that didn't last long because I...because I—" She broke off and drew a long, shuddering breath before she could continue. "Then I remembered how you wanted me to introduce him to you. How you used me—*seduced* me—into doing what you wanted."

"Sara, please—"

"No, Gideon. I don't want to hear it. Were you ever going to tell any of us? Or were you just going to use us all?"

She hadn't given him an opportunity to answer, and he supposed at this point she wasn't really interested in anything he had to say, anyway.

He considered leaving. He even went so far as to dig his duffel bag out of the closet. It didn't seem right to stay around when Sara was so hurt and angry at him. She would feel better if he moved on and got out of her life.

But as he reached for the bag with his one good hand, he hesitated. He was always assuming people would be better off without him, that they would prefer him to vanish from their lives. And always, when he felt that way, he moved on.

But maybe Sara *wouldn't* feel better if he left. Maybe that would only confirm for her that she had meant nothing at all to him. Maybe it would harden her belief that he had simply used her. Maybe it would humiliate her every bit as much as George's defection years ago.

Maybe Sara Yates needed somebody to stick around and fight back. Maybe she needed some proof that he'd forgotten all about using her long before he had made love to her. Maybe she needed to know she meant something to him, meant enough that he would stick around through the rough times.

Slowly he sank onto the edge of his bed and thought about it. Maybe Sara needed from him all the things he had always wanted for himself.

All the things he didn't believe in.

Sara had thought that George had taught her what it meant to be hurt. Now she knew better. Nothing on earth could possibly hurt as much as Gideon's betrayal. Her throat felt as tight as if a noose were tied around it, and she was sure she would never dare speak again for fear of bursting into tears.

Sorrow tightened her chest, too, like a vise, and made even the simplest act seem difficult. From her bedroom window she could see Gideon crossing the meadow to where Zeke and Chester were building the sweat lodge and wondered if he would tell them of his deception. He had used them all.

Etched in acid on her brain was the memory of Faith Parish this morning on the sidewalk, her baby in her arms, bubbling cheerfully and obliviously about how wonderful it was that Micah and Gideon had found one another, how simply fantastic that Micah had a whole family he had never even met. How, if Gideon were any example of the Oklahoma Lightfoots, they would all be wonderful people.

And how she herself had stood there listening to Faith, frozen almost to ice in the middle of a day that had turned into a nightmare. How she had since wondered how many other secrets Gideon was keeping. A wife, perhaps? A dozen children? Maybe that was the real reason he was a "tumbleweed."

And then the horrible, horrible realization that she had been used. That Gideon had sought her out because she worked with Micah.

She drew a long, shaky breath and tried to tell herself it didn't matter. This had merely been a reinforcement of a lesson she had learned long ago, and she had only herself to blame for giving her heart to a drifter. At least he'd warned her about that much. At least he hadn't tried to make her think he would stay.

In fact, she admitted with bitter honesty, he hadn't promised her one damn thing. *She* was the one who had given him more than he had ever asked for. If she had heeded his warning, she wouldn't be hurting half so badly right now.

Like so many women before her, she had fallen into the oldest trap in the world, she thought miserably. She had been foolish enough to think her love could make a rolling stone stay. Foolish enough to think that he would become what she needed him to be.

Lies or no lies, what she was feeling right now was all her own fault.

That knowledge didn't make it one bit easier to take.

By midafternoon Zeke and Chester had nearly finished the lodge. Neither man had any buffalo skins, which would traditionally have covered the frame, so trade cloth was used.

"Tomorrow," said Chester finally, nodding approval. Then he got into his thirty-year-old pickup truck and departed.

"Now," said Zeke, looking at Gideon, "you'll make your *Chanunpa,* your own sacred pipe."

Gideon shook his head. "I've got other things on my mind, Zeke."

For a long moment the old Shoshone regarded him intently, with black eyes as piercing as arrows. Gideon knew that look and felt as exposed as an upended turtle. "Zeke, Sara is...furious with me. With good reason. And right now I just don't want to think about sacred pipes and vision quests and sweats."

"I don't want you to *think* about sacred pipes or any of the rest of it," Zeke said. "I just want you to *do* it. So I'll give you the pipe I started for you, and you can finish it."

"I've only got one arm."

"It's enough. You only need to do a little carving. I even have the knives for you to use."

"Zeke..."

Zeke silenced him with a wave of his hand. "You do it, boy. You carve something on the pipe and it'll be yours. Do it. And while you're doing it, stop thinking with your head. It's been getting in your way for as long as you've been here. I'll get the pipe."

Frustrated, Gideon stared after him and resigned himself to his fate. It appeared he was going to carve a pipe whether he wanted to or not.

Several paces away, Zeke suddenly halted and faced him once more. "Ironheart."

"Mmm?"

"Sara's thinking with her head right now. In a little while she'll start thinking with her heart. Be sure that *you're* doing the same."

Thinking with head or heart, what was the difference? Gideon wondered irritably. Either way, Sara would be furious, and any explanation he could offer sounded pretty pathetic, even to his own ears. What had made so much sense two weeks ago right now seemed to fly in the face of all common sense.

Zeke showed up ten minutes later with the damn pipe. Settling on the bunkhouse step beside Gideon, he removed the hide wrapping from the half-made object. There were two pieces, the long, straight wood stem, and the red stone elbow that was the bowl.

"I drilled out the center of the stem and carved the bowl for you already," Zeke said. "I figured you wouldn't know how to do it."

"I don't know how to do *any* of this, old man."

Zeke chuckled softly. "You'll learn, boy. You'll learn. This first pipe you don't have to make entirely by yourself. When you make your next one, I'll show you step-by-step, including finding the right ash branch for the stem and getting the red stone for the bowl. Did you know there's only one place on earth where you can find that stone?"

Zeke shook his head. "Never guessed."

"White men call the place Pipestone, Minnesota. The Lakota say the buffaloes died there and shed their blood so that we could live. But I'll tell you all that at another time. Or better, get Chester to tell you. He knows a lot more than I do.

"Right now, all you have to do is carve something on the stem. A buffalo, or an eagle. Maybe a turtle. Whatever. Choose something not too difficult. All that matters is that you make it yours."

Then he picked up a second bundle and brought forth another pipe. In spite of his sour mood, Gideon drew a long, appreciative breath. This pipe was a work of art, intricately carved, decorated with feathers, stained and painted in beautiful colors.

"I made this," Zeke said. "I spent many, many hours on it when I was lonely, after my wife died, before Sarey needed me to come here. The work helped me to see with my heart when my head would only grieve. Someday, Ironheart, you will make a pipe this beautiful. But for now, just make a pipe. Any pipe. Tonight."

Gideon picked up his pipe stem and moved it around until he figured out how best to brace it so he could work on it. Anything, he told himself, was better than doing nothing.

Sara had already started dinner when Zeke returned to the house. Industriously, she was chopping and peeling and dicing for stew. Zeke paused to wash his hands at the kitchen sink.

"I'll do that," he said.

"I'll do it. You worked hard this afternoon on the sweat lodge."

"And you work hard all the rest of the time."

Sara turned and pointed at him with her peeler. "Sit down, Grandfather. Have some tea."

The old man smiled. "Yes, Granddaughter. How very respectful of your elders you are."

"I didn't say one disrespectful thing."

"No, but you were thinking of it."

Sara's smile appeared reluctantly. "Go on. Relax."

He didn't speak again until he was seated at the table with a tall glass of ice tea. "Joey's taking longer than I thought he would, fixing that fence."

"Where'd he go?"

"Up by the falls." Every spring, snow runoff softened the ground and made the fence near the falls sag, and every spring it had to be shored up again.

"Well, he probably got hot and decided to take a little dip. Or just to play hooky." It wouldn't be the first time.

"Maybe."

"I wish he hadn't gone up there by himself."

Zeke sighed. "Sarey, we can't live like prisoners because of what has happened. Besides, whatever they were looking for is something they expected to find in the house or one of the cars. And they always come in the dark. There's no reason why they should bother Joey when he's mending the fence."

True, thought Sara, and let it go. She was only trying to distract herself, anyway, from thoughts of Gideon's betrayal, from noticing how badly she hurt and how empty she felt. "Did Gideon tell you about Micah?"

"Yes."

"You don't feel used or betrayed?" She turned to look at her grandfather.

"No. I can see why he wanted to keep his secret until he was sure of the kind of man Micah is."

"But he used me to meet Micah!"

Zeke's expression never changed. "Did he? Did he really?"

Frustrated, Sara turned back to making the stew. Zeke could be absolutely infuriating when he got into one of his inscrutable moods. Sometimes she felt as if she were living with Socrates and was caught up in some kind of philosophical dialogue. It was maddening!

A little while later her thoughts wandered over to the bunkhouse, and she wondered what Gideon was doing. Packing his suitcases, maybe. And that made her think of the trunk of her grandfather's belongings.

"Grandfather? Why do you keep all your things over at the bunkhouse? Why did you pack your wedding picture?"

"Those things are keepsakes for you and Joey. They're meaningless to me."

She turned and looked at him. "How can you say that?"

"Because it's true. All that is important is in my memory, but the past is the past, Sara. One learns from it, perhaps cherishes it a little, but then must leave it behind. I loved your grandmother, child, but I cannot allow my grief over her death to color all the remaining days of my life. No one should allow the past to govern the future."

Sara swiftly turned back to her task, while a niggling little voice in the back of her mind asked: was that what she was doing? There seemed to be no answer beyond the uneasy sinking of her stomach.

Gideon looked down at the pipe stem in his hands and decided that the damn buffalo head looked as much like a buffalo as it ever would. At least the horns, however crooked, were identifiable. He set the knife down and brushed wood chips from his jeans, realizing with a sense of shock that several hours had passed. Now it was supper time.

He wasn't sure he should go up to the kitchen. Sara, he suspected, would be relieved if he didn't, and given his sense of iniquity, he wasn't sure he *ought* to. On the other hand, he was feeling more strongly than ever that he really needed to stick this one out, that for once in his life he shouldn't bail out of a relationship without making a stab at repairing the damage. That it was time to stop skating on the surface and face the currents underneath. Time, perhaps, to face the possibility that someone might need something from him . . . and that he might need something from them.

On the other hand, he found himself thinking, Sara hadn't even given him a chancc to explain what he'd done, which just proved the premise under which he had always functioned: people were fickle and wouldn't hesitate to drop you at the first provocation. She had drawn all her conclusions without asking him his side of the story.

And it hurt. Closing his eyes momentarily, he admitted to himself what he'd been refusing to face for two weeks now. He cared what Sara Yates thought of him, and it hurt that she had judged him without even asking his reasons. Not that his reasons justified his actions, he admitted with painful honesty, but if she cared about him, wouldn't she at least want to hear his side of it?

All of which led him right back to where he had begun years ago. Caring hurt, so he didn't want to care too deeply. And *love* was a word people used to manipulate one another. He'd fallen into that trap long, long ago. So long ago that the woman was only a dim memory of a blond, blue-eyed hussy he'd initially likened to a fairy princess, only to discover she more closely resembled a succubus.

Part of that mess, he acknowledged now, had arisen from his own youth and an overwhelming desire to be . . . loved. The word nearly stuck in his mental craw. Love had turned out to be a blond bimbo who was taking him for every cent he earned and ridiculing him to her friends. One who, when he had overheard her denigrating him, had turned on him with a scornful smile and proceeded to inflict verbal wounds to his soul. One who had come to know him well enough that she knew exactly what to say, exactly how to hurt him.

He had thought himself well past that episode until the other night when the words "half-breed savage" had spilled out of him. Some wounds, it seemed, never healed.

They were the legacy of love.

Sara Yates wasn't anything like that blond bimbo from twenty years ago, so he'd fallen into the trap again, he realized, the trap of wanting to be loved. And it was obvious now that she didn't love him. Not with the kind of love he'd always longed for and never believed in. If she had loved him that way, she might have been angry at his deceit, but she wouldn't have turned her back on him.

He looked down at the rough pipe he held and fit the stem into the bowl. The bowl represented Woman, Zeke had said, and the stem represented Man. The Tree of Life.

Sometimes they sundered, Gideon thought, separating the pieces and looking at them. And when they did, they were incomplete. Useless. No one could smoke a broken pipe. But he had never found the glue that could hold the pieces together.

And once again he faced the dark possibility that it just didn't exist.

Joey appeared at dinner with a dark bruise mottling his cheekbone.

"What happened?" Sara asked immediately.

Joey shrugged. "I wasn't paying attention and tripped, that's all. Forget it."

"Did you get that fence all braced?" Zeke asked.

"I need to go up again in the morning. I'll have it done before lunch." He shifted irritably and stabbed at a pea with his fork. "It'll get done. You don't need to ride me."

"No one's riding—" Sara broke off at a sharp gesture from Zeke. Silence reigned for a couple of minutes.

"Where's Gideon?" Joey asked suddenly.

"Guess he's late," Zeke remarked.

Joey looked at Sara. "What did you do? Drive him off? Every other guy who's ever—"

"Joey Yates, you be quiet right now," Sara said sharply. "It's none of your—"

"It's my business, all right!" Joey shouted, causing Sara and Zeke both to stare at him in astonishment. "Ever since George dumped you, you treat men like rattlesnakes. Even me! You never believe me! Never! You're always so damn sure a man is lying or cheating or—"

"Silence, boy," said Zeke. It was a tone that cut through Joey's tirade and brooked no argument.

"You never even *listen*," Joey shouted and jumped up from the table, heading toward the door.

"Joey." Zeke's voice stopped him. "Ask Gideon to join us. Then come back here and finish your supper. I'm giving you ten minutes."

Joey stomped out without answering.

Sara looked at Zeke, aware that her lower lip was trembling and that she wanted to cry again. This day had been hell, and she felt as if she was losing everything she loved. "You should have just let him cool off," she said to her grandfather.

"It's time he learned self-control," Zeke said. "High time."

Sara nodded, knowing he was right about that. But... "What do you suppose he meant, that we never listen? That I don't believe him?"

"I guess one of us didn't hear something we should have. And maybe we'd better ask him when he calms down."

Joey found Gideon still sitting on the bunkhouse steps with the pieces of the pipe in his hands. Gideon looked up and greeted him with a nod.

"You argue with somebody?" he asked the boy.

"Tripped."

Gideon seriously doubted it, but he let it go. Joey sat beside him.

"Grandfather talked you into making a pipe?"

"Your grandfather is an irresistible force."

A soft snort escaped Joey. "Yeah."

Gideon held up the pieces. "My carving leaves a lot to be desired."

"It looks like my first pipe," Joey said. "Actually, I think mine was a lot worse. The bowl wasn't as straight."

"Zeke carved everything except the buffalo."

Joey leaned over for a closer look. "Oh." Then he snickered.

Gideon chuckled in spite of himself. "Yeah, I know." He picked up the square of hide in which Zeke had originally kept it and wrapped the pieces.

"I'm supposed to bring you back for dinner," Joey said.

"I wasn't sure I ought to show up."

"I wondered. What happened? Did Sara give you hell over something? She's impossible. I think George made her hate men. Or at least never trust them."

And I made it worse, Gideon thought. "Well, I gave her cause," he said to Joey. "I wasn't exactly up-front with her."

"So?"

Gideon looked at him, a little startled. "So?"

"Well, it's not like you've known her for years or anything. It's only been a couple of weeks. It takes longer than that to tell somebody everything, especially the important things." He shrugged. "Not that she would have listened, anyway."

Gideon turned to look straight at the boy. "What didn't she hear you say?"

Joey looked down at his scuffed, dusty boots. "Oh, hell, it doesn't matter now."

"Sure it does. That's the second time you've mentioned it to me. What was it, Joey?"

Joey hunched his shoulders. "I told her I didn't steal that damn car. I didn't even know it was stolen. I thought it was Les Walker's car. He said his dad gave it to him, and he let me drive it. But nobody believed me. Everybody believed Les when he said he never saw the car before."

"Why do you think that happened?"

Joey shrugged, then finally looked at Gideon. "Probably because I'd been cutting up so much at school and Les never got into trouble. Probably because I look like a punk. Probably because I was the only one in the car. But *Sara* should have believed me. *Grandfather* should have believed me."

"And what about Les? Why did he set you up like that?"

"Because of Daisy Halloran. She said she'd go to the prom with me, and Les thought she was going to go with him. He was pretty pi—ticked off about that. We even had a fight over it in the school parking lot. I won." He shrugged. "Daisy went to the prom with him."

So much for love.

"I believe you," he told Joey.

The boy turned and looked doubtfully at him. "Why? Just because I said so? Nobody else did."

"Just because you said so."

Joey almost grinned. Gideon could see it. Then the boy suddenly looked away and scuffed nervously at the ground. "Maybe we better go up for supper. Grandfather only gave me ten minutes."

"Let's go, then," Gideon said, rising with the pipe still in his hands. He felt a little like Daniel going into the lion's den, except that Daniel had had virtue on his side. And Daniel had only had to face a lion, not an angry woman.

Chester Elk Horn spent most of the next morning by the sweat lodge, praying. Gideon looked over to that end of the meadow a number of times and had the eerie feeling that he could feel a gathering of forces in the air. The hair on the back of his neck stood up a little even as he tried to tell himself his imagination was running away with him.

And then the mustangs showed up, hours earlier than usual. The mares, as always, hung back by the trees, but the stallion came prancing right over to Gideon and butted him gently on the shoulder.

Touched by this display of unequivocal trust, Gideon reached up with his one good arm and patted the horse awkwardly.

"It's hell sometimes, boy, isn't it?" he heard himself whisper huskily to the horse.

He'd had plenty of time during the long, dark hours of the night to face the unexpected loneliness of Sara's absence. Plenty of time to consider how much misery he was suffering from an emotion he didn't believe in. Plenty of time to wonder how he was going to cope with the emptiness from here on in.

He'd been ripped up before in his life. Hell, it was the primary reason he tried not to care. Barney's death, he had thought, had completely gutted him. Now the loss of Sara showed him he hadn't been gutted, after all. There was still enough feeling in him, still enough caring, to ache for that woman. God, he thought, pressing his cheek to the stallion's sleek neck. God, it hurts so bad.

The mustang nickered softly and then pulled away, trotting off toward his mares.

Gideon watched him go, wishing he were a mustang rather than a man, and then turned toward the bunkhouse, intent upon working on his pipe. He wanted that buffalo to look like a buffalo before he offered the pipe to Chester later.

Because he *was* going to offer the pipe. He was going to do the sweat and seek a vision, because he needed answers and direction, and neither seemed to be coming from the meanderings of his own mind. Minute by minute he flopped back and forth between trying to force Sara to listen and waiting until she calmed down enough to be willing to hear reason. He could understand that she felt betrayed. If that had been the sum of it, he would have known exactly what to do. But that was only half of it. The other half of it was that Gideon was feeling betrayed, too. By her.

Instinct said to turn his back on the whole mess and walk away right now. His heart said otherwise. Sara Yates and her soft brown eyes had somehow become more important to him than protecting himself.

And it was time to figure out just what that meant.

"Gideon! Gideon!"

Sara called to him from the yard, and the insistent, almost panicked note in her voice brought him across the meadow at a full run from where he'd been listening to Chester explain the strips of colored cloth, called *Shina,* that he was hanging over the altar in the lodge.

His first thought was that the mugger had returned in broad daylight, but then he realized Sara would hardly be standing in the yard shouting for him if that were the case. His long legs ate up the ground as he ran down the hill to her, ignoring the pain in his shoulder and arm as his cast bounced in the sling.

"Joey's gone," Sara said just as soon as he got within talking distance.

"Gone? You mean he went someplace?"

"I mean *gone*." Her eyes were wide, worried. "Zeke took him up to the falls this morning to finish fixing the fence."

Gideon nodded. "I know."

"Anyway, Zeke left him working there and went out to check on another section where we have trouble sometimes and the mustangs might get out. When he came back, Joey wasn't there." She bit her lip and shook her head. "There's no place he could have *gone*. Not by himself without a vehicle. Not from there. Zeke said his hat and gloves are there by the fence, along with all the tools. Zeke called and called and called...."

Instinctively, he reached out and drew her into his arms. She came without resistance, surprising him. "Where's Zeke?"

"Inside calling the sheriff. Oh, Gideon, I'm so worried!"

After the other things that had happened, so was Gideon. Especially after his conversation with Joey last night. He really didn't think the boy intended to get up to any mischief right now. "Micah will be able to tell if he wandered off—"

She shook her head, interrupting him. "Micah's up in the mountains looking for that woman who disappeared from her campsite yesterday." It would take hours and hours to get him out of that wilderness and back to Conard County, she thought. Too many hours. They had to find Joey before nightfall, because if he was hurt and out there all alone, exposure might kill him before morning. The nighttime lows were still falling into the forties and fifties, depending on altitude.

She refused to even consider the possibility of abduction.

"Take me up there and show me the place," Gideon said after a moment, feeling an overwhelming need to do something. "My eyes are better than Zeke's. Maybe I'll be able to see something he missed."

Sara hesitated only a moment. "All right," she said. "Just let me tell Grandfather."

At that moment Zeke stepped out onto the porch. His expression was impassive. Too impassive, Gideon thought. Sara, who had just turned from Gideon, froze when she saw him. "What are they going to do?" she asked.

"Not much," Zeke said. "It's not as if the boy has never disappeared before. One of the deputies is going to come up and look things over, but without some evidence that he didn't just walk off on his own, they're not going to do a damn thing, Sarey."

Chapter 12

Gideon found the blood. It was spattered across the grass and brush not ten feet from where Joey's gloves lay. There had obviously been a struggle of some kind, judging from broken branches and trampled grass. Deputy Charlie Huskins agreed, and by midafternoon search parties were combing the vicinity for some sign of Joey or his attackers.

By nightfall, nothing helpful had been discovered. The search parties returned to the command post that had been established near the place from which Joey had disappeared, all with negative reports. Nor could the search continue after dark. Important clues might be trampled, but just as importantly, someone might get hurt stumbling around in terrain full of gullies, crevices, gorges and boulders.

Gideon and his search partners returned to the command post just as the last light faded and turned dusk into night. Sara had been manning the communications base station at Nate's insistence and despite her own overwhelming urge to participate in the search.

"It's better this way," Nate had told her. "This way you'll know everything we find the minute we find it. You won't have to wonder."

So she had stayed, and now she watched as Gideon's party, the last to return, emerged from the shadowed woods into the light of kerosene lanterns.

"We'll start again at dawn, Sara," Nate promised her before he left.

Gideon approached and stood beside her as they watched the last of the searchers pack up and drive off. A few minutes later they stood alone in the eerie silence and darkness of the deserted wood.

"He's got to be all right," Sara whispered, as much to herself as to him. "He's got to be all right."

Unable to offer any other comfort, Gideon turned her into his arms and stood hugging her as night drew more deeply around them. He didn't want to think about how it was already growing chilly up here and would grow even colder before dawn. He didn't want to think of Joey lying unconscious somewhere out there and dying of exposure. He didn't want to think of Joey already dead and buried in a shallow grave.

And Sara was surely thinking of those things herself, right now, as she shuddered in his arms. He would have given anything to spare her this anxiety.

"Come on," he said presently. "Let's go back. Zeke's probably going out of his mind wondering if we found anything."

"He would know."

Gideon tipped his head back and looked down at Sara. "He'd know? How?"

She shook her head distractedly. "Zeke always knows. Sometimes I think the wind whispers to him. Oh, God!" she exclaimed in a burst of utter frustration. "Oh, God, I'm so scared! What if he's out there somewhere? What if he's hurt and..." She couldn't even make herself complete the thought.

"Come on," Gideon said after a moment. He squeezed her and urged her toward the truck. "I haven't eaten since breakfast and I bet you haven't either. I don't know about you, but my head works better when I'm not starved."

Stupid, he thought, to discuss food at a time like this, but necessities had to be dealt with, even when they felt out of place.

As he helped her into the passenger seat of his truck—a formality that she accepted awkwardly, as if it embarrassed her—a huge fist suddenly gripped his heart.

"Sara?"

She turned her head to peer at him in the dark. The moonlight cast mysterious shadows over her delicate features, darkening her eyes to bottomless wells. Catching her chin gently in the palm of his hand, he turned her face up just a hair.

"I'm sorry," he said.

"Sorry?"

"For not telling you—"

She covered his mouth swiftly with her fingertips. "No," she said.

"No?"

"I don't want your apology."

Until that instant he hadn't realized just how much he had been hoping she would forgive him. Hadn't realized just how much he had been counting on it. With those words she ripped hope from him and left him standing in an icy void of the heart unlike any he had ever imagined.

Slowly, suddenly feeling very old, he dropped his hand from her chin and closed the truck door. *I don't want your apology.* That said it all, didn't it? The words, the denial in them, cast him back into his solitude with a pain so old it seemed part of his skin. With a pain so new and so huge that its magnitude was beyond comprehension.

His feet felt like lead as he walked around the truck and climbed in behind the wheel. He would stay until Joey was found, he told himself. And then he would move on.

When they returned to the house, they learned that Chester had hurried up his timetable and was just about to begin *Yuwipi,* the ceremony to ask for help.

"He's going to ask where Joey is," Zeke told Sara and Gideon. "Come if you want, but once he starts, you mustn't disturb him."

Chester had taken over one of the rooms in the bunkhouse. Everything had been moved out, and the floor had been covered with sage. In the center, a square had been marked out by small twists of cloth all tied together on a rope. Inside the square stood a can full of dirt with a red-and-black stick poking up out of it. Tied to the top of the stick was an eagle feather. Beside that were a buffalo skull and some gourds, and some other items that were difficult to see in the poor light.

By the illumination of a single lantern, the arrangement looked eerie. Not even moonlight penetrated the room, for the windows had been covered by blankets.

"Sit against the wall," Zeke said, motioning Sara and Gideon to one side. "Keep your thoughts pure and don't be afraid."

Chester was bundled mummylike in a blanket, and tied inside it by Zeke, who then rolled him over so he lay facedown on the floor.

"Okay," said Zeke. "Now it begins." He doused the lantern.

Gideon wondered how Chester could even breathe. Beside him, he felt Sara shift restlessly, and then, causing his breath to catch in his throat, she leaned against him. Closing his eyes tightly against an unwelcome uprush of emotion, he wrapped an arm around her shoulders and waited tensely for her to stiffen or pull away. But she didn't. Instead, she snuggled a little closer, and his heart nearly stopped.

For a long, long time, the room was silent. Then the drum began to beat, steady and low, and Zeke began to sing.

It was hypnotic, Gideon thought. Slowly, gradually, tension seeped away, and in its place came a sense of restful expectancy. And little by little he felt himself going into the silence.

* * *

The climb was long, arduous. The air grew thinner with every step, and overhead gray-green thunderheads boomed and rumbled as they swallowed the sun. The sound of his own breathing was loud in his ears, and from time to time he slipped on loose rocks.

There were no shadows, he realized as the sun vanished in the leaden clouds. It was the Black Light, the light that cast no shadows. Around him, trees swayed and groaned in the wind, and then he left them behind. Ahead, above, there was nothing but rock. And a red buffalo that stood far ahead, looking back at him as if it was waiting. Waiting.

Calling.

Fluttering wings brushed his face, invisible wings, the wind, yet more than the wind. From behind, someone pushed him forward, a silent command to climb. Glancing back, he saw nothing but darkness. Even the trees and the slope below had vanished into the pit of night.

Ahead, the buffalo looked back at him, glowing now, a red as brilliant as fire, as beckoning as flame on a cold, empty night.

"Come," whispered the voice of the breeze. "Come see."

Pressing forward, he toiled upward, struggling against gravity, against the slippery rock, against the force of weariness that dragged him down. The air seemed to grow thick, fighting him, too.

And always, always, the buffalo stayed exactly the same distance ahead.

But finally, aeons later, he reached the pinnacle, a small point of land high above the sea of night below, and there the buffalo awaited him. The beast looked at him with sad, knowing eyes, with a sorrow beyond words, and said, "Ironheart, below you lies the sea of your making, and in the midst of the void you stand alone. You have been given all the colors of the universe, yet you have chosen to paint your world in only one tone. Take out your palette now, and paint the colors of the rainbow into your void."

As the buffalo spoke, the black sea below began to shimmer, at first like the dim rainbow colors of an oil slick. But as he watched, the colors blossomed into brilliant, blinding hues of gold and red and green and blue, colors so bright they drowned the stormy sky and made his eyes sting.

"These are your colors," the buffalo said. "Take them with you."

He watched the buffalo turn away, and the great beast began to walk off into the rainbow colors as if they were a road made for his feet.

"Wait!" Gideon cried. "The boy. Joey!"

The buffalo glanced back. "The deer will show the way."

Just then a huge wind blew, toppling him from the narrow peak and throwing him down the rocky slope. He bounced against rocks and felt the bite of their sharp corners, felt the tearing of his flesh and the breaking of his bones. Only when he lay again in the dark void did the pain cease. But this time, inside him, he felt the rainbow.

Turning, struggling to bring the colors inside him back out into the world, he saw the deer.

The pounding of the drum was loud, seeming to reverberate from the walls. Zeke's singing had long since stopped, and now the drum fell silent, too. And into that silence came the rattle of the gourds, a hissing sound like a rattlesnake. First it came from here, then there, seeming to fly around the room. Light flashed near the ceiling, a small blue burst. Another flash burst near the floor, revealing Zeke and the drum for one blinding instant.

Sara curled closer to Gideon, frightened at the strangeness of all that was happening. Lightning seemed to have come into the room with them, lightning and thunder and the rattle of hail. These were powers her grandfather and Chester had spoken of all the years she could remember, but not until now had she truly tasted them.

And then, as abruptly as it had begun, it ceased. Silence reigned for several minutes; then came the flare of the match as Zeke lit the lantern. Chester now lay unwrapped within his square of tobacco ties. Sara wondered how he had gotten untied. A glance at her watch told her the night had passed, and that dawn was less than an hour away.

Chester sat up, and he and Zeke sang softly. Sara looked at Gideon.

"I know where Joey is," Gideon said quietly. "I saw him."

Sara caught her breath as her heart climbed into her throat. "Saw him?" She hardly dared believe.

"I saw him," Gideon said again. "He's hurt, cold and hungry, but he's alive. Up the mountain. Near a tree that was blasted by lightning and then grew into two, like a *Y*."

"I know that place," Sara said excitedly. And there was no way on earth Gideon could have known about that tree. It was on one of the most remote parts of the ranch. She started to rise, in her eagerness, but her grandfather motioned sharply. His meaning was clear. She was to stay until he finished the song of thanks and farewell to the spirits who had aided them.

And for the first time in her life Sara Yates honestly felt she had something to thank the spirits for. Slowly she turned to look at Gideon. This man had had a vision during the night, and even as he spoke of it and prepared to act upon it, he didn't look very happy about it.

"Grandfather said you have power," she murmured.

"We'll see how much damn good it does anyone," he muttered back. "It hasn't ever done *me* any good that I can see."

Impulsively, she lifted her head and stretched until she could brush a kiss on his cheek.

The kiss struck Gideon like a bolt of lightning. Why was she kissing him? Because she thought he was going to find her brother? Was this the same woman who had told him just last night that she didn't want his apology?

"Ironheart." Chester had come over to them, and now he knelt facing Gideon. "The blasted tree is a power place. The boy is alive because of it. Don't break your neck trying to get there. He'll be alive."

A half hour later, with dawn just a faint gray line of promise at the horizon, Sara and Gideon started up into the mountains on horseback, to a place they could get to no other way.

"Except on dirt bikes," Sara said.

Gideon glanced at her. "What? Did I miss something?"

"I was just thinking that the only way to get to this tree is on horseback. Or on dirt bikes."

"Yeah. Well, I kind of suspected our dirt-biking friend might be involved. The question is, what is he after?" Feeling almost helpless against himself, he watched Sara, who was riding to one side and just a little ahead of him, as hopelessly as any sixteen-year-old in the throes of a major crush. The crystalline light of dawning day began to wash across the world, bringing sharp-edged clarity and color to their surroundings.

Watching her, he drank in every graceful line of her face, her neck, her thigh. Thought how lovely she was. How achingly, sweetly lovely. How badly he wanted to hold her again and tell her just how much she meant to him. To admit that she had become the only rainbow in his colorless world.

"Sara?"

She glanced back at him and smiled, just a small smile, but one that warmed his soul. Considering that she had been up all night, she looked awfully fresh, he thought.

"Sara, I really want to apologize for not telling you about Micah."

"That's not necessary. I told you that last night."

"But I . . ." Not necessary? How was he supposed to interpret that? "Of course it's necessary."

She shook her head. "In the first place, it's none of my business how you choose to handle your personal affairs. In the second place, it was presumptuous of me to think I had a right to know anything so personal about you."

"Presumptuous?" Now that was a word he hadn't heard anybody actually use in his entire life. He looked at Sara, taking in her crisp khaki uniform, the sage nylon jacket, the tan Stetson and the .45 riding on her hip, and thought what a unique delight she was. A black-satin voice in a black-satin woman who hid behind a tough-as-nails veneer.

"Now wait one minute," he said, heeling his mount forward until he was right beside her. "Spending a few nights in my bed gives you certain rights." Damn, he thought, feeling a little shocked at himself. Was he actually saying that? "You can't be presumptuous."

"No?" She glanced at him, and from somewhere in the depths of her anxiety over Joey came a glimmer of humor, just a faint sparkle in her brown eyes. "Well, it doesn't matter, anyway. I accept that you had your reasons. I shouldn't have gotten mad."

He frowned at her, feeling off-center and unsure of what was happening. "You had every right to get mad."

Sara shook her head. "Not really. The truth is, I wasn't really mad at you. I was feeling...uncertain, I guess. Scared. Afraid that I was making a fool of myself again. Sort of a knee-jerk reaction because of George. After he left, I always wondered how many secrets he'd had that he never told me about. I guess that was part of the worst of it, besides the humiliation. Thinking I had known this guy, and having it turn out that I didn't know him at all."

Everything inside Gideon winced as he realized the magnitude of the wound he had dealt this woman. "Mouse—"

"Let me finish. Please?"

Meeting the uncertainty of her gaze, seeing her determination to say difficult things, he nodded and fell silent.

"My reaction to you was filtered through my experience with George," Sara said after a moment. "When I calmed down enough, I realized that your being Micah's brother wasn't just your secret. It was Micah's secret, too, and you had no business sharing it with anyone before you shared it with him. And I got to thinking about how I would have felt in your shoes.... Honestly, Gideon, I'm not at all sure I would have done anything different from what you did. When I really thought about it, I saw how complicated and scary and difficult it would be, and why maybe you wouldn't want anyone at all to know, ever.

"And that business about using me? Well, when I thought it over, I realized that you asked me some questions about Micah, but mostly I did the talking, and *I* was the one who came up with the idea of introducing you. So you weren't even being bad in a big way.''

Feeling terribly shy, terribly afraid, Sara dared a glance at Gideon. She had realized, somewhere in the hell of the last thirty-six hours, that she had jumped off the cliff all on her own. Gideon hadn't pushed her, hadn't abandoned her, hadn't done a damn thing except keep an intensely personal secret. And she, who had promised herself that she was going to love him regardless, had succeeded only in showing him once again that you couldn't trust the people closest to you, because they could turn on you at the slightest provocation.

Gideon thought his heart was going to burst. Emotions locked his throat tight, made words impossible, as he looked at Sara's shy, uncertain face and realized she didn't think there was anything to forgive. That kind of acceptance had been so rare in his life that he could count on one hand the number of people who had given it to him. He swallowed hard and managed some gruff words. ''After we find Joey, we'll talk.''

She nodded, then pulled her sunglasses from her pocket and slipped them on. The morning sun was strong now, dappling the open spaces between trees with a brilliant golden light. Gideon found himself remembering his dream, his vision, or whatever it had been. The red buffalo had spoken his grandfather's words, he realized now—that business about colors.

But his life hadn't been colorless, he thought. At least, not until Barney's death. Maybe he hadn't painted it in *all* the colors of the rainbow, but he sure hadn't painted a black void. There had been Barney, of course, and good times, and plenty of excitement and thrills. Some of the colors had been missing, though, he admitted now. And since Barney's death, there hadn't been any color at all.

Until now. It almost seemed the world was glowing from within this morning, as if trees and grass and even rocks were brighter than ever before. As if edges were clear and sharp and perfectly etched. As if he had suddenly donned a pair of new glasses that brought everything into focus. As if such beauty had always been there but he had simply failed to perceive it.

"How much farther?" he asked Sara.

"Another hour or so. We can't make a straight line because of the terrain, so it takes a long time to get to the tree."

"I imagine you know every inch of the Double Y."

"Just about. Exploring was one of my favorite pastimes as a kid. I never much wanted to hang around the house, and once I got my own horse, that was all she wrote. As long as I got my share of chores done, Dad didn't seem to mind, and Mom gave up all hope of turning me into a cook and housekeeper."

"I can't imagine you as a cook or housekeeper," Gideon said after a moment. "I didn't quite know what to make of you when I first saw you, though. Not because you were a cop—there're women cops everywhere nowadays—but because something . . . didn't quite fit. It was as if you were trying to be tough when you really weren't."

"Well, I was," Sara admitted on a small laugh. "I always feel a little like an impostor in this uniform. And with a brawl like that night at Happy's . . . I don't know what I would have done if somebody had argued with me. Some of the guys I work with would have waded right in and enjoyed the free-for-all. Not me. And I didn't want to pull the trigger on that shotgun, either."

She turned in the saddle and looked at him from behind her mirrored sunglasses. "It's harder around here, I think, than it would be in a city, because all these guys know me. They remember when I was too tall, too gangly, and tripping over my own feet all the time. They remember when I forgot my lines in the junior play, and when Chuck Mangan made me cry by pulling my braids. It's kind of hard to be tough around that."

"You did a pretty good job of it," Gideon said with a smile. "None of those guys gave you a hard time, did they? If you ask me, they've got a lot of respect for you, and it would never occur to them to challenge you."

"Except you." Tipping her head, she looked at him over the tops of her glasses. "Your exact words, as I recall, were 'Who made you afraid to be a woman?'"

Gideon winced. "I deserved a pop in the nose for that."

"I considered it." Clucking softly, she heeled her gelding, urging him up a steep, rocky slope. "I didn't know I was so transparent."

"I think it was more wishful thinking than transparency on your part."

She tossed him a glance over her shoulder. "What do you mean?"

"Mouse darlin', from the instant I heard your voice my hormones started howling. It was kind of a crisis for me, in a way, because it had been a long, long time since I'd felt that hot that fast, and it kind of made me uneasy. So there I was, my insides getting stroked into a frenzy by your voice—thinking of black satin sheets, if you want to know the truth—and the person who was causing all that uproar was waving a shotgun, wearing a badge and talking as tough as Saturday night wrestling."

"Ouch."

"Ouch was exactly how it felt. I'd never been into dominance, you know? Especially from the submissive end. And all of a sudden I was panting for this tough... Ahh, forget it. This subject is a loaded gun, and I'm going to shoot myself in the foot if I keep on."

Sara almost told him that he was doing just fine and not to worry. Hearing again that he'd been turned on by her at their very first meeting gave her a thrill like none she had ever imagined. After a decade of believing herself to be a failure as a woman, it was music to her ears to hear someone say that he didn't think she was.

She tossed him another look over her shoulder. "Does this mean I can tie you up with my black silk stockings?"

For a split second Gideon simply stared at her in disbelief; then his laugh rang out, bringing a new kind of light to the sun-bathed woods. "Anytime, Mouse," he assured her. "And bring your .45."

* * *

Their humor didn't last long, however. It had served to distract Sara for a little while, but inevitably her thoughts turned to Joey. They moved as swiftly as they could over the rugged terrain, but fast wasn't fast enough. Farther down the mountain, the search parties would already have set out, looking for any evidence of what had happened.

Sara could have told Nate to hold off, and he might actually have done it, but she wasn't quite ready to risk Joey's life on a single roll of the die. If Gideon's vision had been wrong, it could cost Joey his life.

But she didn't think he was wrong. She was here because this man had turned to her with certainty and told her that he had seen Joey. Because he had known of the blasted tree. Because in her heart she recognized the power in the beliefs of her grandfather and his friend. Because she had felt the power in Gideon.

It was beyond rational explanation, but matters of the heart and soul always were. *See with your heart,* her grandfather had always said. She was doing that right now, following her heart on one of the wildest gambles she had ever taken.

When the terrain leveled out a little, Gideon astonished her by reaching over and covering her hand with his. "I missed you, Mouse," he said.

"I missed you, too," she admitted, and felt a prickle of tears in her eyes. Eventually he would leave, but for now... for now, she was following her heart.

The blasted tree rose in the center of a clearing. It rose straight and true to the height of a man, and there, from a blackened, twisted spot, suddenly split into two perfect trunks which, after curving slightly away from each other, rose just as straight and true as the original. High above, twin crowns stirred gently in the morning breeze.

Gideon could easily see why Chester considered this a place of power. There was an unearthliness to the clearing, a sense of something different, that he had felt in only a couple of places in his entire life. It made the back of his neck prickle. All morning he'd been trying not to think of his vision of this place and what it meant that he had seen it in his mind before he had seen it with his eyes. Now he didn't want to think about the power he felt here, as if the strength of the earth below their feet were somehow magnified and broadcast here.

"I don't see Joey," Sara said, her voice tight. She, too, felt the power of the clearing, and it reminded her of the hush in an empty church.

"He's around." Gideon was even more sure of it now that he had actually come to the place he had seen in his vision. If *that* could happen, then Joey was here.

Slowly he rode around the edge of the clearing, gradually becoming aware of the sound of rushing water over the rustle of the wind in the pines.

"There's running water here?"

Sara pointed. "Over there, just the other side of those trees."

Guided by instinct, Gideon dismounted, and Sara followed suit. They tethered their mounts and then walked into the trees.

"It's maybe twenty yards," Sara said, reaching back into her memory. "There's a deep gorge. . . ."

They emerged from the trees onto the edge of the gorge with almost startling suddenness. Gideon took one look at the rushing water thirty feet below and his vertigo hit him right in the face.

Spinning, splintering blue sky . . .

"Gideon!" Sara grabbed his arm and shook him. "Gideon!"

He drew a long, deep breath and opened his eyes. He was facing the gorge, facing the demons that haunted him.

"Are you all right?"

He turned, looking into her concerned face. "Yeah. Just got dizzy for a second."

"Let's get you away from here."

But he shook his head and looked across the gorge. "Is there any way to get over to the other side?" Something was compelling him, pushing him, just the same as something had compelled him to climb the mountain in his vision last night. Something was . . . guiding him.

"The easiest way is to go north from the ranch house and avoid the worst of the gorge altogether. This is the same creek that feeds into the glade where we picnicked."

He nodded, beginning to see it in his mind. "They brought him up the other side, then. He's over there, Sara."

She stared up at him, opening her mouth to ask how he knew. Then she thought better of it. There was no explaining how anybody knew something like this. "It'll take hours to go back down and come back up the other side," she said tightly. "Hours. Joey . . ."

Gideon turned, looking up the gorge, then down. There had to be a way. Then he saw the felled tree, maybe eight inches in diameter, that lay across the deepest point a hundred yards farther up. "I'll cross up there."

Sara followed his gaze and drew a sharp breath. "Gideon, no! You can't! Your vertigo—"

"My vertigo can go hang," he said roughly. "That boy is over there, Sara. If I can't get over there to help him, then I deserve to fall."

Her hand shot out and clutched his arm until her nails dug into him through the thick wool of his shirt. "I'll cross. I don't get dizzy. . . ."

"And I used to do this eight hours a day, babe. I have a better chance of doing it in one piece than you do." Bending, he astonished her with a hot, wet, almost savage kiss.

"But maybe he isn't—"

"He is." There was no doubt in him. He had the feeling that this was a moment of destiny, then dismissed the notion as nothing short of absolute lunacy. Too much time with Chester and Zeke, he told himself. Those two old Indians were turning him into a mystic. Just what he needed, another crazy quirk in his mind.

Sara climbed the rugged slope beside the gorge right behind him. She had insisted he wait until she retrieved the knapsack with the blankets and first-aid kit from the saddlebags, and now he carried it slung over one shoulder, taking the climb as easily as a mountain goat while she stumbled behind. It was not the first time she had noticed how surely he moved, leaving nothing to chance. But if a man were going to walk narrow beams nine hundred feet above the ground, he undoubtedly had to assess each step before he took it and stay perfectly balanced as he moved. For her part, she slipped a couple of times, but he was always there to help her up, or to catch her with his good arm.

Finally they stood at the point where the fallen tree made a narrow bridge over the deepest part of the gorge. The drop at this point was thirty-five or forty feet, and the cleft was narrow, almost straight-sided. Gideon kicked at the fallen tree, testing whether it would roll, and found that it had been there long enough to have settled fairly well. A scan along its length told him it was not yet visibly rotted anywhere. As good as he could ask for, under the circumstances.

"Oh, my God," Sara whispered suddenly. "Gideon... Gideon, I see him! There's Joey!"

He turned and looked where she pointed. The opposite side of the gorge was a foot or two lower than where they now stood, and at first all he could see were the low-growing shrubs and grasses that took root in any sunny crack in the ground. But then he saw the dark shape beneath one of the trees, a huddled bundle of denim and leather.

"I see him. I'm going over."

With Sara's help, he ditched his cowboy boots. They were meant for riding, not footwork, and their slippery soles and high heels would be a definite danger in what he was about to do. The he slung the knapsack over his good shoulder and put his bare foot on the end of the log.

The world seemed to shift as if from an earthquake. For a wild, terrifying instant he felt as if he was swaying back and forth on a falling swing, as if he would tumble end over end with the sky splintering above him. Cold sweat beaded his brow, his stomach heaved.

"Gideon... Gideon, don't. Let me."

He turned his head and looked straight into Sara's frightened brown eyes. "I'll do it," he said. Because if he didn't do this now, he would never be a whole man again. Because he couldn't let Sara take the risk.

He stepped up onto the log, every instinct screaming at him not to do it. Then, with his eyes straight ahead, he stepped out over the gorge. Arms out, making minor adjustments for the weight of the cast and with all the grace he had learned over the years at the top of the world's tallest buildings, he walked the length of the tree.

Twice his balance suffered as his mind deceived him, trying to convince him that he was falling. Twice he caught himself with instinctive ease. If Sara said anything, her words were drowned by the rushing cataract of the water below.

And then he was over. For an instant the whole world seemed to spin and he thought his knees would buckle. Almost as soon as the weakness assailed him, however, it vanished in a flood tide of rediscovered confidence and strength. He'd done it. He'd faced the demon and won. He gave himself a moment, a mere moment, to savor his victory, then hurried over to the huddled heap that was Joey.

Kneeling, he touched the boy's shoulder. "Joey? Joey, do you hear me?"

Joey groaned and shifted a little. His face was swollen and bloodied, and it appeared that his nose had been broken. It was then that Gideon saw he had been chained to the tree.

"Sonofabitch!" he muttered. Dropping the knapsack, he rose and cupped his hands to his mouth. "Sara! He's alive, but he's chained here. I'm going to have to try to break the chain."

She waved, signaling her understanding. Then he saw her lift her hand to key the radio mike that was attached to her collar. He hoped her transmission would reach the base station.

They'd chained him here. Gideon thought about that as he hunted up a heavy rock to use as a hammer. Chained him here to die of exposure, or to make dinner for one of the bears in the area. Damn! He couldn't believe that kind of mind. Couldn't even finish their own dirty work.

He found a good-size rock, maybe ten or twelve pounds, that he could hold in his one good hand and swing down against a length of the chain. Then he hunted up another rock, a flat one this time, to place beneath the chain.

For a man accustomed to swinging a sixteen-pound hammer as a normal part of his daily activity, smashing the chain was relatively easy. Fewer than a dozen blows weakened the link enough to shatter it.

The sound roused Joey to a kind of foggy awareness. He was a little hypothermic, dehydrated, tired. Maybe bleeding internally. It was impossible for Gideon to tell. He was just grateful that the boy surfaced to a semiconscious state.

"Joey? Joey, I'm going to have to tie your wrists together so I can carry you over my shoulders. Joey?"

"'Kay."

He had to be content with that. First he wrapped the boy mummy-style from his armpits to his ankles in the wool blanket that was in the knapsack and tied him into it with a length of rope. The wrapping would serve the double purpose of warming him up and keeping him still while they crossed the gorge. Then he took a roll of gauze bandage and bound Joey's wrists together.

He slung the boy over his shoulder, one of his arms over Gideon's good shoulder, the other arm under Gideon's other shoulder. With his hands bound, there was no way Joey could slip away from him.

"Now, don't move, Joey. Just keep still for a few minutes." Only a faint groan answered him. Gideon scooped up the knapsack and started over the gorge. Sara stood on the far side, hand pressed to her mouth as she watched.

Joey jerked once, on the way across, and Gideon did a quick little tap dance as he regained his balance. He managed to give Sara a grin as he steadied himself and finished the crossing.

"Piece of cake," he told Sara when he stepped off the log on the other side. "Piece of cake. Let's get this boy down the mountain."

Chapter 13

Gideon stood quietly in the far corner of the hospital room while Sheriff Nathan Tate questioned Joey. Sara stood near the bed, her hands tightly clasped as she listened. Zeke occupied the room's one chair.

Joey looked a lot worse for wear, Gideon thought. His face was so swollen and bruised, it was a wonder he could even talk. His nose was broken—evidently the cause of the spattered blood Gideon had found—and one eye was so blackened he couldn't even open it. Other than bruises, however, he had suffered no real damage.

The story he told wasn't very edifying. He'd been angry and hurt because no one would believe that he hadn't stolen the car. He had, he admitted, wanted to get even somehow. On a school field trip to the atmospheric research center at Boulder, he had run into a couple of guys who convinced him that he could make a lot of money by selling drugs.

"I wasn't thinking too good," he told the sheriff now, his voice muffled by all the swelling. "I was drunk."

Sara gasped. Gideon instinctively moved to her side and took her hand, squeezing it reassuringly.

"You were drunk on a school field trip," Nate repeated evenly. It was not a question, but the statement of a man who had just heard an unpalatable fact.

"Yeah. Me and a couple other guys."

Nate rolled his eyes. "God have mercy. Where were your chaperones? No, never mind. Just get on with this story. I'll deal with the school later. So you thought you could sell drugs?"

"Only when I was drunk. They said I could take the stuff and pay them their share after I sold it. Later I got scared shi—you know."

"I know," the sheriff agreed. "I take it you didn't give the drugs back?"

"No. I was already on the bus home. I didn't know what to do about it. Finally, I buried the stuff. I figured they'd never find me, you know? I didn't give them my real name, and I never said I was from here. Somebody else must have told them."

"Must have," Nate agreed. "For the moment, I won't ask why the hell you didn't tell your sister or me."

"Because you didn't believe me about the car! None of you! None of you except Gideon!"

"Shh," Sara said, stepping to the bed and taking Joey's hand in both of hers. "Hush, Joey. We're listening now. I promise." Oh, yes, she was listening, and she wanted to gather him into her arms and tell him it would be all right, but she couldn't do that anymore. Nobody could promise this mess would be all right.

"When Sara told me Grandfather had been attacked," Joey continued finally in answer to Nate's prompting, "I was afraid it was them, but I didn't see how it could be. Anyway, I started getting real cooperative so you'd let me out of jail. I figured if I was home, and it *was* them, they'd come for me, not Sara or Grandfather."

Nate nodded, and Gideon felt a strong surge of respect for the boy. He hadn't turned tail but had come home to face the problem in order to protect his family. It was the decision of an adult, not a child.

"Then Gideon got hurt," Joey said. "I knew then for sure it was them. It *had* to be. Nobody else would keep coming back. That's when I decided to go out and work on the fence alone. I figured they'd know I was home by then and would come looking for me. I kind of hoped they'd take the dope and leave me alone." He fell silent.

"So they found you," Nate pressed.

"Yeah. They beat me up a little, even when I told them I'd give them the drugs. I took them to where I'd buried the stuff and dug it up. I thought that was it, but they came back yesterday morning. They beat me up some more and left me chained to the tree. I guess they had second thoughts that I might tell somebody, so they decided to get rid of me."

There was more, but Gideon stepped outside into the hallway and went hunting for a coffee machine. He had plenty of his own baggage to deal with, he thought, starting with a brother he had just found, and ending with a vision he understood all too well. And that didn't even take Sara into account.

It was kind of an unsteady feeling for a man whose balance had always been perfect, he realized. He had always known where he stood on things, had always identified himself in certain ways. For years he had been Gideon Ironheart, ironworker, tough man. Cherokee half-breed who was ready and willing to make an issue of it. Yeah, he'd always seen himself clearly, and if he'd had to draw a picture, it would have been of him standing alone on a beam at nine hundred feet, steady, sure and untouched.

What a farce. Grimacing at his own foolishness, he dropped change into the coffee machine and then headed back toward the room with a cup of burned-smelling brew.

Coming from the other direction along the corridor was Micah Parish. Micah looked tired, and a layer of mud still covered his boots and splattered his uniform.

"Joey?" Micah asked.

"He's okay. We found him a couple of hours ago."

"I heard he was missing, and somebody said he'd been brought here, but nobody knew for certain what had happened."

"He's okay, Micah. Beat up, bruised, but okay. Sara and Nate are with him right now. You found that missing camper?"

"Yeah. Grizzly got her. She was in pretty bad shape when we got to her, and she'll probably need a lifetime's worth of plastic surgery." He stared past Gideon for a moment, seeing something in his mind, then shrugged it off. "You're looking ragged yourself, man."

Gideon smiled crookedly. "It was a long night for everyone."

"Faith said I was to ask you and Sara to come to dinner Saturday. Think you can make it?"

"I can't speak for Sara, but I'll be there." Gideon hesitated. "Guess I have a niece I need to visit."

Micah, who seldom smiled, smiled then. "You sure do. And you and I have a lot of missed ground to cover."

Gideon looked straight into Micah's eyes, eyes so very like their grandfather's, and saw an acceptance there that warmed him. "In case nobody ever told you, you're the spitting image of our grandfather."

Micah gave a small chuckle. "Knew it had to be somebody, and it sure as hell wasn't Dad."

Together they strolled down the hallway to Joey's room, arriving there just as the door opened and Sara, Zeke and Nate came out. Nate collared Micah immediately, drawing him aside for a low-voiced conversation.

"Ready?" Gideon asked Sara. She nodded, looking up at him with bruised eyes. "Okay," he said. "Just let me say goodbye to Joey."

The boy was staring up at the ceiling when Gideon entered the room, and he managed a crooked smile when he saw the older man. "I was stupid, huh?"

"Yep." Gideon shook his head as he looked down at the boy. "I doubt it's the first time a guy your age has done something stupid, though. Seems like I've done a dumb thing or two, even just last week. Did the sheriff say what he's going to do?"

"He said he hasn't seen any drugs, and he figures finishing out my probation on the car is enough. He made me promise I'd testify if they catch the guys who beat me up, though." Joey half shrugged, wincing as a bruise protested. "He also said he can yank my chain hard anytime I get out of line, so maybe it's time I straightened up."

"How do you feel about that?"

"Like it's time I straightened up. Gideon?"

"Yeah?"

"Are you going to stick around?"

Impulsively, Gideon touched the kid's shoulder. "You bet, Joe. And this summer we'll go do the Sun Dance together."

"You mean that?"

"I mean that. Now get some rest." He turned to leave and found that Sara was standing right behind him. Judging by that funny shine in her eyes, she'd been listening to every word.

Gideon hesitated, nearly overwhelmed by an urge to scoop her up and hug her to death, but then he eased by her and left her to say whatever she needed to Joey in privacy. They had to talk, he thought, but not here.

"So when are you going to do the sweat and the vision quest?" Zeke asked as they neared the ranch.

The three of them were crowded into the cab of Gideon's truck, Sara in the middle.

"You just don't quit, do you?" Gideon remarked.

"It's important, boy."

"I'm still trying to absorb what happened last night."

"And I keep telling you to stop thinking with your brain. You don't need to *absorb* anything. Your heart understands what happened."

It seemed to, Gideon admitted to himself, but he wasn't in any mood to give Zeke the satisfaction of his agreement. Nor was he in any mood to discuss sweats and visions. He had more important things on his mind.

"Leave him alone, Grandfather," Sara said. "Gideon will do what's best for him in his own time and in his own way."

When, Gideon wondered, was the last time someone had defended him? Not caring what Zeke might think, he reached out and squeezed Sara's thigh. "You got that straight, Mouse." From the corner of his eye, he saw her blush. "We'll talk about it tomorrow, Zeke," hc addcd as they jolted up the last few feet of rutted driveway and into the yard. "Tomorrow. Sara needs her sleep."

When he had parked the truck, he climbed out and reached back in for Sara, scorning the cast on his arm and the sling he'd long since abandoned. He ignored Zeke as if he had vanished, and turned with his woman in his arms and headed for the bunkhouse.

"Gideon . . ."

"Hush, Mouse. I'm a man in need."

She looped her arms around his neck and pressed her cheek to his. "In need of what?" Her question held a shiver that seemed to touch his nerve endings with fire.

"Of you," he said huskily as he climbed the steps. "I know you're tired. We'll just sleep, but, God, I need to hold you."

Sara's throat clogged with tears as her own yearning for this man filled her, making her ache with a longing so strong it hurt. "Oh, Gideon," she whispered brokenly. "Oh, Gideon."

He set her on her feet beside the bed and began to remove all the "tough" layers of her rumpled uniform. The tough side of this lady delighted him, but right now, in ways he couldn't begin to describe, he needed the soft, gentle side of her. The Mouse who had come to mean so much.

He threw her gun belt onto the dresser and pulled her shirt over her head without unbuttoning it. "We can wash up later, after we sleep," he said. He probably smelled like horse and sweat, but he didn't care. Sara smelled a little horsey, too, from their ride earlier, but he hardly noticed it compared to the sweet, warm fragrance of woman that emanated from her. "God, you smell sweet," he told her hoarsely. "You smell like heaven."

He got her naked beneath the quilts, and moments later he joined her, taking care not to bang her with his cast. He tucked her soft bottom against his loins, wrapped his arm around her waist and dropped a kiss on her ear.

And suddenly, for the first time in his entire life, everything felt absolutely *right*.

The digital clock on the dresser said it was just after midnight. Moonlight poured through a crack in the curtains, a slender beam of silver that found its way to Sara's shoulder. Gideon lifted his head and kissed that silvered spot.

"Mmm..." Sara stirred and twisted onto her back. "Gideon..." It was little more than a sigh. Reaching up sleepily, she looped her arm around his neck and pulled him closer. "Love me...."

The sleepy, husky request electrified him. Every nerve in his body woke to sizzling life. Love her? Yes. Absolutely.

She didn't want foreplay. When his hands began to wander, she caught them and tugged him closer. "Now," she whispered in his ear. "Like this...."

With her still warm and cuddly from sleep. Feeling soft and dreamy as if all the hard edges were gone from life. He sank into her slowly, oh, so easily, until he was buried completely in her welcoming warmth. There was no urgency in him, or in her, but rather a gentle, tender heat. He slipped his arms beneath her shoulders and pressed his face into her neck and began to rock them both like babies in a cradle. Soft. Warm. Easy. And oh, so good.

Together they climbed the pinnacle slowly, almost lazily, and when they tumbled over the top it was in a deep, satisfying haze of golden warmth.

"Zeke's going to come looking for me with a shotgun."

Sara laughed softly and grabbed a handful of Gideon's long, silky hair. Dawn's light was easing its way around the curtains now, a fragile, pink glow. "Not likely. His view of these things is decidedly unconventional." She tugged gently on his hair and for her efforts received a gentle kiss.

"I need to feed you," he said. "When was the last time we ate?"

Sara shrugged a smooth, naked shoulder. "Who cares?"

"I thought so. Too damn long. And the chores.... Damn, I clean forgot them last night. Zeke—"

"Zeke handled them," Sara said. "The same way he handled them before you arrived. Gideon, are you trying to get away from me?"

He froze just as he was bending to nibble her shoulder. Trying to get away from her? Was that what she thought? Was that how he sounded? But the truth was, he was scared she wanted to get away from him, and he was trying to sound as if he didn't care.

Slowly he lifted his head and looked straight into her eyes. The vulnerability in those soft, warm depths made him ache. She had asked the difficult question and now was awaiting his judgment. Sara Yates, who had never wanted to be a fool again, had just stepped out onto a limb and handed him a saw.

"Sara Jane Yates," he said, his voice cracking with unaccustomed feeling, "I don't ever want to get away from you."

Her breath caught, and her eyes filled. "Ever?" she repeated brokenly.

"Ever. Do you... want to get away from me?"

"Never."

Never. That one whispered word was the answer to a lifetime of prayers he hadn't even known he was making. "Hug me, Sara. God, just hug me and hold me... forever."

Two weeks later, surrounded by Gideon's relatives from Oklahoma, his new relatives in Wyoming, and by Sara's friends and neighbors, they faced each other across twenty feet of meadow up behind the ranch house. Aromas of roasting meat rose from below, where Jeff Cumberland was supervising the barbecue.

Sara still wore the white peasant blouse and prairie skirt in which she had married Gideon that morning at Good Shepherd Church. Gideon, too, wore white. White denim, white shirt, and a white head band to hold back his hair.

Sara held a blanket and an ear of corn. Gideon held a blanket and a string of jerky.

Then Sara and Gideon walked toward each other, slowly, one step at a time, marking the solemnity of what they were doing. This morning they had made solemn vows. This afternoon they made an equally solemn gesture in the old Cherokee way.

When they stood only a step apart, Gideon handed her his blanket. Sara folded his blanket and hers together, then handed him the corn. He handed her the jerky.

Chester stepped forward and shook a gourd rattle. "The blankets are joined," he announced, and cheers filled the meadow.

"I love you, Mouse," Gideon said huskily, so full of the feeling he thought he would burst. In finding Sara, he had found himself, and now he was embarking on the adventure of a lifetime.

"I love you, too," she murmured back, her eyes shining with joy and wonder.

"Good," said Zeke, throwing one arm around each of them. "Now we'll have new life and laughter around here."

Gideon glanced at him and grinned. "You better believe it, old man."

"Lots of great grandchildren," Zeke continued cheerfully. "All that an old man could ask for...except one thing."

Gideon turned and looked down at the old man. "Not now," he said.

"You really need to do the vision quest, boy. *Before* you do the Sun Dance."

Gideon sighed. "*First* I need to do a honeymoon."

"When you get back, then."

"Yes, damn it, when we get back!"

Sara's laugh suddenly pealed out gaily, and Gideon looked at her. "He did it, Gideon. He did it!"

"Did what?"

"Got you to agree. When we get back, you said."

Suddenly Gideon was laughing, too. "I always knew he was going to get his way. He's an irresistible force."

"Like you," Sara said, leaning close as the whole world seemed to recede. "Like love."

Gideon hauled her into his arms and hugged her until she squeaked. "Thank God for that, Mouse. Thank God."

* * * * *

INTIMATE MOMENTS®

Silhouette™

CONARD COUNTY

continues...

Come back to Conard County, Wyoming, where you'll meet men whose very lives personify the spirit of the American West—and the women who share their love. Join author Rachel Lee for her fourth exciting book in the series, IRONHEART (IM #495). Gideon Ironheart didn't expect his visit to Conard County to embroil him in a mystery...or entangle his heart. But the magnetic half-breed with a secret hadn't counted on wrangling with Deputy Sheriff Sara Yates. Look for their story in May, only from Silhouette Intimate Moments.